Exodus

Journey to the Promised Land

To Thomas
thanks Family !!
Peace & Power

T. H.

Exodus

Journey to the Promised Land

Obadiah Holder

Edited by Norris Ford III

Printed in the United States of America

Edited by Norris Ford III
Cover artwork by April Shelton

ISBN: 978-0-578-18336-7

Library of Congress Control Number: 2016912394

P.O. Box 111733
Carrollton, TX 75011

website: www.exodusofthepeople.com

Facebook: exodusofthepeople   Instagram: exodusofthepeople

This is dedicated to my family.

Acknowledgements

I would like to thank The Creator, The Spirit, The Light of Life. Thank You for the vision and the Spiritual kick in the butt to get this done. I would like to thank all my inspirations over the years. The Million Man March Movement, Hip, Hop, comic books, Cedrick Muhammad and Black Electorate, Daniel Marks, Kwon Adon, Michael Djangali and C52G, Kevin Woods, Brandi Holder, Jireh Holder, Aisha Adams, Kola Boof, and several others. Over the 10 years that I have written this novel I have come in contact with great people, great inspirations and great ideas that have added to the texture of this story, and I am so grateful for every Spirit that has touched this creation. Thank you.

A Vision Worth Sharing
a forward by Jiréh Breon Holder

Around ten years ago, Obadiah Holder and I were enjoying a hot Nashville summer when out of the blue, he asked me a question. "Nephew, what do you think would happen if all of the Black people in America moved to one state and took over?" Little did I know that he had been mulling over that question for a long time. We spoke at length. Who would move? How they could afford it? Which state might be the most advantageous? He shared the best-case scenario and worst-case scenario. We pondered if the plan would even work. Not long after, I received Part One of Exodus: Journey to the Promised Land. Years later, I am honored to offer an introduction to my uncle's work.

In Exodus: Journey to the Promised Land, the Black community is facing a war not dissimilar to the one we face today. Right now in 2015, we have the power to fight back with technology, protests, and campaigns like #Blacklivesmatter and #sayhername. However, in Holder's story the fight has reached a point of desperation. It has one solution: a mass exodus led by the Bishop family. As the Bishop's moves through their exodus, they are led by a series of dreams that collect and unfold much like the text itself. In a time of exceptional racial turmoil, Holder's words serve as a vision told with concise clarity.

Exodus: Journey to the Promised Land is at once a warning, a fairytale, a history, and an invitation. Holder nudges sleeping consciences with a reminder of what an entire race of people is capable. Reminiscent of Aaron McGruder and Sam Greenlee, this text is as buoyant as it is impactful. The words come straight from the heart and fall on the page like a mixture of hip-hop and calligraphy. It is a genuinely thrilling offer from a writer of exceptional thought and research.

With an undeniable freshness, a generous helping of imagination, and the resonance of a village elder, he journeys to an America not quite fantasy and not quite science fiction. It is a mirror of our America, a reflection of what may come. He maintains his storytelling with the ease of a griot.

As with most stories, this should be read with your ears wide open. I hope you enjoy this story as much as I have.

Jiréh Breon Holder

July 18, 2015

Exodus-Journey to the Promised Land

Book 1

Prologue

Early spring, winter still lingered so there was still a chill in the air and the house was quite cold. Robert Johnson slowly awoke from his slumber. He always rose around 4:30 in the morning. It was nothing new. He had no idea why, it happened automatically and had been happening for the last year now. Just another early morning in Milwaukee, Wisconsin. As always, he quietly crawled over his wife and peeked in on the twins before heading to the wood-burning stove to build a small fire. But this morning as he headed to the den he saw two SUV's slowly moving down the street, with their headlights off. The headlights being off was not the first thing that struck him as odd. It was the fact that gas powered vehicles were rare since the economy got so bad and gas became scarce and very expensive. As the automobiles came closer, Robert peered out the corner of the window curtains to investigate further. The truck's glass was tinted, but through the windshield he saw pale hands. Immediately he ran to phone Brother Lucas at the community security office located in the police precinct. Obviously, the town's outer layer of protection had been breached.

"Yeah, who is this? There's two SUV's on MLK and I think they…" Before he could finish he heard a rumbling explosion. "Marian, get the girls and stay in the room!" Robert yelled as he grabbed the Smith & Wesson revolver he kept in the umbrella stand near the door.

He stepped into the front yard and looked down the street to see the high school two blocks over in flames. Mere seconds later, BOOM! A rocket-propelled grenade was launched at the 1st Baptist Church, one of Milwaukee's oldest churches. This peaceful community was under attack and neighbors from both sides of the street were waking up and coming into the street, armed with pistols, shotguns, or whatever they owned!

Suddenly the SUVs roared back down the street at break-neck speed while firing M16's from the windows. Robert found cover behind a nearby bush and took aim at the lead vehicle's tires. The last thing he wanted was for the assailants to get away. He knew there would be no police investigation or arrest so it was up to the community to defend itself. Something they had become used to. Direct attacks weren't common, though according to news reports, they were increasing.

Most of the neighbors were reluctant to shoot, which was intelligent. Missing the vehicle could end up leaving one of their friends across the street wounded. But Roberts next door neighbor was a war veteran; survivor of Baghdad's angry streets. He knew exactly what to do. He dashed across the street scattering a box of nails in the vehicle's path. The first car hit the swiftly laid trap and immediately lost control, swerving recklessly into one of the yards as it flipped over onto its side. The other SUV did a 360 and halted in the street.

Swiftly, the neighbors moved in to apprehend the passengers. Others ran to the overturned truck to do the same. As they moved in on the wrecked SUV in Robert's yard they could see that the driver had been thrown from the vehicle; his body in the street 50 feet away. The other four White occupants had been killed upon impact. Then Mr. Wilson saw, near the rear tires, Robert's lifeless body pinned underneath the vehicle. The out of control driver had run him down during the crash.

"Oh Lord," Mr. Wilson said, considering the wife and children inside the house.

Before he had more than a second to think, he heard a scream coming from the other incapacitated truck. "Die you Niggers," A wounded and weak, but very hateful voice yelled out. And with that, the lone living gunman in the back of the SUV pulled the pin of a grenade and blew himself, the truck, and several nearby neighbors to their end. Mr. Wilson, along with several others was blown off his feet and lay unconscious near Robert's front door.

The so-called Milwaukee police and fire department arrived hours later, after the wounded had already been attended to by the neighborhood clinic, and the fires had been put out by the community fire department. No one paid the MPD any attention. What good were they now? The community security team had already collected evidence pointing to a branch of the Madison KKK called the "Madison Militia for White Pride" as being the culprits.

And so it was that the Milwaukee community of Westhaven became the fifth all Black community in the last two months to be attacked by racially motivated extremists. No attack the same, yet, no attack thoroughly investigated by those one would expect to be leading an investigation. As Dough Boy said in "Boyz in the Hood", "Either they don't know, don't show, or don't care about what's going on in the hood…"

CHAPTER 1

What a lovely sight! As Clifford watched from a distance, his wife Tina walked hand in hand with their two sons, Ryan and Marquis, and their daughter, Denise. Sweat beaded their brows as the hot summer sun shone upon them. However it did not deter their obvious happiness. Behind them were thousands…no, millions of followers—Black and Brown followers of all shades. Where they were going, he couldn't tell. Though he knew they were all going together. Clifford's chest reverberated with a feeling like heavy bass lines of at a hip hop show. Yet, no music blared from any instruments. Only the humming of "We Shall Not Be Moved" from the throngs of marchers. They carried their children, and belongings. And though the pain of a long journey was evident on many faces, so was a certain determination. A determination to finish what had been started, in search of something better. Something promised…

"Good morning baby," Tina said as she noticed Clifford's slow arousal from sleep. "You smile so much in your sleep lately! I wish I was in there with you."

1

"Oh, you are," he tells her while gently kissing her lips. "You are."

A new day was getting into motion as this small Virginia neighborhood embraced a rainy spring morning. As Clifford read The New Times online newspaper from his laptop he knew it is going to be another trying day. Although the online paper concentrated on the good things happening in the new progressive Black communities, they also reported on the new wave of violence as well. It had only been a few weeks since the Wisconsin incident.

Clifford Bishop was a strong man. Not weight-lifter strong. More like axe and hammer lifting strong. He had a naturally powerful physique not always common for men in their early fifties. He made sure to stay in good health. Cliff had seen both his father and grandfather live long, sickly twilight years due to their wild lifestyles of smoking and drinking. He kept his hair cut short and sported a well groomed mustache and beard. Although he lived a stressful life, the pressures of time were not written on Clifford's face. His hard, callused hands let you know he was no Rhodes scholar and that he was not a stranger to hard work. Still, he certainly looked younger than his years. When Cliff was a boy, he had heard the stories from his great grandfather. Growing up in the rural South, his grandfather had seen the unimaginable and he always shared his memories with Cliff, in hopes that the young boy would always respect the progress Blacks had made. A young Clifford learned to respect the resolve that his ancestors had to stay strong and get ahead.

"Lynching! I cannot believe I am reading about lynching in Two-Thousand Ninety Nine." Dropping his fork, Clifford was done with breakfast. His appetite gone, he sat staring at the table's flower arrangement. Cliff was not only aware of the Black community's short fuse toward such unprovoked violence, but he was also aware of the short temper of the Council of Medina-the governing body for the Million Man Movement Association. The Council was made up of spiritual and community leaders from across the country. They had centralized operations because communication was often difficult. Cliff and his wife spearheaded the council. Nonetheless, the council was often torn by opposing views. Half wanted to make peace with White America. Invite them in and share all that the Black community had developed since the second Great Depression. The more belligerent leaned toward war and hostile takeover. They felt that if the Polar Bears had so much trouble running the country then it is time for The Gorillas to step in and take over, by any means necessary. It had been one hell of a balancing act to keep these two sides neutral and patient as proper measures were being decided and Cliff and Tina both knew that neither side would tolerate much more unprovoked violence to their loved ones.

"Thanks for breakfast luv."

Tina smiled, "You know we gotta have our energy to deal with our brothers and sisters today."

"Don't you mean every day?" Clifford smirked.

"You know I do, baby," Tina laughed. "Breakfast and prayer! Go on and lay out our prayer rugs. I will be in as soon as I clear the table."

Tina, a former professor of African American studies, was not only well studied in her race's trials and tribulations, but she made a special effort to learn of the behind the scenes lives of Black leaders and their wives. She knew how to reconcile being wife, and mother, and be a leader in her own right. Short and fiery with dreadlocks that hung just short of her elbow, Tina was determined to be an ideal wife especially in such a precarious position and in such dangerous times. The Council members knew not to underestimate her petite stature. For in her big round brown eyes brewed a fire. When provoked, those salt and pepper locks would start swinging, the veins in her neck would pop into view and her body language would tell anyone in arms reach to watch out!

And this is how the Bishops started their days for the last thirty years. Before the madness. Before the children. Breakfast and prayer had kept their heads level and their spirits ready for whatever the day presented. Today was no different.

CHAPTER 2

*M*an, everything smells so good!" Marquis thought as he peered out over what he figured was history's biggest cookout. On the lush green landscape, tents were posted, blankets were laid out, and grills were fired up. "I only wish I could taste a little of everything!" As far as the eye could see, brown faces were smiling, talking, and sharing. Not a soul hungry. Not a soul sad. And it seemed like millions of them! Children ran and played without a care in the world as they climbed trees, played tag and generally were able to be kids. A group of men noticed Marquis observing from the hillside and started a chant, "Harambe! Harambe! Harambe!" The chant caught on and it seemed that everyone in sight was chanting. Even the children paused their games to throw up a fist and shout their appreciation. Marquis could not imagine what he had done to deserve this, but he politely waved to the crowds and shook one proud fist into the air. Two little girls ran up the hillside and brought him a plate. Grilled bar-b-que chicken, corn on the cob, mustard greens and baked beans. A little boy followed with a blanket for Marquis to sit on. As Marquis took his rest and *prepared to tear into the scrumptious meal, an elder came and offered him a glass of lemonade.*

"You and your family have done an honorable thing, son" The old man said, "Not only are we proud of you, but we are also deeply grateful. Our people will forever be grateful. You have changed lives and made history!"

"Thank you, sir." Marquis said, wiping sauce from his mustache. "But what exactly are you grateful for?"

The old man laughed! "And such modesty!! Your dad would be tickled right now. Seeing this day finally come and you still act like a silent observer to it all."

"How late are you going to be today, hun?" said Marquis' wife, Renée, as she banged his head with a pillow. "I guess your breakfast will be 'to go', again!"

"Aww baby, don't trip," Marquis said with a yawn, "you know even when I am late I am always on time." But as he glanced over at the clock, Marquis realized that it was a little later than he expected. "That breakfast will need to be 'to go' though," he said with a smile. Mark rose from bed and into his slippers to avoid the cold wooden floor of their two level townhouse. Marquis was always cold and figured he may be anemic, but Renée said it was because he didn't have enough meat on his skinny bones. Tall and rail thin, Marquis had the family height. If basketball were still a big entertainment force like it used to be, Mark would have been a pro. Except he never had hoop dreams. That wasn't an option in this "New America."

"Go get in the shower," Renée ordered to her husband. As he passed her, she slapped his ass. "I will get the boys ready."

"Yes, mama." Marquis said with an embarrassed grin as he headed into the bathroom.

Marquis was the oldest of Tina and Clifford's three children. He now had two boys of his own-Brandon and Justin. Teaching at the community school gave Marquis many opportunities to teach his sons and prepare them for this new world. Marquis would be the first to admit that he never knew what each day would bring. The dreams he had been having lately led him to believe that a major change was on the horizon.

"Good morning, daddy," his boys both said in unison. Renée had them dressed, fed, and ready for the stroll to school with their dad.

"Mornin' boys. Y'all ready to carry me to school?"

"Daddy, you're too heavy for us to carry!" said Justin.

"Not for me," Brandon said as he went over and unsuccessfully tried to pick his dad up.

"Whoa, son! Good try, but you are not quite there yet."

It looked like the boys would grow to be thin and wiry like their dad. The thought made Mark proud. Looking at his sons was like looking at younger versions of himself and Ryan, his brother.

Renée handed Marquis a bag with an apple and a bagel inside and Marquis got his coffee mug from the table and off they went.

"Wait daddy. We gotta pray," Justin reminded. A family tradition, no day ever started without prayer.

"You do the honors then, Justin"

"Almighty Creator, thank you for this day. Thank you for my family, even my stinky brother. Keep us safe as we go out today and bless Grandma and Grandpa. And protect us from the mean people out there, amen".

"Good job J," Renée said, as she gave her three big men goodbye kisses.

The three of them walked toward the school on a beautiful morning. The earlier clouds had cleared but the fresh smell of rain lingered and a rainbow graced the sky. Marquis waved and spoke to several of his neighbors as they stepped outside to start their daily routines. Many of the other children had not yet started their walks to school. Marquis had to arrive early to ensure he was prepared, so by default, his sons arrived early as well.

"Daddy," Brandon began, "what's going on today? Any more bad news? The White people still after us?" Being the older of the two, Brandon always showed a greater awareness of current events. His curly baby Afro seemed to represent question marks for all the questions that swirled in his head.

"It seems that they are, son. No more bad news though."

"Did they find those four little girls in Alabama yet?"

"No, not yet. I guess there isn't any good news either."

"Have granddaddy and the council people decided what we gonna do?" Justin asked. "Is it gonna be a war? Cause I'll fight if I have to!"

"Me too!" added Brandon.

"That's good to hear boys, but I don't think there is going to be a war. I have a feeling there will be another way to handle things. That does not mean that it won't be a fight. Y'all willing to fight to keep your freedom?"

"Yeah, daddy, we willing to fight! No struggle, no progress, right?"

"That's right boys, no struggle, no progress."

The Fredrick Douglass Community School for grades K-12 used to be a middle school. Children were no longer bused all over town anymore. Now classrooms took on the feel of a time well past. Like it was done in the old days. One building for all grade levels. With several grade levels being taught all in the same classroom. Even though Justin was in the sixth grade, and Brandon, the eighth, they both went into Mrs. Robinson's room.

"Good morning, Mrs. Robinson," Marquis said to the short, full figured woman.

"Good morning, Mr. Bishop, and hi boys."

"Hi Mrs. Robinson," they sang.

"I will see you two later," Marquis told the children as he kissed their foreheads and headed for his high school classroom.

As Marquis headed down the hallway, he suddenly felt nauseous, as if he had eaten something foul. He recognized the feeling as something he had felt in the past when heading into a negative setting. Marquis hated to imagine negativity in his classroom. When he reached the door he offered up a prayer and once inside walked with lit incense to rebuke the negative energies. Nevertheless, Marquis knew that his class would have some issues that needed talking out.

When the bell rang and the students started coming in he could see the stress on their faces. And this morning they all were avoiding eye contact. They filed into the warmly lit classroom and solemnly took their seats, something they hardly ever did. Not many days went by that Marquis didn't have to take an extra minute or two to get the teenagers under control. It wasn't disrespect. It was just the high spirits and energy of their youth. Marquis had a great group of kids, and he loved them like his own.

Mark never took roll. He knew all these kids personally. He scanned the room to make sure everyone was there. He noticed that fraternal twins, Kevin and Keisha Smothers were absent. "Where are the twins?" he asked.

"They're missing, Mr. Bishop," one student spoke up. "Last time anyone saw them was last night at a little house party. They left and they were cutting across Byrd Park. This morning someone found Keisha's shoe and Kevin's Walkman in the park."

"What?" Marquis asked in surprise. "Kevin's Walkman stays glued to him!"

"We know! That's what worries us! If them Klan devils got them, what we gonna do? Cause they gon' do Keisha and Kevin real bad!" Some of the girls in the class started crying. Marquis walked the room handing out tissue.

"I will have to find out what we are going to do. If they have been taken from the neighborhood, it will make finding them a challenge--but not impossible." He didn't pause his speech. Not wanting the room to focus on the negative. "Everyone listen, we live in extremely dangerous times. There are those that despise us simply because we carry on moderately normal lives while they struggle. We may be on the brink of civil war. My parents and the Council are working to determine the best course of action for our protection. Now, as we have studied, during any racial unrest, there are casualties. From this day forward, after dark, I want you rolling in packs no less than five. Stay out of the park. Stay on main, lit streets. We have to protect one another. DO NOT go outside of the community looking for your friends. What I find, out I will let you

9

know. I will say this: at all times, remain vigilant! And spread the word to everybody -- we need to stay in groups. Kids and adults. Y'all got it?"

"Yes, sir," the class acknowledged.

With a troubled heart, Marquis worked to disguise his fear. *What if those were my kids missing?* he thought. But he made sure to keep a brave face in front of the class as he began the day's lesson...

CHAPTER 3

Aside from the park in summertime, the library was the second most popular central hangout. It was akin to the student union building of a college campus. For the younger crowd, the basement served as an entertainment area complete with pool tables, ping-pong, cards, chess, and the like. On the main level, quiet was maintained, but there were study rooms where adults would congregate and talk, play games, knit, or whatever. The second floor had been converted to City Hall, with the largest meeting room reserved for the meetings of the Council of Medina. The room was mostly lit by its floor to ceiling windows. The walls were lined with municipal paperwork, historical records, census filings, and deeds of trust. The Council convened around an enormous round oak table. The Council of Medina consisted of thirteen men and women who represented what was widely known as "Black America". At the head of this thirteen body board sat Clifford and Tina Bishop. Many on the board would rather have Clifford and Tina only be mere figureheads. Voices and faces for the masses to identify with, but with no true power; the celebrities of the group, if you will. In truth, Clifford and Tina were the rocks; the foundation upon which most of the board, and all of Black America relied upon and trusted. They had motivated and laid plans for the organization of new Black communities. And they did it with an orderly method that was easily mimicked and reproduced across the nation. Essentially, they franchised a commercial design similar to McDonalds put forth a plan for opening restaurants and it allowed cities from Rock Hill, South Carolina to Seattle, Washington to organize and thrive.

The Bishops never allowed the MMMA to stray from the initial principles laid out by Minister Farrakhan at the first Million Man March. These steps were set forth not to place blame, but to foster personal and communal growth, first and foremost: The Eight Steps of Atonement.

1. Point out the wrong.
2. Acknowledge the wrong.
3. Confess the Fault.
4. Repent.
5. Atone.
6. Forgive.
7. Reconcile and Restore.
8. Perfect Union with God.

Although some Council members didn't like it, they realized once the Bishops disclosed the plan to combat the new wave of violence sweeping America, their recommendations would be the course of action taken. But until something was announced, nothing kept the Council from quarreling and debating in a play to sway and influence the Bishop's thoughts.

The Council had two dominant arguments in regard to a course of action. One, fight Whitey to the death, and take over the country by force. Two, beg the government for help and protection while providing them complete communal access, if required. Neither of which were acceptable to Cliff and Tina. Until they announced a proposal of their own, they had to listen day after day to these two arguments.

"You MUST make a quick decision! The violence will only get worse if we don't do something about it. It's already spread to our own community! Soon it will be too late and our towns will be overrun."

"We have to appeal to the government as soon as possible. If we don't, when things get worse they will turn a deaf ear to us and let our cities be burned and our people killed. They may even try to place us back into slavery."

That is how outrageous the arguments could get. Clifford would listen attentively, but Tina would normally tune the bickering out and speak to Clifford mentally. Through their years together, they practiced speaking telepathically, and after a while, it clicked.

"Why do we subject ourselves to this, Baby?"

"Because we have to be diplomatic," Clifford would say. "You know they are depending on us. We HAVE to listen to them."

Tina frowned. *"When are any of them going to get off of the same two ideas? It would be different if they were coming with something fresh, you know?"*

"Do we have anything to tell them yet? I know I don't."

"I know" Tina replied. *"Same here, and I know you are right. It is best to keep our mouths shut until we have something constructive to say."*

Clifford looked Tina in the eye, "Exactly," he said out loud.

"Exactly what, Brother Bishop?" one of the board members asked. They hung on every word spoken by Cliff and Tina.

"Oh, nothing," Cliff said. "I was speaking to my wife."

"She didn't say anything…"

Clifford stood up, "Look everyone, all we keep getting is the same options. Does anyone have any fresh ideas?" The room was silent. "We do not yet have the Army to fight. Plus, we are spread too thin and would be picked off easily. It is a god-awful shame what they did to the Smothers children, but why go begging a government that has never done anything in the past to help us? Was it not city and state police that turned water hoses and dogs on us in the past? I know that me and my wife are not providing a solution today, but we simply can not go with either of these ideas and feel like the Black community will be in a better position. Let us adjourn for the day. Better yet, for the week. Talk to your neighbors; your families. Get their thoughts and let's see if we can get some fresh ideas flowing. I give you my word that me and Tina will work to give you our ideas next week. And as you know, if it does not come from the Creator, we are not going to just throw it out there. Because it will be doomed to fail."

As they stood and all held hands, Tina offered up a prayer of cohesive thought, patience, love, and unity throughout the group. Whenever she prayed, it left everyone with a sense of calm and optimism. Nevertheless even with prayer, some of them still harbored fear.

***

As Ryan and Denise played chess, they listened to the radio. The Hip Hop songs, one after the other issued messages of neighborhood protection, self defense, peace, power and unity. Ever since African Americans began to unify more rappers began making their music purposeful and cohesive to the needs of the day. And until the Bishop family said otherwise, what was needed was for cooler heads to prevail nationwide. Music reinforced the message. Just like when there was a need for Blacks to centralize in certain areas in respective cities, and when it was time for Blacks to collectively drive out drug dealers and drug users, music was the messenger. Once known as the CNN of the hood, Hip Hop, today, truly was the way Black America passed along coded instructions. Like drums in the Motherland. So much so that the Pentagon had teams of agents who deciphered lyrics daily in an attempt to keep the pulse of what was going on with Black and Brown folk.

The songs told of the raid on the engine factory in Detroit and noted the bravery of the men and women who worked there. It also paid homage to the dead, but spoke nothing of retaliation. "I guess momma and daddy ain't gave the 'kill the crackers' order yet," Denise commented.

"Right. It's all in the music," Ryan said. "It ain't like we won't be the first to know when they do though."

Denise reached for the remote and changed the station from the hip-hop show to a more mellow instrumental flow. The band was complimented by an 808 bass line and a Creole hypnotic voice whispering love rhythms.

"You think it's gonna happen? Think we will declare war on the polar bears?" Denise asked.

Ryan contemplated as he moved his knight in place to take Denise's bishop. "Hard to say. Not like daddy ain't got the balls to do it. But he ain't gon just jump out there irrationally. If God tells him its war, then its war."

Denise nodded as she moved her bishop out of harms way. "Has God been telling you anything Ryan? I mean...I mean I feel like he has been telling me something."

"Speak on it then, sister." Ryan said, encouraging his sibling.

She looked at him from over her glasses and shifted herself in her chair. "Well bro, I have been having these dreams. And in most of 'em momma and daddy are walking and holding hands, and it's like, a billion Black people following them. In some of the dreams momma is walking and holding our hands. And we are all going somewhere. White people are just standing on the side of the road looking at us. Some are yelling, but I don't know what they're saying. Some try to join in with us, but they get pushed out. We won't let them march with us! And it seems like..."

"Every Black person in America is walking with us," Ryan finished his sister's sentence. "Funny thing is, I have been having dreams like that too. In mine we all get somewhere and everybody goes straight to work. A lot go to these factories. Some go to the fields and do farming. Others build houses, but everybody is doing something! And happy about doing it! It is like all our little towns become one big city." He moves a pawn, hoping to set something else up later. "So you think we're getting a message, D?"

"Now that you tell me you are having the same kind of dreams, it makes me think so," Denise said as she moved her queen. Ryan was going to lose a rook or a bishop. There was no way to save them both. "Have you talked to Marquis to see if he is having dreams too?"

Still perplexed by the last move, Ryan moved his knight in hopes of protecting his two other soldiers. "Not yet. Let's bring it up Sunday. Cause if this is not just me and it is not just us, then we may all have the answer that momma and daddy have been waiting for to take to the council. Why you think we don't keep seeing daddy though?"

Denise says, shaking her head, "I don't know Ry, I don't know. I don't even want to think about that part." She sat thinking for a second more with a grin spread across her face that exposed her beautiful White teeth. Then, in excitement, she exclaimed, "Checkmate!"

CHAPTER 4

Every Sunday had time set aside for the family. Still, there were too many dinner invites. Too many people that wanted to reach out, and be heard. Not just by Tina and Cliff, but some wanted the children's ear. Yeah, the people were pretty smart. A lot of them knew that one day the children would be the leaders, so it was beneficial to try and get in good now. Some provided words of encouragement; some asked for help or advice, and some tried to plant seeds of negativity within the family. Nevertheless, there was no way the family could just up and leave after service. Years ago, when the kids started their own families, it was agreed that as long as they were in the same city everyone would meet at the parents house two hours after church. Of course, dinner was always prepared at the house for anyone who was able to get to the homestead early. Which meant that Denise, Marquis and Ryan never had dinner cooked at their homes. Why cook when you knew where a perfectly good meal would be?

As usual, Ryan was the last to get there. The family was puzzled as to what always delayed his arrival being that they all lived within blocks of each other. No one ever said anything because he was always still on time by somebody's watch. And if not, he would have so many excuses that it wasn't really worth the argument.

Anyone and everyone who wanted to raided the kitchen for leftover dinner rolls, chess pie, or any kind of cake they could find then they all gathered in the great room. The great room used to be called the living room. It is where the good furniture was. Dark brown leather couches, loveseats, and chairs all with a suede paisley design accenting every angle. The floor was hardwood but there were plush Indian rugs for the comfort of anyone sitting on the floor. The ceiling to floor windows were covered by fine maroon curtains and in the evening, the sun shone through and gave the room a glorious red aura. Although all family members were allowed to attend these meetings, it was usually just Clifford, Tina and their siblings who spoke. Though everyone's opinions were welcome. The gathering included Marquis' wife and his kids, Denise's daughter Zenobia and her husband Lamar, as well as Ryan. Everyone had properly flavored their favorite coffee or tea and the kids were settled with their coloring books, games or other lessons and it was now time for some real talk. Nothing was off limits at these meetings. Sometimes the children had to be excused if the subject matter was too adult. If one of the couples was having marital problems it might be discussed. If any of the children had issues at school or at home it would be handled in this village environment. Not all of the in-laws liked their home life always being discussed but no one could argue with the results. Today though, no one had to worry about discussing personal problems. Today's agenda covered a much larger issue. Cliff was in his Lazy Boy throne and Tina always rested on a tan chaise. There were big pillows strewn around the floor that the children and whoever else would lounge on.

"Daddy," Denise spoke out first, "what's the news?"

As Cliff prepared to speak, he threw his chair into stretch mode and let out a long breath. "The council has no new ideas. And me and your mom are still meditating. We really have been waiting until today because we want your opinions. Y'all know what the arguments have been: look for government assistance or take up arms and strike preemptively. And some even want to let the Whites come in and live with us."

"What do you think, daddy?" The children weren't used to providing input on such important matters. Mr. and Mrs. Bishop's ideas were always so on point that the kids usually just told them how good their thoughts were. But issues of this great magnitude didn't come up very often. Over the years there had been a few. Like taking back their communities and moving dope dealers and junkies out. Even the Bishops had to turn their backs on some cousins, uncles and aunts who were strung out and didn't want help. The children pushed their father for his opinion rather than jump right in offering up their own.

"I want a long term solution that involves an evolution forward, not a rescission backward. I want something new, something unexpected. It isn't my will, though,"

"BUT GOD'S WILL!" the whole family said in unison. Cliff ended almost every speech with the phrase.

"Pop, I don't want to go against your wishes," Ryan spoke out, "There is something I want to bring to the discussion that may be signs of the answer." Ryan glanced over at his sister. Before he could continue his mother interrupted.

"Are you having dreams?" Tina asked suddenly.

Ryan's surprise was evident on his face. Denise's eyes widened as well. Other than Cliff, the rest of the room looked confused.

"Yeah, I have had a couple, ma." Ryan eventually stammered out. "Denise has too. And we wanted to know if anybody else was having them."

"What kind of dreams, uncle? Denise's four-year-old daughter asked. "Momma, you having bad dreams too?"

"They aren't bad dreams, Zenobia." Denise said, comforting her daughter. "They are quite marvelous, actually! So," she looked at her parents and brother, "tell us, momma, daddy, Marquis, are y'all having dreams of a huge gathering?"

19

An uncanny energy instantly touched each of their souls and they knew. They knew they were sharing the same vision.

"Family," Cliff concluded, "I would like y'all at the council meeting in the morning. I think it's clear to us what needs to be done and we will share it with the elders." The younglings were thoroughly confused. They had no idea what had just transpired and were too young to share the visions. But their parents, Cliff and Tina's kids knew. None of them knew whether to smile, frown, or cry. Everyone left that night kind of in a daze, feeling the gravity of what was about to be put into motion…

***

It was shortly after 1am when Denise awoke to realize that Lamar was not laying beside her. During their six years of marriage they hadn't slept apart often. When they did it was never a restful night of sleep for either of them. She peeked out the window to see him in the back yard gazebo swing. That was her first guess. It was his favorite place to chill and think. Also, knowing he wasn't allowed to smoke in the house, Denise figured he might be outside. She could see his cigar's faint glow. After putting on her robe Denise went to the kitchen, poured two glasses of tea and went to join him.

"Hey baby," she said as she sat down, handed him the tea and took the blunt from his hand, taking a small puff herself.

"What's good, luv?" Lamar asked. He tried to sound upbeat and happy, but his voice betrayed him. D could hear the worry and stress that weighed on her husband. They had been together a long time and she knew his tendencies.

"Talk to me. What's on your mind?"

Fireflies circled them and filled the yard with yellowish green flashes of dim light. Lamar's eyes followed one in particular as he watched it land on his wife's leg. He gently swatted it away, making sure not to kill the tender life force. Taking the blunt back, Lamar took a long pull before answering. "I am just thinking about the meeting tomorrow and what's about to go down soon. It's all just so big, ya know? I never imagined being a part of the most important family in America! And I don't want to hold you back, but I want to keep you and my daughter safe as well. Plus, I want to do my part."

"You said a mouth full just now," Denise answered. "In these strange days, I am so glad to have you by my side. I know you'll always be there to keep us safe. That's why pop likes you so much."

"Don't worry baby, I ain't going nowhere. We're all in this together. I once heard a saying 'I would rather struggle on my feet than live on my knees.' I know we have to do what we have to do."

Denise smiled. "Come on back to bed, baby. We got an early start tomorrow and you know I can't sleep if you aren't there."

Satisfied by their tea and their doobie, the couple enjoyed a long kiss and embrace before heading back to the house. Only hours away from the Council meeting, it was important to get some rest. Before they got to their bedroom Lamar stopped at Zenobia's door and peeked in on her. Denise watched with loving eyes. She thought that Lamar's sensitivity and care for his daughter was so sexy. She grinned at the thought. When Lamar turned around he saw her.

"What are you smiling about, woman?"

"You baby," she said as she wrapped her arms around him in the hallway. "I'm smiling about you."

Obadiah Holder

CHAPTER 5

The room was separated into distinct groups. Those who wanted war, those who wanted peace, and those who supported any decision the Bishops made. All were growing impatient with the lack of direction. Just over the weekend alone, a Black family was found dead in Alabama and an execution style slaughter of six was discovered in Illinois. The talk was turning toward ousting Clifford and Tina as leadership and simply making a decision based on a majority vote. One of the Council's most outspoken was Deacon Mayberry. The deacon had known Tina Bishop since they were teenagers. He had introduced Cliff and Tina to each other in high school. Cliff and Mayberry pledged Alpha together their sophomore year at Howard. He was about as close to the Bishops as anyone could get. Practically an uncle to the kids. If he was jealous of the Bishop's power it wasn't evident. Mayberry was Cliff and Tina's right hand man. Third in charge. And he was loyal to the family despite having his own opinions. Deacon Mayberry wanted peace with the government and White people as a whole. He and his contingent were more than ready to turn over to the government any and everything they requested for "protection" by the National Guard. He endorsed sharing the masterful plans that allowed the harnessing of solar power and its new uses: Lights, heat, cooling, and automobiles. All fueled by the sun! Great minds in the Black community had toiled on these systems for over a decade. And finally, "Black people learned to truly utilize the Sun's power," Tina always used to say. She admired people like George Washington Carver, Lewis Latimer, Elijah McCoy and Norbert Rillieux. Historic Black inventors that blazed new trails of discovery, regardless of what society said.

But Deacon Mayberry would sell his grandchildren's souls, let alone their solar technology, to have stability and safety once again. He wanted to live his senior years in peace. For so long, he had been fighting for equal rights, and now, he was drained. The deacon grew tired of his friend's indecisiveness. His discontent was contagious.

"Should we go ahead and start this thing?" Mayberry impatiently offered. "Who knows when his and her highness are liable to get here? Let's take our seats."

"Now who are you to start things up without our leaders present and accounted for?"

"I'm the one saying we're not a body with one head! We have brains, we have power, and we can make decisions! I don't know why we have sat around for so long now! Acting like we can't act unless King or Queen Bishop says so…"

Before the arguing could escalate any further, the heavy wooden double doors swung open and Tina and Cliff walked in, hand in hand. They were followed closely behind by their children. "I am glad to hear your eagerness, Deacon." Clifford stated. "Sounds like you're ready to hit the ground running. Let me take my seat then, and the floor is yours. A man so passionate should be heard." Cliff and Tina sat and the children stood behind the heavy oak throne-like chairs.

"Um, I am glad you cold make it, we were a bit worried for your safety." Mayberry stuttered. Obviously shaken by being overheard. "And it is always a pleasure to see the children, but I am curious. To what do we owe this honor today? They are not always in our council meetings. Nor do any of us ever bring our children."

"Don't worry they won't speak. They are only here to confirm and observe. We invite you to bring your children in to observe too. How else can we train the next generation?"

"I give the floor to you then, mister and missus." Mayberry conceded. "It looks to me like you two definitely have something on your minds today. I am sure everyone is as eager as I am to hear what it is."

Tina began, "Today is special because there is a vision of the future that we have all seen in our dreams. We see it as an answer to our question of what to do. Though, as my husband said, Deacon, we will let you speak first."

"With all due respect, sister Bishop," it was Mother Jones, the Council's oldest member, "but we have been waiting to hear this from you two for some time now and I think that the good brother Deacon still has the same ideas he had weeks ago. Let me know if I am wrong brotha Deacon."

"All I wanted to say is…"

"That's what I thought." Mother Jones interrupted. "Nothing different." Deacon Mayberry scowled with embarrassment. "Children, y'all go right ahead. I am sure Mayberry will be letting us know what he thinks anyway. Hell, we have been waiting for a word from y'all for too long now anyway!"

And with that, Deacon Mayberry took his seat and Clifford Bishop rose to address all those assembled. "Brothers and Sisters, this may sound cliché, but WE have a dream. And I mean that literally. Me, my wife, and our children have been sharing different aspects of the same dream. Therefore making it more of a vision. A vision that moves our people to an even greater level of unity. A vision that brings us closer and centralizes our power. A vision that allows us to watch each others backs like never before. Now, there are easier paths than what we propose, but our question is: where will those paths lead? Brother Malcolm always said that we have to be willing to pay the price for freedom. And we have been doing it. It's been a fight to get to where we are. Now we are getting too big for our polar bear brethren. It's like the world done turned upside for them and we are sitting high on the hog. They are scared and they should be. Like we were when we were broke and living day to day. Before the violence gets out of hand, we have to move. We have to pool our resources and do it! Our vision gives us control, stability, and probably the power to run this country. And for that reason alone, our vision comes with a heavy cost and an uneasy burden. Not everyone will see it to fruition. Many will bleed. Many will die. But history tells us that the greatest changes come by means of bloodshed."

The room's aggressive contingent grinned to themselves. It seemed that they might get their way.

"No, we are not going to war. We do not have to. With this course of action, the war will probably be coming to us. As simple as the plan is, that makes it that much more difficult. And I have not come to tell you that it is all mapped out. Still, I would be doing you all a disservice if I held my tongue and gave you no clue. Because now is the time for us to come together and make it happen. The plan: we are moving."

The room remained silent as everyone waited for Clifford to explain further. Yet, he said nothing.

"Who is moving, brotha? You and your family?"

"We all are," Tina rang out. "Black America will claim a state for ourselves, develop it and govern it. At the right time, Black people will leave from wherever they are in the country and establish a new home in a designated place. Like Cliff said, this will NOT be an easy task. There are several logistical nightmares to be tackled. People must have jobs, housing, food, protection, and the list goes on. Today, we wanted to express the idea. And before you ask where, we are not yet sure. The dreams tell us Texas, but we can't be sure just yet.

The whole family could sense the thoughts ricocheting throughout the room. They made a conscious effort not to read any minds. They had agreed, long ago, not to intrude on people's thoughts. Plus they would start speaking their minds soon enough.

"Move? All the Black people in America are gonna move to Texas." Justin Phillips said in disgust. "And you think Black folk are gonna go for that? Hell, you think WHITE folk are gonna go for that? Let alone the government."

"This is just leading lambs to slaughter!" Sean Simmons added. "There will be gangs just waiting to see a group of brothas and sistas thinking they are headed to some Promised Land."

"Oh, we won't even have to worry about that." Deacon Mayberry began, "I doubt if that many Black folk will be eager to leave their homes to go to who knows where and deal with who knows what? I just don't see it happening. Maybe we can see if we can get a plot of land from the government that they will let us settle. Then we can get their protection to get set up."

"And what good would that do Brother Deacon?" Denise spoke out angrily. She hated how the council members always wanted to run to the government for help. Asking for handouts was not her way at all. Not only that, but as a history buff, she knew the country was founded not by voting and asking for handouts from Europe, but from unifying and fighting for what they wanted. "If anyone wanted to hand us a plot of land then they could 'a done that back in the nineteen seventies. Don't you realize the struggle it took for White people to get independence in this country? They had to fight! And Black people had to fight for the right to vote. What makes you think they are just gonna start handing out land to people who are doing better than the majority of the country? It's unrealistic."

"Thank you for the history lesson, Ms. Denise, but you realize how many people died then too, don't you? Child, don't think that those same White people would have any qualms about wiping us off the face of the map."

"EXACTLY!" Clifford bellowed. "That's exactly why we have to make such a drastic move. How can you want to ask the government for help and be afraid of them killing us off at the same time? It's contradictory. Looking back on history once again think about what the government did to the Native Americans. Gave them diseased blankets and alcohol! What makes you think they wouldn't give us diseased land? Or even give us a plot of land just to surround us and destroy us! This is our time! We will develop factories for our solar powered transportation. Our people will have jobs producing cars. We will get agreements from our clothing designers. Get them to quit having their clothing made overseas and get it produced here! Truly For Us by Us! We will buy up the land and provide housing. We will organize our military veterans and hardened street brothers and sisters and they will become our police force. They will protect us. We will develop and cultivate the land the way it is supposed to be done. Rotating the crops every seven years and allowing it the chance the rest, like the Creator intended. We will spread businesses across the country in our own way. We will educate our own. Our community model will become what America will mimic to get back on its feet! We will lay a foundation for a NEW America! But we will not do it for America. No! We will do it for the benefit of our people! Self-preservation and development! And no, we are through asking! We are taking it, by legal means."

"Brotha! It sounds nice, but how in the world are we gonna do all that?"

Clifford spoke almost in a whisper. "We are gonna do it carefully, meticulously, and prayerfully. There will be much work to do. It'll be a while before we make the move. Please believe, we aren't jumping into this endeavor haphazardly. We have to make sure the I's are dotted and the T's are crossed and then we have to think about every possible roadblock that could work against us and come up with contingencies for most of those. Makes my head spin just to think about it. But what is right is right, and no amount of hard work will deter me and my family from putting the full force of our energy into making our dream a reality! This is what I want to do for the rest of the week: I must convene with my family. We will further analyze our vision and lay out an informal outline of an action plan. When we bring it back to the council on Monday, we will need to get your input to fill in the gaps and point out problems we haven't thought of. And from there we will have to see what is next. We will have to disperse teams across the country to spread the word and lay the foundation. Now, me and my family look forward to the task ahead. This is the GREAT WORK meant for our generation.

And even if none of us make it to the other side, we will still complete a work that will impact our people and our world for generations upon generations to come!"

The room burst with applause! Member after member standing to their feet in adulation. Even those who disagreed, which were not as many after the speech, stood and faked it. Most could understand the power in centralizing and the importance of what was to come.

CHAPTER 6

As the meeting adjourned, several council members came up to shake hands with the Bishop family. Everyone realized the challenges ahead but there was a soothing sense of confidence because now they had direction. A goal. A mission. Marquis scanned the room with curiosity noting who was talking with whom. He noticed Randy McFarland, one of Deacon Mayberry's supporters, whispering to his underling, Howard Sherrill. Shortly afterward, Howard rushed from the room. Marquis had long suspected spies and leaks within the council and he took every chance to look for signs of disloyalty. Looking out the window, Marquis saw Howard take to the street. "What you see, Markie?" Ryan asked, joining him at the window.

"You see Howard? McFarland told him something then he rushed out. I want to know where he is going. I think they are telling what little they know. Punk motha…"

"Any way of knowing for sure?"

"I have a plan in place." Marquis removed a pen light from his pocket and blinked the beam three times out the window.

After seeing a young shortie emerge from a tree top and give chase behind Howard, Ryan asked, "Is that my nephew out there?"

Sherrill scampered for four blocks, not knowing that he was being followed. He raced by neighbors doing yard work and children playing in the street, acknowledging no one. It appeared that his mind was on one thing…His trip ended at an abandoned gas station that sat just barely within the protected zone's parameters. It was a secluded building, owned by Deacon Mayberry, that no one ever ventured to. The windows were boarded tight and the pumps were rusting. Yet Howard removed a wooden plank that covered the back door and entered easily. The young spy surveyed the whole scene from outside. Though he had no way of knowing what was going on inside. He simply waited outside concealed from view. About twenty minutes passed and Sherrill reappeared, walking in a relaxed fashion back toward the town square. The youthful undercover agent did not bother to follow Howard again. He figured it would be much more valuable to find out what was in that building. After waiting to make sure Sherrill was well out of sight, the youngster crossed the empty street and entered the station. Taking his time, he allowed his eyes to adjust to the dark room. The only light came through the few spaces and cracks in the boarded windows. He moved about, tripping over debris strewn about the floor. But he didn't run into any cob webs. This space had been frequented recently. Finally, he came upon what was probably the office. Still stocked with a desk, chair and filing cabinet, there were fresh hand prints on the dusty desk. Placing his hand on the print, the young investigator tried to assume the position that Sherrill most likely had been in. Which appeared to be seated behind the desk. Once, seated he began to rummage through the drawers. Most of the drawers were empty, save for a few old receipt books and random papers. It didn't take long to find the hidden treasure. A satellite phone. Although cell phone activity was still abundant, this was the type of phone used in very limited circles communications. Not something that the average person possessed. Though his curiosity made him want to push the redial button to find out who would answer, Brandon was more afraid of messing something up. He didn't want this to be the last mission he was trusted with. Quietly, the boy placed the phone back where he found it and carefully exited, while taking care not to be spotted. Once outside, he made a mad dash for home. He was sure his dad and grandparents would be interested in what he had found.

Arlington

The building that sits in view of an empty Interstate 395 is called The Pentagon. A designated area of park benches remained silent. There used to be a continuous gurgling of water at the Pentagon's 9/11 Memorial. Now the lights were darkened and the water dried. Who could afford frivolous electricity use? Inside one of the many golden tinted windows, Corporal McNulty hung up the phone and headed down the dingy carpeted hallway. Reaching a door that read Captain John Vanguard, he entered and asked the secretary to make his presence known. "Word from Richmond, sir," he informed the Captain, standing stiffly at attention.

"Is that so, Corporal? Do tell. What is this news from Richmond?" Capt. Vanguard sat down the top-secret file he was studying and listened intently to the young man's report.

"Sir, the Blacks plan a massive move. They want to centralize their power somewhere. It is not yet clear where."

"They are gonna up and move." The captain pondered as he rocked back and forth in the old noisy leather office chair. "They mention taking their asses back to Africa? That would be nice."

"No sir, they didn't. The details are sketchy. Our source says that we should receive more intel by next weekend."

That is piss poor." The captain grunted. "Are we supposed to make plans around that shit? Are we?" The Corporal said nothing. "Keep me posted, Corporal. Good job. I guess it is still more than we knew before. Dismissed." As Corporal McNulty vacated the office, Captain Vanguard sat up, relit a half smoked cigar, and scratched at his scruffy chin. "Just what exactly are those niggers up to?" He picked up a phone that had no buttons. Yet, without dialing, he was automatically connected to who he was trying to reach. "Yeah, it's me," he said. "Put the Chief on…"

"Clifford! Brother Bishop! Come on up here, brother. Come on to the mountain top." Far above, two shadowy figures stood at the top of the mountain. Clifford thought that from this distance there is no way he should have heard the voices so clearly. "Come on up, brother. Your destiny lies with us. Come witness your good works." Clifford found his grip. He found his footing…and started to climb.

Tina awoke, nearly in tears. Her startled jerk woke Clifford. "Baby," he halfway yawned, "what's wrong?"

"Dreams, luv," she answered. "It's always the dreams."

"Dare I ask?"

"No baby, don't." Tina cut him off. "Just hold me. Hold me tight."

As Tina lay back in bed, she crawled into the safety and comfort of Cliff's arms. Clifford kissed her forehead, then each eyelid, as he felt the tension temporarily leave her body.

"I love you so much, Cliff."

Tina said into his powerful chest. "You will always be my warrior."

"Always." Cliff confirmed. He raised Tina's chin so that their eyes could meet. "I will always be your warrior. And let my strength always be yours." He kissed his wife before he shed a visible tear. They both knew that tough, maybe fatal times lie ahead. And without speaking, at that moment, they made a pact to thoroughly cherish every quiet moment they had together. Tina rolled Cliff to his back, straddled him, and gently kissed his neck and chest. Cliff's eyes closed in pleasure and he ran his hands through Tina's locks. His strong hands caressed the stress from her shoulders. They made love to each other's body. To each others mind. And to each other's spirit, with a passion reserved for newlyweds. One would not think they had been married almost thirty-five years. Their lovemaking was an example of what being in love truly means. As Tina moaned, tears of ecstasy streamed down her cheeks. She gently bit his shoulder as he pulled her head closer to his mouth. Cliff whispered both sexy and naughty nothings to his wife and reminded her that she was all that he would ever want and need, making her feel like the most beautiful chocolate sista on the planet earth. Afterward, they smiled, played in each other's hair and giggled like school kids.

***

Ryan, Denise, and Marquis all nosed around the kitchen looking for something to eat while they waited for their parents to come downstairs. Marquis shared what Brandon had found.

"A SAT phone?" Ryan questioned. "Deacon Mayberry is talking to the Feds!"

"We don't know that for sure, Ryan," Denise spoke up. "We don't know that it is really Mayberry's doing. We have to be careful before we start pointing fingers."

"D," Ryan interjected. "Mayberry's assistant led the boy to the phone. Isn't it obvious who is giving the orders?"

"And what orders are those?" Tina asked as she and Clifford entered the kitchen.

Over breakfast, the children updated their parents on what their grandson had discovered, and that they had kept a lookout on the old gas station ever since.

"The debate right now," Denise continued, "is whether or not Deacon Mayberry is the mastermind or if someone else is behind the snitching."

"It is good to have surveillance on the station," Cliff noted. "But we are gonna have to smoke the snake out of its hole. Once we reveal more of our planning, they will definitely have something to run back and tell. We will have to let them spread misinformation. Can't have them giving out our true itinerary. We will have our guys stationed inside the spot to hear the phone call. And whoever makes the call will be snatched up and interrogated. I think we should keep them from reporting back so that they don't give it away that we are on to them. Also, once we make them disappear, it should lead someone else to the gas station. At that point, we snatch them up and interrogate again until we find out who the head is."

"Dag, pop!" Marquis said in amazement, "Do you just come up with this stuff on the fly?"

"Yeah, I do, son. It just comes to me. Any other suggestions, though? There could always be a better course of action." The room fell silent. "I guess that's that…"

The council convened and the atmosphere felt positive. Through the opened windows a mild spring breeze fluttered the drapes. The meeting table had extra chairs for the full Bishop family. Fresh fruit, vegetables, sandwich fixings and coffee sat on the table in the corner. Chances were, everyone would be there for a while. The family entered and everyone took their seats. "Alright brothers and sisters," Clifford began, "here is what we have come up with so far. Write down your questions, as I am sure there will be many. We don't want any of them forgotten. And I don't want to lose my train of thought, so let's save the questions until I at least finish the first part of what we have come to share." Many members picked up pencils and jotted down questions that they already had. But by the end of the session a lot of those questions would not even have to be asked…

The sun was setting when Jerome's phone rang. He didn't have to answer it. He knew it was a signal that the meeting had ended. He left his cozy cover in the bushes and he headed into the old gas station. Because he had previously explored the room, Jerome knew exactly where the phone was stashed and where he should hide out to listen to the call. A former Force Recon sergeant, Jerome was the ideal operative for the Bishops to enlist as spy and muscle in this situation. Jerome eagerly anticipated detaining the caller and roughing him up. From his days in the military, Jerome had developed an appetite for violence that he didn't get a chance to feed too often. Twenty minutes passed before the shadowy figure entered the dark building. By the figures build he discerned that it was a teenage boy. Long, skinny and lanky. Jerome would have to be careful not to kill him…too soon. The boy sat at the desk, got the phone and placed it to his ear. "Hello, Corporal? Yes, this is Howard Sherrill I have information from today's meeting."

Jerome listened attentively.

Obadiah Holder

CHAPTER 7

Pentagon Ready Room

General Rudolph slowly scanned Captain Vanguard's report. He knew it would be the next order of business in today's debriefing. To his left was Secretary of Defense Scott Richards. To his right sat Director of Homeland Security, Bill McCregg. The remainder of the table was filled with various members of the Joint Chiefs of Staff. President Calvin Reynolds sat at the head of the oval table and Vice President Walter Campbell was present via two-way monitor. "OK General Rudolph," the President voiced, "what do you and McCray have for us?"

"Thank you, Mr. President," the General began, "our intel informs us that the African American population plans a staggered move to Oklahoma City, Oklahoma. They want to re-establish towns like Black Wall Street. Our source tells us that they will start migrating in six months with the eastern population. About nine months later, southern Blacks will move, and lastly groups from the west coast. The migration is estimated to take a year and a half. They plan to continue their community practices and they hope to protect themselves better if they can centralize. The Blacks predict that with a high arrival of coloreds to the area the White population will naturally move away, as they historically have. They feel that Oklahoma has good land for farming, a decent climate, and access to the river system. Though it still leaves them land locked, making them easy targets."

"And what are their chances of success?" the President asked.

"Moderately good," Rudolph replied. "If they can successfully organize the move and the militias and Klan don't run them back home, then the initial group could colonize the area. The other groups, actually, all the groups including the first, will make it only if we let them."

"And do we want to let them, Mr. Director?"

"Well, sir, it depends on our goals. If we want to centralize and eliminate the Blacks, this is an excellent opportunity. On the other hand, they have some very advanced technology right now. It would be easier to obtain if we keep them divided. There are pros and cons either way.

The President had heard enough for the day. "Very good, gentlemen. We will follow up in three days. I want a proposal outlining how we keep this move from happening. And someone review Memo 46. See what revisions might be needed for us to use it in this situation. That strategy has worked before. Who's to say it won't work again? Dismissed....hold on. Just for shits and giggles, somebody go ahead and take a look at the benefits of allowing this to happen. I seriously doubt that that will be our course of action, but we need to be thorough and look at this thing from all angles. In the world's eyes we could be made to look even weaker as a nation if we show absolutely no control of our land or our citizens. We have to spin this right. Either we crush the plan or we make it look like it was our idea."

***

"Yes sir. Thank you." Howard had barely ended his call when he felt a screaming pain in the back of his head. Jerome smacked him pretty hard with the Blackjack. He wanted to make sure he had Howard's attention. Sherrill wasn't even able to yell in pain. Jerome's huge mitt quickly covered his mouth.

"Shut up and relax." Jerome hissed. "You might not die today. Then again, act a fool and I guarantee you will not see the sky again." Jerome took the duct tape that he carried religiously and taped Howard's mouth, then his hands and feet, binding him to the chair. Howard was petrified. In the dark room all he could tell was that a hulking figure, three times his size, was manhandling him. He could tell that the sun had almost set and all Howard could think about was never seeing it rise again. Without warning, Jerome tore the tape from his mouth.

"Oww!" Howard yelled.

"Believe me, that's the least pain you will feel tonight if you don't cooperate." Jerome really had no plans to kill the kid. Unless he was ordered to. He normally wouldn't kill anyone under eighteen. These were different times and different circumstances. Jerome began, almost flippantly, "Why are you giving up our info lil' buddy?"

"I don't know what you are talking about." Howard rebelliously answered. Jerome rapt Howard's knuckles with the Blackjack, breaking two fingers. He didn't actually think Howard would have the heart to try and hold out. His reluctance gave Jerome a slight bit of respect for the youngster. Though he did consider Howard a bit dumb.

"You do realize I was here for your whole conversation don't you? I already know who you were talking to. Ain't no secret! I actually don't care why you are doing it. I want to know who is giving you your orders and who is giving them their orders. You better come clean youngster. Otherwise Mother Sherrill may have seen her oldest son for the last time…"

***

Randy McFarland was worried. He should have heard back from Howard over an hour ago. If he had time, he would've headed over to the station to investigate. But Randy had people to meet. Standing at the wood's edge, Randy could see the dim light of a lantern in the distance. Because of recent events, this meeting felt different from previous meetings, and that made Randy anxious. There was never any light when he met with the contact. Matter of fact, if they had never met in the daytime, Randy would not know what the man looked like. And tonight, as he approached, he saw a second man digging a hole. Randy considered turning and running like hell, but he knew that there was no running from his destiny, whatever it may be. Randy was about to speak but the man he came to meet held up one hand. "Let me talk," he said. "You don't know anything that I don't know. Plus, I figure I have a thing or two to let you know. Your little runner got the info to the Pentagon, but the family is on to him."

"No way," Randy objected. "I made sure…"

"Shut up, McFarland," the man snapped. "I told you I am talking. Your man never left the gas station. From what I can tell, he is still in there. No doubt he will give you up." Randy noticed that the other man had stopped shoveling and faded into the darkness. "Next they will be after you. Naturally."

McFarland spoke, recognizing the moment's urgency, "There's no way I would give you up! What we are doing is way too important!"

"Damn right, it is too important! Downright life or death shit! And our exposure has to be limited." After hearing those words, Randy's head felt like it exploded. He fell to his knees and was on the edge of consciousness. The man with the shovel re-appeared from the shadows behind Randy. He had taken his best baseball swing and hit a homerun against Randy's skull.

"Please Ar---!" Before he could say the name Randy was struck again with the shovel.

"And that's why you gotta go, bruh," the man said to the unconscious figure. The men didn't even bother to kill Randy. Instead they bound his hands and feet and tossed him in the hole. Randy began to stir as dirt splattered his face, but he was helpless, bleeding and dizzy. By the time he had somewhat gathered his wits, there was no sign of the lantern or the two men, even though he could hear their voices. Randy could not move or breathe. Walking into the meeting, he never thought it would end like this. In the past, he thought about escape routes, quick ways to remove himself from the situation in a hurry. He never expected things to escalate so quickly. He never got a real chance to speak, beg, or negotiate for his life. And now, buried alive, Randy had time to think about where things had gone wrong …before he took his last dirt-filled breath.

CHAPTER 8

Tina brought the bread from the kitchen and placed it on the table, completing the spread: Baked chicken, collard greens, candied yams, green beans and of course, hot water corn bread. This would be the last family dinner for a while. If their plans were to come to fruition, the children had to be major contributors. And for that reason, dispatching them to different regions was absolutely necessary. There was a lot of organizing that needed to be done, and not a lot of time to do it.

The family ate in silence. Clifford taught the importance of infusing your food with positive energy and ideas and then to ingest every single bite, making that positivity a part of you. Mealtimes became more ritual than just a time for filling the belly. And after the meal was complete it was time to discuss the serious matters at hand.

"The time has come," Clifford began. "Time to consolidate our people. Divided we will all perish. And there is no doubt in my mind that the hateful devils in this country would rather see us all killed than to see us living better than them. As the old saying goes, 'united we stand, divided we fall'. We have discussed the objective. We have seen it in our dreams, discussed it at this table, and acknowledged that this is not a mission we have decided on ourselves, but it is a divine mandate assigned to this family and designed to purify this country. Like the floods in the days of Noah. Like the exodus of Yahweh's chosen in the days of Moses. The time for our exodus has come. Time to rally our people and lead them to the Promised Land."

Denise could no longer contain her excitement, "This is so awesome, daddy! Having our own, for our own!"

"I know that's right," Marquis added. "And it ain't like we ain't already doing it anyway, for the most part. We just spread across the country. Once we bring it all together I think the rest of the nation eventually is gonna have to give our people the recognition we deserve. Everything is so tore up now. With gas the way it is and transportation so jacked up most everybody is just doing for self. It is a shame that things got so segmented that people can't work together no more."

"And it's a shame that it took all that for Black people to finally trust each other and work together." Ryan chimed in. "Now the only safe and functioning communities are Black communities."

"That won't continue to be the case if we don't get our plan into action," said Clifford as he stood and once again took control of the conversation. "Hatred is making the enemy strong again and they ain't going to have us being stronger than them. They would rather have no strength at all and wait for the government to do something. Even when we consolidate to Florida it will be of the utmost importance for us to have our own army. That is why we will be reaching out to the gangs, starting in LA. Our gang members, former prisoners, and former military are the battle tested, street hardened soldiers we need. And this plan is from God! They may give us some push back, but in the end, they can't say no!"

Tina always loved to hear the emotion in Clifford's voice and see the fire in his eyes. Even after so many years of marriage, seeing his passion always rekindled her love.

"Even though each of you will be touching base with the gangs in your designated areas, it is your job, Ryan, to have the sit-downs with the heads in LA. And then to quietly spread the word nationwide. That's a big part of your responsibility, but your primary mission is to convince our Left Coast family to even participate in this. They have the furthest to travel and may be the most reluctant to do it."

"Denise, you have the real estate side of it. The realtors for the MMMA have already been scooping up most of Florida. Which has not been that hard since the storms wiped out so much. I need you on their asses about rebuilding and getting those factories up. The business people I am going to contact have to see manufacturing infrastructure in place and ready to go. And our people are gonna have to see that we have jobs for them.

"Marquis, your job is organizing communications and logistics through our connections in the mid-west. This will be a long journey and not everyone will survive. We have to have all the vehicles we can, all the safe houses we can, and all the protection we can. Our movement will be like the Underground Railroad times ten! And no doubt it will mostly be done on foot, but when we can move groups by vehicle, by god we will!

"Me and your mom will be meeting with business heads to convince them to move their operations from overseas and bring the jobs back to our people. Like I said, once they see our plan and that we will have the facilities I am confident that they will buy in. We will also be back and forth to DC talking to the lawyers and politicians. Once we announce this plan it is gonna be a hell storm coming at us and we have to have all our ducks in a row on all fronts."

As Clifford looked at the serious and concentrated faces of his family he could not help but smile. To see this level of readiness and commitment from his own flesh and blood made him feel like the proud parent of a magnificent tribe.

Denise knew that smile. "We love you too, daddy," she said. "And we are proud of you as well."

Though the seriousness of the time was still in the air, the Bishop family was once again all smiles, as they looked each other in the eye from their respective seats at the table. And they reached out, holding each other's hands uniting an unbreakable cipher.

Book 2

*I*t was the night of the winter solstice and the Bishop family slept. They were connected in a dream. And they didn't know it.

Each stood at different locations on the West Coast of Africa. Marquis was in Benin, staring at the location of Albreda. In Ghana, Denise stood at St. George's Castle. Ryan walked through Salaga, and Cliff toward Cape Coast Castle. In Senegal, Tina stood on the beach at Goree Island.

They were absorbing the importance and impact of their locations when their attention was grabbed by the receding surf. The waters were dividing, like the Red Sea of Scripture. The family, in their own respective places, walked closer to gaze into this great watery divide. For reasons unknown to them, they were compelled to walk in the path.

Before entering the watery walkway, each looked back at their starting place and reflected on the pain and inhumanity of the slave trade. They thought about the total disregard for families and lives as numerous Africans were put on ships, never to see their home again.

As the family walked their paths, it didn't take long before they saw a human skeleton. Their thought was that the skeleton was from a stolen African who was able to jump ship, or who had died and was thrown overboard. Cliff, Tina, and the kids thought about the skeleton, then continued walking. Shortly after passing the bones, they heard someone behind them. In some cases it was a Black man. In others, it was a Black woman. But they stood where bones once lay. And they stood naked, staring and smiling at the Bishop who had passed by. Then they spoke: "Peace," and turned to run back toward Africa, never looking back. The Bishops were astonished! As they each passed the next set of bones they waited and watched to see what had happened last time. What they saw were organs, tissue, and skin re-form on bone, and a Black body come back to life. "Peace," they would say, and then head back toward the Motherland.

The watery pathways eventually merged. Marquis emerged first. He looked down the path beside him and saw Denise! Before he could look down the other pathway,

Ryan appeared, then Tina, then Cliff. Denise saw her family gather and rushed to join them. They embraced, but didn't speak. They just studied the path before them.

Then they continued the walk through... Along the way they saw more bones and as they passed, the same thing happened. They watched as groups of Africans ran back toward Africa, splitting at the crossroads and heading back toward their homes.

Cliff and his family surfaced on a sandy beach and watched as the parted ocean began to settle. A signal that the resurrected bones, now fully formed people, had completed their journey. The sun was setting in the west and they all turned, checking out their surroundings. Ryan saw a sign on the back of a hotel and touched his dad's shoulder to get his attention. They all looked toward the sign. It said, "Welcome to Florida."

"What do you mean misinformed?" barked the President.

"It seems that was their intention, sir," a nervous attendant continued. "They were on to one of our insiders and used them against us."

"What do we have to show for the last couple of months? Diddly squat?"

"Oh, not at all sir. We actually know that the Bishop sons were deployed. One to California and the other to the Mid-West. Either Oklahoma, North Texas, or Kansas. You know where the parents are, and we have eyes and ears with Mrs. Denise Hargrove and family in Florida."

President Reynolds smiled. "Finally," he said, "a piece of good news. That's enough for now. Make sure the chiefs know I want updates in detail when we meet later."

"There is one more thing, sir. Our intelligence says that the African American population, as of now, is not in favor of a move. And that the chance of even getting this off the ground is slim."

Reynolds sat there staring into space, appearing lost in thought. "Is that all?" he coldly asked.

"Yes, it is, sir."

"Thank you. Dismissed."

Obadiah Holder

CHAPTER 9

Mid Summer

According to reports coming in from all across Florida things were going really well. The soil tilling in North Florida was getting the land ready for planting season. Manufacturing facilities in Central Florida would be on line as scheduled. Textile and entertainment complexes were being built in Southern Florida. Commercials ran openly on the radio advertising housing and work in the state. While also delivering inspiration about what was to come. Almost daily, groups of men, young and old crossed the Georgia and Alabama borders to enter the state, excited about what potentially lay ahead for themselves and their families. Buses waited to take them to areas that needed their expertise or their muscle. Everyone was well aware that they were expected to arrive at their locations prepared to work in any capacity necessary.

It was a noisy scene. Bulldozers pushed debris from the street and into gigantic piles. Rotted wood was thrown from buildings as they were gutted, sometimes down to the very frame. And other structures were demolished completely. With the scraps being used to re-build the few salvageable buildings. Men came and went, leaving a tinge of musk in the air. Miami was no place to be right now if you were trying to be pretty. It was a place to work pretty damn hard. And work they did.

In the midst of all this "manliness" stood a woman. She wore jeans, a tank top that left her shoulders susceptible to sunburn, and a hard hat, like everyone else. Her steel-toe Negash boots had miles of usage on them from her travels from worksite to worksite. She poured over maps, grids, blueprints and layouts. Denise Hargrove had all her focus on this one city, for now. It was her sole responsibility to revive and transform the place. Her mental blueprint was an image of a place out west called Las Vegas. Nestled in the desert, it once became a haven for travelers, vacationers, families, and the like. A claim to fame once held by Miami as well. That's the rejuvenation part. She also was out to transform the city into a new and improved Hollywood. A virtual music and media Mecca for the world.

Denise looked at the maps with Marvin Wheeler, a fifty year old civil engineer from Tuskegee, Alabama. The wrinkles in his face and the gray in his hair spoke volumes about his life experience. He was the expert and made most of the recommendations. Denise didn't have a problem with that because if she wanted something done, then Marvin better have a good reason that it needed to be done differently, which he always did. After giving approval to Wheeler's plan for trash recycling, which involved converting the waste to energy and goods, she headed off to her next meeting in Liberty City.

Denise was glad to close the Land Rover's door, muting the ruckus surrounding her. The driver already knew the location and proceeded. After looking in a mirror and frowning at her appearance, Dee wiped her face with a wet wipe to remove the caked dirt from her pores and then stretched out on the leather seat to catch a quick nap. With her long days and nights, Denise caught a moment of sleep whenever she could.

Her husband Lamar was just as busy. He was very hands on at the construction sites, working alongside everyone else. That is, until he was pulled away by some other responsibility. Every day for the last month, he never slept in the same city he awoke. He was in constant motion.

Lamar did not want to let his wife or her family down. Therefore, he just figured it came with the territory when you rolled with the Bishops. Other than industry and farming, Lamar's major concern was security. Everyone coming into the state was screened for military and gang training. Most came across the border with weapons. And those that didn't were given weapons. Only if they had adequate experience. Housing areas were handled at night like a military base: Fire watch. Two to four bodies up rotating on an hourly basis. Ensuring awareness and vigilance at all times.

Later that evening, after a long days work…

"I know Marvin," Denise said into the phone to her lead engineer. "You know I can't leave anything to chance." Her neck cradled the phone awkwardly, yet Denise appeared comfortable with it. Her hands were full of hair from the seven-year-old sitting between her legs. "Sit still, girl! No, not you, Marvin. I'm doing this child's hair. Alright then, but give it some more thought tonight. Talk to the levy and bridge people and I will see you around nine-thirty. No, I will be up. I'm going with the other mothers in the morning to do a walk-thru of the school." Denise laughed out loud, provoking Zenobia to look up.

"What's so funny, momma?" Denise ignored the child.

"OK Marvin, see you tomorrow." In one motion, she lifted her head, allowing the phone to fall. She caught it and pressed the off button. "One more plait, Zee, and I'm done." Her hands ached and her body longed for sleep. The early mornings, the long days, and the late nights took Denise well beyond the aggravation stage.

She knew of the whispers about her looks. Being on construction sites every day in sweltering heat and dust taught her not to primp and try looking cute. Plus, her man was on the other end of the state, so what did it matter? Still, the grandmothers at camp had pulled her aside more than once just to slow Denise down, make her take a short break, and counsel her about staying healthy. "Chile, if you don't take care of yourself, you won't be any good to none of us," they would tell her.

"I'm fine, Mother." She called all the older women Mother. The obvious truth, though, was that she had lost more than twenty pounds that she didn't need to lose and her hair had been breaking off. So she shaved it down to a baby afro. Denise was glad Lamar couldn't see her. Not like this.

As if on queue, Zenobia asked "Can I call daddy?"

"The phone is by your leg. Go 'head." Zenobia felt around, found the phone and dialed the familiar number.

"Hi, daddy!"

Denise could feel the warmth of Zenobia's smile, and her love for her father. "Ouch! No, mommy is doing my hair."

"Be still, girl!" Denise hissed.

"Yes, sir. No, sir. Yes, well Kimmy and Jubilee said that by Christmas y'all should be down here."

Denise stood up. She held up her hand with her fingers spread signaling to Zenobia that she had five more minutes to talk while she put away the grease, berets, and combs. "Mommy, daddy said he will see you in your dreams." With her back turned to Zee, Denise smiled and walked into the bathroom.

"What does that mean, daddy?" Zenobia asked her father.

Denise lay in bed thirty minutes before she had to wake. She lay there gently rubbing her legs together. Eyes closed and head back, she inhaled deeply. She was intoxicated by the smell of her man. Denise opened her eyes and there he was, above her staring her in the face. When she saw the adoration and lust in Lamar's eyes she felt bashful. He always had that effect on her. Making her feel the puppy love of a school age crush. She reached out to outline Lamar's lips with her fingers. But he began to fade as a soft chime invaded Denise's ears and her dream. Slowly, she opened her eyes. Realizing where she was and that she was alone, Denise whispered softly, "damn." She both hated and loved the dreams, which she had quite often. Any chance to see a glimpse of her man was a welcome one. Though the disappointment of waking to find him not there was also a let down. The only thing she could do to keep the feeling going was to call him. Still lying in bed, she rolled over and grabbed the phone. After dialing and hearing the first ring, she waited in anticipation to hear his voice. "Hello?" she said. "Hey baby, it's me. Nothing's wrong. I'm just missing you…"

***

After the long and difficult trip to Oklahoma, Marquis and Renée took the first week to get themselves and the boys settled. It was very different being so far away from the coast. The community in which they resided was on hundreds of acres of farmland. There was a main house and several smaller homes. Renée imagined that this is how plantations probably looked. Children ran freely through corn fields and played in open spaces. Marquis knew it would be good for the boys, though he noticed that his oldest, Brandon, was becoming more and more serious minded, even at fourteen years old.

There were trade stores right in the community, but there was also a town square that served as a central point for other surrounding communities. The town square held more shopping, barber shops, beauty shops, shoe stores, etc. One thing that Marquis found really cool and probably useful was the mixture and camaraderie that existed between the Black people, Latinos and the Native Americans. The Cherokee nation was deep in Oklahoma and it appeared that there was no problem with them and the Black and Latino communities having each other's backs.

The Bishops were well received. When they moved into the home prepared for them, the fridge was full of food, complete with cooked meats that they could just warm up. The boys had a separate room. There were radio and Internet connections available for communication with the outside world. With the family content, Marquis began thinking about his mission.

The small contingent of men and women consisted of elected community officials. The gathering was slated as an opportunity to meet Marquis and his family, and to find out why he was there. Though he was used to standing before classrooms full of children, Marquis was embarking on a new type of public speaking. He was nervous but confident. He told himself, "I just have to get the first words out."

After a brief introduction, Marquis took the podium and began, "Um, good afternoon. I am Marquis Bishop, son of Clifford and Tina Bishop. I am joined by my wife, Renée, and my sons, Brandon and Justin. We are all aware of the violence that has plagued Black communities across the country." Marquis looked across the audience. He had everyone's full attention. He even saw some smiles; which set his mind at ease. "We have defended ourselves well, but there continues to be a need for long term solutions. My family has had a shared vision. We have seen, in our dreams, a land that we inherit, cultivate, and thrive in. A safe place where we raise our children and provide technology for ourselves and the whole world. That place is Florida. All of Florida." The audience was buzzing. Marquis could see some smiles, some frowns, and a lot of whispering and personal commentary. This was not the time to entertain questions. He paused, then continued.

"We have purchased land in the abandoned state. Farming will begin soon, and my parents are lining up factory jobs and mass media so our people have places to work. In essence, we will be calling for a mass exodus to the state. All that will be announced later. I am here to scout the best and safest routes to travel. We expect severe, possibly violent opposition, so we are now mapping out the paths of least resistance. What I ask for today is help locating those paths and help finding those willing to open the doors of their homes to be used as rest stations and hideouts. I request the help of any and all who will venture north, east, west and south to locate enemies, learn their patterns and determine the best routes to avoid confrontations." Marquis got into his flow and spoke for another fifteen minutes.

After he finished and the applause died down, several attendees stood to voice their support and thanks. Some had specific questions about the exodus, but Marquis couldn't answer such questions. He reminded the group of his mission and informed them that as he received word from his parents, he would pass it on. One person who started to speak was Bobby Crying Wolf. He was a representative for the Cherokee nation.

"On behalf of Cherokee Nation and Chief Johnny Longfeather, you have our aid in finding the right paths. We have constantly monitored the White men and we know of several campsites to avoid. We also have alliances in other states, which will probably help."

"I thank you, your chief, and your tribe as well, for your expertise," Marquis said. "It has been a joy to witness how closely y'all work together. Thanks, again."

***

Ryan had to get used to the Cali heat. The dry air kept his lips crusty, and his nose bled when he awoke. He was acclimated to the humidity of the South-East, but he did feel like he could learn to enjoy the palm trees and cooler breezes. Los Angeles was the capital of what was called the Brown Nation. In California, Blacks and Latinos had set aside their differences and began cooperating. The Whites that still occupied the state had moved to the northern regions. On his way out west, Ryan had been briefed that California was the prototype for their vision of Florida. They had it on lock. Security, jobs, agriculture, all on point. And absolutely all of the hard drug culture had been pushed to designated areas. Since demand for narcotics was so low, the Mexican border wasn't getting much dope into the states. One thing you could find in abundance in Cali was marijuana. Though it was predominately grown for personal use and industrial hemp products.

Ryan had given himself a day to adjust to the time change. Today, he would begin touring the city, getting intimate knowledge of their operations, and then he would present his dad's plans, with hopes that the well-organized Californians would join them.

The phone rang in what sounded like five rooms of the suite. Ryan was staying in the Sunset Tower Hotel and he didn't recall requesting a wakeup call. Then again, the hotel wasn't really a "hotel" anymore. It was now free living quarters for those in need. Ryan rolled over to grab the phone, ready to curse out the caller. He knocked the phone to the floor, then had to completely fall out of bed to pick up the receiver.

59

"Mr. Bishop?" the feminine voice on the other end said. "This is Kimberly with the CCAN. I am your guide today and I will take you to meet Ms. Scott. How long before you are ready?"

"I'm still in bed," Ryan said groggily. "No one told me when to expect you. Give me like, thirty minutes."

"I will see you then. What would you like for breakfast?"

"Eggs, better yet, a veggie omelet if possible. And some turkey bacon. Can I have a coffee to drink?" Ryan asked.

"Certainly," Kim replied. "Everything will be here waiting for you. See you in thirty." The call disconnected and Ryan got up from the floor, shuffled to the window and parted the Black-out blinds. The brightness of the rising eastern sun made him wonder what time it was. It didn't matter though. Time to get rolling. He headed to the bathroom for a shower; the hot water helped clear his head. The current massaged the back of his neck and shoulders like a million hot fingertips jabbing into his skin. He knew it would take him more than thirty minutes to make it downstairs. The softness of the water was like taking a shower in lotion, and he couldn't pull himself from it.

Although Kimberly was very shapely and very beautiful, Ryan did not react to her good looks. She was a chocolate sister with afro puffs and a hoop ring in her nose. He did not even notice her lack of a wedding ring. His demeanor remained businesslike and undeterred. Since she was waiting by the elevator when he exited, Ryan had no question as to who she was. His mind on the day ahead, he forgot that he'd ordered breakfast, which Kim was carrying in a brown take-out sack.

"Good morning," Kimberly said pleasantly. She didn't mention the fact that Ryan was almost twenty minutes later than he said he would be.

"Good morning," Ryan replied with a warm smile.

"I picked up your breakfast," Kim continued. "It might be a little cold now. We can have a seat over here." Gesturing to a grouping of tables, she led Ryan to a lounge area near the hotel bar.

"You're not eating?" Ryan asked.

"I already ate. Thanks for asking, though."

They sat and Ryan opened the sack. Kim asked Ryan, "Do you mind if I talk while you eat? I just want to give you a run down of our itinerary. You don't have to say anything."

"That's cool," Ryan said with his head down and preparing to tear into his breakfast.

"Today, we will tour the city's manufacturing district. Then, the retail and grocery zones. Tomorrow, we will meet with Shawn Scott. She is basically LA's Mayor. She will have you for a day or so. Later this week, we will visit the military base and training site."

"She is the leadership on the West Coast?" Ryan questioned.

"Ms. Scott? Actually, no," Kim responded. "There is a head for each major township, and you will meet two or three of them. Our commander-in-chief lives further south."

"That's interesting," Ryan remarked. "Shawn wears the public mantle of leader. Even though she's not the real leader?"

"It's for security purposes," Kim continued. "History has taught us to be very careful. Have you ever read up on the Black Panthers?"

"I've studied them."

"Our systems are largely based off their foundation. We have taken it to the next level. And we've included our Hispanic population. We work hard to keep from being systematically dismantled like the Panthers were."

Ryan rubbed his scruffy chin and nodded. "I see. What is his or her name?"

"Who?" Kim asked.

"The head."

"Oh," she said. Then Kim hesitated. "I'm not at liberty to say. I'm sure you will find out. Maybe Shawn will tell you."

"OK. I won't buck the system right now," Ryan said. *Too early to be arguing,* he thought. "Factories, stores, and base. What's after that?"

Kim continued with the itinerary. "The whole city, actually, the whole state admires your family, so we were hoping to go into some of the neighborhoods so they can meet you. If that's ok with you."

61

"Well," Ryan responded, "I ask that y'all don't make any announcements or anything like that. Let's just see how the day goes. If not today or tomorrow, definitely sometime this week. Deal?"

"Agreed," Kimberly said with a smile.

Harlem

Tina wearily fell across the bed of her and Cliff's temporary abode. Even short trips like this one from Richmond were taxing due to the numerous security measures that had to be in place. Scouts had to be sent out days in advance to map the route and then those routes had to constantly be monitored to confirm that they remained the safest way to go. Distance was never a factor. If it took traveling nine hours out of the way for the sake of staying alive, then so be it. The Bishops were in town to meet with a group of influential Black business leaders. Most of whom inherited their fortunes and empires from their grand and great grand parents. Big wigs back in the 1990's, their ancestors were rappers, singers, and clothing designers. Yet, through that legacy of entertainment their children's children now sat upon billion-dollar clothing, textile, and computer industries. Industries able to stay afloat by producing their products overseas and selling almost primarily to foreign markets. It had taken a month to organize this gathering. None of the attendees liked being in the same room together. One, they were highly competitive and two, they feared assassination. But upon the Bishop's call, they agreed on a time and place to hear the revered brother out.

"How much time do we have to rest before we get going again?" Tina asked Cliff.

Cliff sat on the bed beside Tina, took her shoes off and began rubbing her feet. "About three hours," Cliff answered. "You have time for a nap. First, we have a public appearance at the Audubon. That should go for about an hour or so. Afterward, we have a late dinner with the New York Medina Committee. They have been out of the loop with some of the plans we have been making in Richmond. Then around midnight Thursday, we present to the business leaders. You are welcome to be there, of course."

"I will see," Tina responded. "I might just pick your brain from here. You know how we do!"

"Yeah, I know baby. You ain't gotta be there to be there," Cliff said with a chuckle.

"How about you do it all this time and I come back and kick my feet up?"

"I don't think so buddy! I thought of it first!" They both burst into laughter as they lay back in bed, enjoyed one another and rested for a minute.

CHAPTER 10

There was a knock at the door. "We will be leaving in fifteen minutes, sir," a voice announced. The setting sun licked orange rays against the White drapes. Cliff and Tina were already dressed. Only their prayers remained. Tina led a prayer for safety and open minds. Going into a corporate meeting could easily bring about clashing egos and hurt feelings. She and Cliff embraced and shared a loving kiss before opening the door.

Outside the door stood six behemoth security guards. Two walked point, one on their sides, and two brought up the rear. *How are we all going to fit into the elevator?* Tina wondered as she looked up at the big offensive linemen. The question was answered when she saw that they were taking the freight elevator. With the lecture only a block away at the famous Audubon Ballroom, there was no need to drive. The walk would be short.

Throngs of supporters lined the hot summer streets. Obviously many could not get seats in the auditorium but still wanted to see the first family. Cliff motioned to one of the interns. "Yes sir?"

"Are there any speakers set up outside of the Audubon?" he asked.

Feeling a bit confused, the intern answered, "Not that I know of, sir."

"Hustle ahead and make that happen. I want the people outside to be able to hear the message as well." The young intern spoke into his hand held radio for a second then he started to jog ahead of the group. By the time the Bishops reached the ballroom four men were running wires to a pair of huge tower speakers placed outside.

Clifford and Tina were welcomed inside with a thunderous applause as they were led directly to the stage. Using his telepathic voice Cliff told Tina, "*I got first.*" She looked at him from the corner of her eye and scowled.

"*You got me,*" she answered. "*That's why I get to go back to the room first.*"

"*Why you gotta rub it in?*" The two smiled at each other as Cliff prepared to take the podium. He spoke to the gathering for about twenty minutes and then gave an introduction for his wife who would give the keynote address. The address would be the same regardless of which one of them gave it. There were no cue cards, or Teleprompters, the two were simply that tuned into each other.

***

Los Angeles

Ms. Scott's office seemed a bit detached from the Movement. Or maybe Ryan had that idea based on the order in which he was being introduced to things. He had met several community leaders within the retail areas. People who got respect. People who solved problems. It threw him off a bit to now be visiting an ivory tower office space. *I guess,* he thought, *the Movement has to touch every aspect of life.* Shawn's office was filled with contemporary African-American art. She had a corner office giving her a panoramic view from the South and West to the Pacific.

A very pleasant secretary walked Ryan in as Shawn stepped out briefly to go to the restroom. The momentary solitude gave Ryan a moment to admire the space. Behind her desk hung a huge scroll with the Black Panther Party's 10 Point Program:

1. WE WANT FREEDOM. WE WANT POWER TO DETERMINE THE DESTINY OF OUR BLACK AND OPPRESSED COMMUNITIES.

2. WE WANT FULL EMPLOYMENT FOR OUR PEOPLE.

3. WE WANT AN END TO THE ROBBERY BY THE CAPITALISTS OF OUR BLACK AND OPPRESSED COMMUNITIES.

4. WE WANT DECENT HOUSING, FIT FOR THE SHELTER OF HUMAN BEINGS.

5. WE WANT DECENT EDUCATION FOR OUR PEOPLE THAT EXPOSES THE TRUE NATURE OF THIS DECADENT AMERICAN SOCIETY. WE WANT EDUCATION THAT TEACHES US OUR TRUE HISTORY AND OUR ROLE IN THE PRESENT-DAY SOCIETY.

6. WE WANT COMPLETELY FREE HEALTH CARE FOR ALL BLACK AND OPPRESSED PEOPLE.

7. WE WANT AN IMMEDIATE END TO POLICE BRUTALITY AND MURDER OF BLACK PEOPLE, OTHER PEOPLE OF COLOR, ALL OPPRESSED PEOPLE INSIDE THE UNITED STATES.

8. WE WANT AN IMMEDIATE END TO ALL WARS OF AGGRESSION.

9. WE WANT FREEDOM FOR ALL BLACK AND OPPRESSED PEOPLE NOW HELD IN U. S. FEDERAL, STATE, COUNTY, CITY AND MILITARY PRISONS AND JAILS. WE WANT TRIALS BY A JURY OF PEERS FOR All PERSONS CHARGED WITH SO-CALLED CRIMES UNDER THE LAWS OF THIS COUNTRY.

10.WE WANT LAND, BREAD, HOUSING, EDUCATION, CLOTHING,   JUSTICE, PEACE AND PEOPLE'S COMMUNITY CONTROL OF MODERN TECHNOLOGY.

Other than the art, the scroll was the only thing that said, "This is a place where Black Independence work is done…"

It wasn't long before he could hear the sound of Shawn's heels clicking against the marble floor. "I am sorry for the delay but when you gotta go, you gotta go," she said as she walked into the room.

"I'm Shawn Scott and it is indeed a pleasure to meet you Mr. Bishop!" Her voice dripped with attraction. And so did her eyes. She studied Ryan's facial features closely. Shawn noticed his freckles and his need for a shave. She admired his shoulders and chest and smiled broadly. After a second, Shawn shook herself back into business mode. "Excuse me," she said. "I lost my train of thought.

"As I was saying, it is a pleasure to meet you and have you here in L.A. I am a huge admirer of you and your family. Of course, I have seen your pictures online but you are much more handsome in person," she said flirtatiously. She rested her chin on her left hand, flaunting the emptiness of her ring finger. But to no avail.

"It is a pleasure to be here," Ryan returned. "You have an outstanding office. I was admiring the art and view while you were away."

She was thrown off by Ryan's deflection of her advance, but she realized that she didn't know his personal situation. At that moment, Shawn decided not to invite Ryan over for dinner. "Yeah," she said, "if there is one thing there is no shortage of is office space. With so many defunct businesses, most of these buildings are abandoned. We picked this one for the view. Amazing what you can see with a pair of binoculars."

"If you don't mind," Ryan continued, "what can you tell me about your position as well as the responsibilities of others in your position? I doubt I will be able to get around and talk to all of you. This is a huge state!"

"Of course, Mr. Bishop." Shawn told Ryan that she and the others were mainly message takers and message deliverers for the real man in charge. She said that the people on the street, the shot callers, were truly tuned in to the everyday dealings. They knew the good and the bad that were taking place in the cities. They were aware of the drug trafficking heading into the badlands. And they stayed abreast of any nastiness that was close to leaking out of the badlands. She said that she had authority to make minor decisions, but anything major had to come out of San Diego.

"I have two questions," Ryan stated. "First, where are the badlands here in Los Angeles?" Shawn grabbed the binoculars from her desk and motioned for Ryan to join her at the window. "Over by that plume of smoke. There, and the surrounding area."

Ryan looked through the peepers and saw huge hillside estates. "There?" he said in surprise. "Those are mansions!"

"Yup," Shawn replied. "Those are the Hollywood Hills. There was a time when those were the most exclusive houses in the state. Most of those residents moved north. When we were deciding where to push the drug business, we figured it would have to be somewhere attractive. Somewhere the dealers would want to be. We pushed them there. It was easy. Plus, there aren't a lot of ways out of those hills. If and when, because it does happen from time to time, they want to come down, it's not hard to force them back up. We found that the community wanted their neighborhoods back. They didn't want to move anywhere else. Hopefully, you will get to see some of the neighborhoods that were so bad back in the day."

"I believe I saw some of them already. You couldn't tell now that they used to be overrun with drugs, gangs and murder," Ryan replied. His voice expressing how impressed he was.

"Ok, just two more things," he continued. "I am sure you know why I am here and what I am asking. Are you able to tell me if y'all will be willing to participate in the move?"

Shawn looked at Ryan empathetically, "I am not able to tell you. I know the answer but 'you know who' said only he can convey that information to you."

"Just as expected," Ryan countered. "Which leads me to my last question that you will not answer: Who IS 'you know who'? Because no, I do not know who and this secrecy is getting frustrating!"

Shawn sat silently. Ryan got the picture. Even though he was supposed to spend the day with Shawn he felt that she didn't have much more to share. He was ready to go. "It's been good meeting you Ms. Scott. I appreciate the insight you've been able to give me. Rest assured, I am not upset with you; so don't take offense. I will be voicing my displeasure to this 'mystery man' when I get to meet him." Shawn came around the desk and faced the now standing Ryan. Instead of a businesslike handshake, he gave her a familial hug. She nearly melted. Ryan understood. We are all family. And sometimes family disagree. At the end of the day, you still love each other.

As she tried to break the hypnotic spell of his scent, Ryan turned and headed to the elevator and back downstairs to Kimberly's awaiting vehicle. He knew there were other things he was still supposed to do in L.A. but all he wanted to do was leave for San Diego.

***

It was another sweltering summer day in South Florida. You could see the heat rising from the red earth into the humid atmosphere. There wasn't a noticeable breeze. And when the wind rose, the gusts were so hot that the air was barely breathable. Later in the afternoon, the full clouds would burst open for the daily thunderstorm, a welcome break from the mid-day inferno. The day work crews were working on rotations, and a lot of the operations were being run at night, even though it wasn't much cooler than the daytime. Denise stood inside the planning tent, one hand on her hip, the other swiftly fanning an old church fan she had found. Back and forth. Back and forth. Not only did she try in vain to keep her body cool, but also her temper. It had risen like the mercury.

"I would move all the shifts to the evenings," she said to the foremen, "if I thought anyone could sleep in this hellish daytime heat." Despite all their efforts to keep the men hydrated, healthy, and comfortable, some still suffered from heat exhaustion, and two had died from heat strokes. Many had stopped showing up for work. Even though the majority of the construction, destruction and excavation projects were ahead of schedule, they wouldn't remain that way for long, if the crews missed too many more days of productivity.

"We've tried rotating the guys who are working inside buildings with the guys working outside," one of the foremen said. "They don't wanna come out in this shit! Who would?"

"It seems you aren't keeping their eyes on the goal," Denise rebutted. "They have their guarantees for plots of land and they may be comfortable with that. We have to keep their eyes on the collective needs!" She stopped short of finishing her thought and pulled a rag from her back pocket to wipe her forehead—which wasn't even sweating.

"Sit down right here Dee." Marvin gently ordered. "Bring her something to drink, and some ice," he yelled at no one in particular. Three men leapt into action. Everyone was quiet as Denise sat and was handed a thermos of water. Her skin was clammy and grayish white. Her hands trembled as she drank several huge gulps like a camel, thirsty after a week in the desert. Then she hung her head, staring at the ground as if she were looking at the Devil himself. Marvin took a handful of ice cubes and ran the frozen blocks across the back of Denise's neck. The melting water ran down her collarbone.

"OK, Dee, listen," Marvin said as he continued working the ice, "me and the guys will work out the schedule for the men. Around the clock, inside and outside rotations. And if they don't wanna do it they have two choices: get the hell out and lose their land, or go up north with your husband and keep working outside anyway. Shit, it ain't like its any cooler up there." He eyed the other foremen to gauge their attitudes toward his idea. Most nodded in agreement but a couple refused to meet his gaze. Marvin continued, "I think they need a pep talk too. For real. You might want to get everybody together for some kind of pep rally, I guess. A revival, whatever you want to call it. Get these boys going again. Get their wives, moms, and daughters, whoever to put a foot in their behinds." Dee nodded in agreement without raising her head. Marvin didn't continue talking about plans. He just studied Denise. Grabbing her chin, he raised her head to look into her eyes. They were glassy and distant, which caused Marvin to worry more.

"James, go get the truck-and have the A/C on blast. Solomon, go tell the Mothers we are bringing Dee in. Something's wrong with her."

Denise didn't object. Once the pickup truck pulled around, two men picked her up as if she were still seated and carried her to the vehicle. Marvin took the driver's seat as James moved to the middle, continuing to fan and ice his overworked leader. The truck sped away, leaving a hot, dry cloud of dust.

***

Brandon sat on the porch watching Justin play with his new friends. As the children played "red light, green light," Brandon wondered when he might get the green light for more responsibility. He felt too old to just be watching kids play. His legs were getting longer, his voice a bit deeper and he was feeling like he was just about grown.

Almost daily he was designated to baby-sit as his mom took care of the house, and his dad ran the "Safe Passage" operation. Brandon admired his father and grandfather and he wanted to play a greater role in the movement like he did when he acted as a spy in the old gas station. Recalling the thrill and excitement, Brandon decided to ask his dad if he could work with him on the day-to-day operations.

Marquis was supposed to be home tonight after spending almost a week in Kansas. Maybe they could talk at dinner. Until then, Brandon decided, he would teach the children some close combat defense techniques he had been taught by his uncle back in Richmond. "Hey ya'll," Brandon yelled to the kids, "come and get some water." They all gathered for a drink. "I know a cool game that the older kids at home used to play," he said, "Ya'll wanna learn?"

"Yeah!" they all yelled.

"It's called 'catch my punch'. Finish your drinks and I will teach you…"

Later that evening…

Marquis got in late, and he was hungry. He kicked his backpack full of dirty clothes under the kitchen table. Fortunately, Renée left food for him to reheat. After going to the sink to wash his face, hands and forearms Marquis turned on the stove to warm up collard greens, corn and cauliflower. Since it was so late he decided to stick to a veggie dinner.

As he sat to eat, Brandon came out from the back room and headed for the bathroom. "Hi, dad," he said as he passed the kitchen.

"Hey, son." Marquis answered.

Shortly, the toilet flushed and Brandon walked into the kitchen and gave his father a hug. Marquis hugged back and gave Brandon a forehead kiss. "I missed y'all," Marquis said.

"I missed you too, daddy. So did mama."

"And what about Justin?" Marquis asked.

"He has so much to get into here, he ain't paid nobody no attention but his new friends," Brandon reported.

"There's nothing wrong with a kid being a kid," Marquis replied. "What about you, son? You got new friends you kicking it with? A little girlfriend or anything?"

"I have some rillas (short for gorillas, slang for Black friends) but we really ain't trying to be playing." Brandon was in a really serious mood now. "We want to be about Movement business. Help to fight off these polar bears. Next year, most of my boys will be at the age that they get manhood training. We didn't do nothing like that at home, though. Can I go to manhood training with them?"

Marquis suppressed a smile, but he was proud to see his oldest son ready to be a man. "Maybe. I have to find out more about it and then talk to your mom."

Brandon looked a little disappointed. "Dad, remember when you had me spying at the gas station? I did good, didn't I?"

"You did great, son. What's your point?"

"It was fun dad! Awesome! And I want to keep doing stuff. Important stuff," Brandon stressed.

Marquis thought for a minute, then he asked Brandon, "Do you and your gorillas practice your hand skills? Slap box a little?"

"Yes sir, a little bit. They don't know what I know though so I am teaching them. I stated teaching Justin and his boys today."

"Very good," remarked Marquis. "I'll tell you what, and remember I have to talk to your mom about this, I will let you start going to meetings with me. And when I go out of town, I might let you go. I will also see if we can organize classes where you can teach the older kids and young adults the Blocks. Because if you go to this manhood training I want you to be a leader. Understand?" Brandon nodded. "You come from a family of leaders so you must be prepared to take up the mantle one day. How does this sound? Want me to get it going for you?"

"Yeah daddy, "Brandon exclaimed. "I just wanna be doing what you doing. I wanna be helping out."

"You got it son. Know that I am gonna be hard on you. And it is only because I want you to learn the right way…what time is it?" Marquis finally looked up at the clock. "Boy, go to bed, as late as it is! Don't make me test your Blocks."

"Break the glass then, daddy! What up?" Brandon said, standing boldly.

"Tomorrow, son." Marquis replied. "We can slap it up then. I will be here. Go to bed."

"Ok, pop. Goodnight."

"Later, son. Sleep well."

***

Back in New York, about five past midnight…

Clifford Bishop entered the conference room at the St. Nicholas Hotel and shook hands with those already present. In attendance were: gold and diamond trader, Percy Miller IV; international real estate developers, Cassandra Jackson and Safir Carter; big time media mogul Sonia Johnson and the famed clothing designer KoKo Lee. Still missing were Lynette and Lendale Combs and Romeo Simmons, all big names in the international clothing sectors. They were infamous for being "fashionably" late. Their tardiness didn't sit well with Clifford, so he started the meeting. "I would like to thank everyone here for being on time. I know that as corporation heads you are busy signing checks and playing golf," he said with a laugh. "I will get right to it. What I tell you here stays between us. The Council of Medina does not even know some of the details I will share tonight.

"In the coming months we are planning a mass exodus of our people and we will settle in Florida. The hurricanes drove the population out but also purified the soil at the same time. We have been buying up land under various business fronts. Ms. Jackson and Mr. Carter, your companies have completed some of the deals. I bet you didn't know that was us! As we speak, homes and factories are being restored. The land is primed for farming and we will franchise grocery stores out to the Latinos and Native Americans across the country.

Cliff paused as he saw the Combs twins and Mr. Simmons enter. "Thanks for joining us," he said in an aggravated tone. Cliff really did not have a lot of patience for the "fat cat" types. "Have a seat. There will be time for questions later."

***

The wee morning hours in Florida...

"No, baby." Denise was trying her best to comfort Lamar. He was alarmed to find out his woman was ill. She hadn't even told him about her sick spell but word still got back to him in North Florida. "I'm fine. I was just dehydrated, that's all." Denise took another sip from the water bottle on her nightstand. She didn't dare lie to Lamar. He would have known.

"Look, baby," Lamar said, "its OK to sit down sometimes. Delegate authority!"

"And how often are you sitting down, Lamar?"

He hated it when she called him by name like that. He felt like a child about to be punished. "You got me," he said. "You think I like hearing that my wife fell out? And I am too far away to even be there for her? You knew I wouldn't be all rosy and happy about this."

Silence ensued for a moment. They both had just made good points. Lamar's bare feet paced back and forth in his Super 8 Motel room and Denise sat in the darkness of her room fidgeting with a lock of her hair. Denise didn't know what to say next, and Lamar didn't want to be too heavy handed to his wife. He missed her so much that his heart ached.

"OK, baby," Lamar started again, "I know what we have to do and I know that it's bigger than the both of us. I'm through fussing. I am just a concerned husband."

"I know, love," Denise said. Her voice dripping sympathy.

Silence again. Lamar had stopped pacing and sat on the bed.

They needed to touch each other. To embrace. To comfort each other non-verbally. The way people in love do. A million words said and a thousand stresses washed away in a release of mute emotions. It had been months since they had such contact.

Simultaneously they said, "I want to see you." Hearing their words echo back through the other end of the phone made them both burst out laughing.

"At least we know we both want the same thing," Lamar said through his laughter.

"Look babe," he continued, "you keep me posted on your health. Seriously. I know we have our assignments, but if things get worse for you down there then I just have to put somebody else in charge up here and come take care of you."

Denise loved it when Lamar talked about taking care of her. As strong as she displayed herself, she still considered herself Lamar's baby. "I will, Daddy. I'll let you know…"

***

KoKo Lee spoke first. Her bangle earrings jingled like bells because of the gyrations of her neck. "You are asking us to shut down our overseas production and move it back to the States? That's a big shift. I was hoping you were just asking for donations. I had my checkbook ready."

"This time we need more than just money thrown at the problems," Cliff answered.

"When we move these people, they need jobs, livelihoods. Not everyone can be a farmer."

"And not everyone here has a business that you can build a factory for," Lendale Combs said. "What would you expect from people like Perry and Sonia?"

"We will still have a need for media. Television, newspapers, movie studios, we are preparing printing presses and production houses, as well." Cliff continued. "We don't want to tell you where to be located. We have ideas of course. But we need your input as to where you want to be. Remember, we are taking the whole state!"

"What about me?" Perry asked. "How would I fit into the puzzle?"

"We need someone who could organize and manage international trade. We want to do business with Jamaica, Cuba, the Bahamas, hell, all of the islands, as well as, with Africa and Mexico. And eventually China. I know you have major connections in all of those countries. Like I said before," once again he addressed the whole group, "this is not an overnight venture. We do not plan to make the move for maybe another year and a half or so. We need to know early on who our allies are."

"I guess you won't be mad if you don't get an answer today?" said Romeo. "We do have boards of directors and contracts in these other places that we just can't walk away from."

"All I want today are your thoughts about how this sounds to you. I am not asking for signed contracts, but I would like to know if this is something you would want to be a part of." There was silence in the room as the Children of the Farm looked around at each other. Eyes rolled. Lips were turned up. From the look on their faces, it didn't seem that anyone thought moving their business would be a good idea.

"Any questions?" Clifford asked, and everyone started speaking at once. Right then, Cliff knew it would be a long night, and rightfully so.

Tina woke at six thirty, surprised that Cliff was not beside her. She stretched and looked around for any signs that he was either in the suite or had been in since the meeting. Cliff could instinctually feel her alarm so he softly communicated to her, *"Come down for breakfast."* Immediately relaxing, Tina started her day with a shower, got dressed in a long purple and yellow sundress and headed downstairs.

Clifford's late night meeting had carried into the morning. He was glad to answer all of the Children of the Farm's questions. To him, it was a sign that they really wanted in. Cliff knew he was being optimistic, but with what he was planning, it didn't help to be any other way. He scheduled one on one meetings with each of them and vowed to do all he could to earn their full confidence.

Tina arrived downstairs just as everyone was about to exit into the stifling morning heat. She only got a chance for brief pleasantries before they were gone. By the time Tina turned to face her weary husband, her breakfast was being placed on the table. "I take it everything went well," Tina remarked as she took her seat.

Cliff sat across from her at the table and rubbed his eyelids and forehead. "It did," he replied. "Ms Jackson and Mr. Carter have already agreed to connect with Denise on the real estate side of things. And I have set up more meetings with them, individually, after I get some updates from across the country. Especially from Denise. So baby, we may be here a month or so." He was looking out into space, still mulling over the questions that were brought up about things he hadn't even thought about.

"That's encouraging," soothed Tina as she reached across the table to take his hand. "These people are a big piece of the puzzle, so it's whatever. Now please, baby, go up and get some rest."

CHAPTER 11

Oceanside

The sight of a very active Camp Pendleton welcomed Ryan and Kim. The personnel all wore red berets. The rest of the uniform seemed to be up to them. Though it appeared the color of choice was Black. Boots, pants, shirts, something, if not everything was Black. *The Panthers*, Ryan thought.

They wheeled the jeep past barracks and buildings until they reached a football field. He noticed the men on the field were separated into two teams. Shirts and skins. They weren't playing a sport at all. They were sparring for close-quarters combat. The style was very familiar: changing levels from high to low, swift return punching off of blocked attempts, faking openings where there were none. "Fifty-Two Jailhouse," he whispered softly. Though it was loud enough for Kim to hear.

"You're familiar," she commented.

"Yeah, we do it out East. It looks like they got some West Coast funk with theirs."

"Huh?" Kimberly didn't understand what Ryan meant.

"They have their own style, that's all," he replied.

A tall dark skinned man broke away from the training and approached Kim and Ryan, who were standing outside of the vehicle. The man was shirtless and sweating. Ryan admired his physique as he approached. Very short crew-cut hair, slender face with prominent cheekbones, and small, cutting eyes. His strong chest leading down to a small thirty-two or thirty-four size waist. And ripped abs like he did crunches in his sleep. Without being introduced, Ryan respected this man, simply based on his physical fitness.

"And who is this?" Ryan asked.

Quickly, Kim replied, "Don't worry. You will find out in about two seconds."

"Kimberleeee," the man's jovial voice rang out. "Come and play in the dirt with us!"

"I don't think so," she replied with attitude.

"Then maybe your big homey will," he said, turning his gaze and smile to Ryan.

"That's on him. Quit trippin', fool, introduce yourself," Kim seemed in her element. She was in full Cali girl mode now.

"What's up, homey?" he said, extending a hand to Ryan. "You are Ryan Bishop. I have been waiting to meet a member of the great Bishop clan!"

It made Ryan a bit uncomfortable for someone to know him without knowing who they were. "And you are?" he asked, still shaking hands.

"My bad homey, I'm Stephen Andrews. I head up hand to hand combat training and I have a similar program for the kids in the neighborhood. Have you been around to the housing districts yet?"

"Just a little bit," Kim chimed in. "I figured you could take him when you go to see the children's group later."

"That's cool with me," Stephen said, looking back at Ryan. "First you have to sit through the rest of our training though."

Ryan responded, "Aiight. We do something similar to the style you are teaching."

"You know Jailhouse?"

"I got a little flavor," Ryan admitted, modestly.

"You mind shooting some right now?" Steve asked. "We got gear to protect your pretty face."

"Yeah, I'm with it, if you got some sweats I can throw on."

"I got'cha, homey." The two gave each other dap again. Steve was smiling at the chance to see how the East coast got down with their hands. He had always heard stories that the best fighters were from the East. "Let me show you where to change."

"I'll show him," Kim stated quickly. "I'm on my way out, anyway. Come on, Mr. Bishop." As she led him to the locker room, she warned, "Be careful. Those guys are good."

Ryan smiled and told Kimberly with a cool confidence, "Thanks, but so am I."

The guys were doing calisthenics in a circle, with Stephen in the middle leading. He nodded his head, directing Ryan to fall into the cipher. Knowing that he needed to warm up, Ryan moved to join. Now, dressed in Black: sweats, wife beater, and boots--he felt like a part of the family. After a few series of jumping jacks, burpees, and push-ups, Steve called the group to a halt. He motioned Ryan to the circle's center. "Take a seat, guys," he ordered. "Today, we have a special guest. Y'all heard of Clifford Bishop, I know," he paused as the group nodded in acknowledgement. "This is his youngest son, Ryan. He is observing how we get down out West. I'm gonna give him the floor. Let him say a few words." The group clapped it up, welcoming Ryan.

"This doesn't seem like an atmosphere for speeches," Ryan began. "I'll keep it short. With so much tension across the U.S., I am glad to be here on the West Coast. Traveling cross country is tough. I never thought I would make it out here in my lifetime.

"At home we practice hand to hand combat, but it's mostly as kids. As young adults we have been training more on guns. It's good to see you brothers keeping your hand game tight. It's about more than the fight. It's about the energy. The flow and the Spirit. I urge you to always watch your brother's back. Protect each other." Ryan offered a courtesy bow and the group clapped it up again.

Once again, Stephen spoke. "Mr. Bishop told me that he practices Jailhouse Boxing as well."

"We call it Fifty-Two," Ryan interjected.

"He is willing to spar with us, so we can see what they working with back East. Any takers? It ain't often that you get to take shots at a potential world leader!" No one raised their hand. "Come on, gorillas! I think he can take a punch."

Ryan leaned over and whispered to Steve, "Who is your strongest?"

Steve smiled, then ordered, "Micah, get over here." Micah looked like Stephen except with cornrows, a little shorter in height, and lighter skin. He carried the same slim, stocky frame.

"You nervous?" Stephen asked Micah.

"No, sir," he answered. "I will take it easy. I don't want to hurt Mr. Bishop."

"Don't worry about that," Ryan shot back. "If I get hurt, I deserve to get hurt. Give me what you got. Don't hold back. That's how YOU will end up getting hurt."

The two men donned knee and elbow pads. Steve handed Ryan a mouthpiece. With a pat on the back, he said, "Show me what you got, gorilla."

To start the fight, Stephen yelled, "Guard your grill! It's about that time! Let's go!" The two men approached the center and both began to circle-walk. The men around them yelled and beat the dirt, creating a cloud that attracted the attention of others nearby. People on the base knew that when the dust started flying, one of the better matchups must be going down.

Ryan and Micah were tentative. Ryan worked to remain calm and feel the rhythm in his head. Suddenly, Micah went into a driving bob and weave as he attempted to close the distance on Ryan. Ryan let him inside, but quickly dropped his forearm on Micah's clavicle, keeping a distance between them. In a single motion, he pushed Micah back, clocking him with a right hand. Ryan pivoted to the right, so that when Micah recovered from the punch, he had to find him. And Ryan knew it. As Micah attempted to square his feet, he ate a left followed by a right. Ryan dropped down, hit Micah's foot, his thigh, his gut, and then threw an uppercut to the chin. They were light punches, demonstrating the flair, style, and skill of Ryan's technique. Obviously dazed by the combo, Micah wilted under the barrage.

"OK, break," Stephen stepped in. "Look at big brother Bishop! Clap him up y'all!" The circle, along with the stragglers who had come over to watch, all clapped. Ryan and Micah shook hands and embraced. No hard feelings.

"Brother B, you got another round in you?" Stephen asked.

"Sure," Ryan replied. "I'm loose now."

"Bet, homey!" Stephen was excited. "Give him some water. Let me gear up."

"Oh, we're gonna get it in?" Ryan asked.

"Fo sho, homey. That cool?"

Ryan smiled. "Gear up, chief. I got plenty more."

"Hey ma! Me and Mr. Bishop are here," Steve announced as they entered the unlocked door.

"OK," Minnie Andrews replied. "Y'all go get washed up, if you need to. The food will be on the table in a minute."

Stephen motioned for Ryan to follow him into the kitchen. "We're fine, Ma. We took showers on base." When the men walked in, Minnie turned to face the footsteps.

"What the hell y'all been doing? Fighting?" she asked after seeing their battered faces.

"A little bit. That was yesterday. It was all in fun."

"Lord," she said, "I thought I taught you to treat guests better than that. You don't fight them! Would you fight Jesus if he was in town?"

"Absolutely," Stephen said enthusiastically.

"Me too, Ms. Andrews," Ryan chimed in. "Just for sport, of course."

"Y'all fools need help," she said with a giggle.

After they all laughed for a minute, Ryan composed himself. "Ms Andrews, I'm Ryan Bishop. Thanks for having me in your home."

"Baby, the honor and pleasure are all mine. I listen to your daddy and momma on the radio every week. Your family is such an inspiration!" She gave Ryan a huge hug. It made Ryan miss his own mother. "Now y'all go and put the food on the table. I got to get the bread."

After dinner Minnie opened the front door and headed for her rocking chair on the porch, where she spent almost every evening. She was used to the street still being a bit busy with people going place to place. This evening was a bit different. "Boys," she yelled back into the house, "y'all might want to get out here."

The guys had cleaned the table and were washing the dishes. Ryan had insisted. Stephen went to see what was up. "What is it, Ma?" he asked as he stepped out the door. Looking up, he saw that the whole neighborhood was standing outside his mother's house.

"Now, boy," one of the waiting neighbors said, "you KNOW we ain't here to see your Black ass. No offense sister Minnie." With that warm welcome, Stephen headed back into the house and to the kitchen.

"Hey big shot, you ready to do another meet and greet with the hood?"

"I guess," Ryan said. "After we finish busting these suds, right quick."

"That wasn't the question, yo," Steve stressed. "Roll down your sleeves and dry your hands. You got an audience out front."

Ryan was puzzled. "What do you mean?"

"Shhh…just listen."

What Ryan heard was a chant: "Bishop, Bishop, Bishop, Bishop."

He looked at Stephen, and Steve just smiled and stepped out of the way like an opening door. Ryan rolled down his sleeves and took his queue.

Stepping outside, Ryan saw a sea of faces. "Looks like people are here from four or five different townships, homey," Stephen said, almost yelling into Ryan's ear. He had to. The roar of the crowd was deafening. The sight brought Ryan to tears. He had no idea of the love his family got from across the U.S. He even noticed a lot of Latino faces in the crowd. He nudged Stephen and nodded in the direction of a Latino group. "Oh yeah," Steve responded. "If you're brown, you're down out here. We can talk about that anytime. For now, make a move man! You gotta give these people something!"

"OK," Ryan said with a smile. "You think your mom would mind if I got on the roof?"

"How much you weigh?"

"Whatever," Ryan replied, laughing. "Enough to have whipped your butt earlier."

Steve whispered to his mom, and then turned to give Ryan a boost to the roof. Once he got up he was once again blown away at the number of people there to greet him. He waved his arms to quiet the crowd. Steve tossed him a bullhorn. "Wow!" he exclaimed to the crowd. "This is overwhelming! I doubt if everyone can hear me so I will try to do something on the radio while I am here. If it is OK with y'all, can I just come down there and hang out a little bit?"

The crowd roared. "Yeah, yeah!"

"One thing," Ryan added. "I want to speak to as many people as I can so I might not be able to spend a lot of time with anyone individually. Just don't be mad at me," he said with a smile. "Oh yeah," he threw up a power fist with his right hand and yelled, "Peace, power and love from the Bishop family!"

The uproar commenced and music started playing. The block party was on. Ryan, Stephen, and a couple of Stephen's broad shouldered brothers made their way into the mix. Ryan felt like a politician: shaking hands, offering hugs and signing autographs. All the while, smiling from ear to ear. And in his mind, he envisioned his dreams. *This is what Florida is gonna look like*, he thought.

CHAPTER 12

The seasons were shifting. Red, brown and yellow leaves coasted effortlessly to the ground. The fall mornings were chilly and the days pleasant. A welcome change from the oppressive summer heat. Deacon Mayberry, who was working with the Movement wholeheartedly, though he still had some doubts, walked into the meeting room fully dressed in suit and tie.

"Good morning, y'all. I have some news," he reported. Word from D.C. is that the President wants to have a sit down with you two. He heard about the move to Oklahoma and wants to see if you all can come to terms on the whole thing."

The Bishops were dressed very casually in sweats and running shoes. They had just finished a light morning workout and sat having breakfast. "We don't have time for him right now," Tina said.

"For real. There's too much to handle here. We aren't about to go to D.C." Clifford added. "It's been a struggle up here in NY and its time to go home for a while. You are headed back to Richmond at the end of the week, right Mayberry?"

"Yes sir," Mayberry said, straightening his posture as he sensed an important mission coming.

"I want you to stop in Washington to see what he's talking about. Tell him we will let him know when we will be available to stop by the District."

"Not a problem, Minister Bishop. I can do that," Mayberry said, hardly able to keep from smiling. "Should my report wait until I get back to Richmond?"

"No, holla at me on your way back. I want to talk while it's fresh on your mind."

Later that week in Washington DC

Deacon Mayberry and his assistant Robbie Taswell beamed with excitement as they waited in the Oval Office for President Reynolds. "I can't believe they let us wait in here!" Robbie said excitedly.

"Calm yourself, son," Mayberry counseled. "Act like you been somewhere before." Deacon Mayberry could hardly hold back his own excitement. *This is the stuff you only see in history books*, he thought. For his young assistant sake, he maintained his composure.

Led by the Secret Service, the President made a regal entrance. "Good afternoon, gentlemen," he began. "Sorry to keep you waiting. I take it you are comfortable?"

"Very comfortable, sir. Thank you." Mayberry replied.

President Reynolds cleared his throat. "Ahem…Deacon," he started, cutting his eyes over to Robbie, "since the Bishops could not make it, I was hoping to speak to you alone."

Deacon Mayberry looked at Robbie and, disappointedly, he took the cue to leave. As the door closed, President Reynolds began. "How are the plans going? It's not like I don't know. I AM the President."

"I am sure sir," Mayberry replied. "I'm not at liberty to say."

"How about I just ask a few questions and you can answer 'yes or no'."

Mayberry grimaced. He was genuinely afraid to deny the President. "Sir, I have only been instructed to listen. I can't speak on anything."

"Fine!" the President said with anger. "You listen then, god dammit." His whole demeanor changed. President Reynolds hated being disobeyed. So he figured he may as well play hard ball. "I am gonna tell you this in two parts. The first part is just for you because I think you have a good head on your shoulders. The second part is for you to go tell your fucking Council." His words dripped with disgust. "Son, I want you to help stop this move shit. Plain and simple, we are not gonna let it happen anyway. It's just a matter of how much blood has to be shed to stop it. And believe me, we are willing to shed your blood. What I want you to do is, get in the ear of your Council to get them to reject this plan. We got operatives nationwide doing the same thing. We also have other operatives in your unit. If you spill the beans, your throat is cut! If you cooperate and do a good job, we can make your life real comfortable. You won't have to worry about a thing. You understand?"

Deacon Mayberry swallowed hard then wiped the developing beads of sweat from his forehead. "Yes sir, I do," he said.

"Now, I want you to tell the Bishops that I didn't give you a lot of detail because I want to talk to them. Let them know that I don't want this move to happen and that I have a plan to protect your homes. Only if they are willing to compromise. Tell that Council that I only want a peaceful solution and no more bloodshed in the Black community. Got it?"

"I got it, sir," Mayberry replied.

The President continued, "There will be eyes on you. And we will contact you whenever we feel the need. Just know that if y'all reject our plan there will be hell to pay! We got ways of putting y'all back in chains without calling it slavery. Do your best son, make us proud. Better yet, do more than your best! Your life depends on it." President Reynolds reached into a wooden box and handed Deacon Mayberry a cigar. "Now get outta here. We'll be in touch."

As Deacon Mayberry stood to leave, he could feel his legs shaking. He felt perspiration, his armpits and forehead visibly wet. His hands shook as he reached for the cigar. President Reynolds noticed and smirked, pleased with the reaction.

When Mayberry exited the Oval Office Robbie quickly asked, "You OK, Deac? You look like you seen a ghost. What did he say to you?"

"I'm fine," Mayberry said defensively. "You would be nervous too, sitting across from the President. When the Bishops know what he said to me, you will know. No time sooner!" He took out a handkerchief and mopped his brow and forehead.

"Fine!" Robbie replied, taken back a little by Mayberry's barking. "Sorry I asked!"

President Reynolds and his Secretary of Defense watched as the two men were led from the building. "I am glad they sent Mayberry," Reynolds said. "He is the weakest link in the chain."

Secretary Richards agreed. "Your plan should work well sir, one way or another."

"As long as we get that solar technology from them darkies, I don't care what happens to 'em. Either the Bishops will hand it over, or we will take it."

***

South Florida

The caravan's trek down the interstate resembled the old pictures of covered wagons and horses making their way out west to mine for gold and build a better life. This group wasn't headed west though. Their next stop: Orlando and the surrounding area. Miami had been "liberated" as everyone liked to call the process. All it meant was that citizens were free to occupy the city. Much work was left incomplete, but Denise's mandate from her parents was: "Don't do it all." Just make the towns ready for their new residents to finish.

Skeleton crew security forces remained to deter trespassers. And any late-comers seeking work were pointed in the right direction to continue their journey. Word was spreading quickly that something big was happening in Florida; and a growing number of Blacks were risking everything to be a part of it.

The cleanup crews had already been in Orlando doing prep work: cleaning roads, scouting likely housing areas, repairing electrical grids and installing solar panels. They stood waving at the caravan as the trucks pulled into town. The parade-like atmosphere ended at a makeshift stage that had been built right at the gates of the old Disney Park.

Denise got out of the third vehicle. The cooler weather did wonders for her health. Those close to Denise were grateful for the season change as well. She had given a lot of people a good scare during the summer.

Zenobia, wiping the sleepiness from her eyes, got out behind her. A hive of activity buzzed around as car and truck doors opened and closed. The people moved close to the stage where Denise and Zenobia now stood. "Gather round, y'all. Gather round." Denise said into a bullhorn. "I will make this quick, but I do need to say a little something."

She reached down and played in Zee's hair as she patiently waited for the crowd to get into earshot. "Beloved," she began, "as the dust settles behind us from a job well done, we get ready to kick it up once again, while laying the groundwork for a new beginning in America. I heard it said that we as a people changed the world once. And we are destined to do it again. Well guess what?" she said with a sly grin. The crowd absorbed her energy and began to hoot and holler.

"Yeah!"

"That's right!"

"Hallelujah!"

A revival was in the works. "I see that you feel it too," she continued. "This phase is almost done. And soon the skeleton we are building will take upon it tissue, veins, organs, skin, and oh yes, personality and soul. Florida will be the soul of a soulless nation. And if the rest of the nation doesn't want to get their soul back, then at least we will be OK because we are a family! And family takes care of their own. They protect their own. And they love their own. Look to someone beside you and say I will protect you...you will protect me...and lets all protect each other! Yes Lord! Now hug somebody!" Denise put the megaphone down and hugged her daughter. Then people stepped upon the stage to hug the two of them.

"I will protect you" was the whisper being told to each and every person. Denise stopped hugging to pick up the megaphone again. "This evening, and tonight, we rejoice. Tomorrow, we begin again on the job at hand. I love all of you! Now let's close this out like they used to do in the church back in the day. Let the congregation all sing…"

Everyone collectively sang out, "Aaaa-meeennn!"

***

Ryan and Stephen rode comfortably in the back seat of the SUV as it sped down the abandoned I-5 toward San Diego. Behind Ryan's dark sunglasses, Stephen could not tell that he had woke from his nap. He continued staring at him.

Obviously, Ryan thought, *Steve doesn't know I'm awake.* Ryan wondered what was going through Stephen's mind. He knew whatever the thoughts were, they would remain with Stephen, as Ryan had no plans of asking any questions. Ryan decided to play sleep a while longer.

He must have really fallen back asleep, because the next thing he knew, Steve was nudging him. "We're almost here, bruh."

"Ok." Ryan sat up in his seat and looked out the window. He was in the suburbs. They passed rows of houses, most of them quite run down and lacking upkeep for obvious reasons. They pulled into a cul-de-sac. It was like day and night. Every house in the cul-de-sac was in the best condition. Lawns were manicured. Paint fresh and bright. There was no doubt that every home here was occupied and probably owned by the Movement.

The vehicle made a bee-line directly into the driveway of the house at the furthest edge of the circle. "I guess we're here," Ryan said, stating the obvious. "Anything in particular I should know, Steve?"

"Well…" Steve said, then hesitated, "you will find out soon enough, so I guess it can't hurt. The man you are about to meet is a former President. The third Black President, actually."

"Theodore Jones?" Ryan asked excitedly. "You can't be serious! Man, he's been incognito ever since he left office."

"Yeah, he's been out of the public eye. But he has been a beast g us out here. He makes appearances from time to time, but you

92

know the media ain't what it was ten or twenty years ago. And we know better than to blow up his spot. It keeps the heat off.

"He's a regular dude. Serious, but regular. Be you. Don't lie. He can tell if you are lying. And just try to not be overwhelmed. I know he will be dropping some major shit on you."

"What do you mean?" Ryan asked.

"Man, we here now," Stephen said with a smile. "All we gotta do is go inside and you'll find out." Stephen laughed and opened his door. "You coming?"

They headed for the front door. "Oh yeah," Steve said, "I forgot to mention. You will have to take your shoes off. I hope your feet don't stink," he said with another laugh, trying to break the tension and ease Ryan's nerves.

A petite, older woman opened the door and welcomed them in. Ryan recognized her as the former First Lady. She wore a simple, but elegant house dress and slippers. He was already in awe, but he played it off. As Ryan removed his shoes, he looked around the immaculate space. There were colorful flowers and lush greenery in every room. The walls were painted in warm orange, yellow, and red hues. The vibe felt tropical. The windows were open allowing the Pacific breezes to blow freely throughout the home.

"Follow me, y'all," she said. "Teddy is downstairs." She led them through the dining room and into the kitchen where she opened a door and yelled down, "Teddy, the boys are here."

"Send the Bishop child down," a husky voice returned. "Steve, keep your butt up there. Don't call us, we'll call you."

Stephen smiled. "Mr. Teddy always gives me a hard time," he said. "I'll be next door or something. Y'all call me." Stephen dapped Ryan and turned to leave, while Ryan turned and headed down the stairs.

"Come on down here, Bishop," the voice urged. Ryan glanced at the old framed pictures on the wall as he went down. Most of the photos looked like they were taken in Virginia, in places he was familiar with. One particular picture caught his attention. He could have sworn he'd seen the exact same photo in one of his mother's scrapbooks.

"There ain't but ten stairs. What's taking so long?" Mr. Jones asked. Ryan broke his gaze and hustled down the last five stairs, dismissing the thought about the picture as just being a coincidence.

A short and solid man met him at the bottom step. His round, bearded face offered a warm smile. Ryan noticed that they both had a few freckles. And looking at Teddy was like looking at Marquis. *Odd*, Ryan thought. He extended his hand. "I'm Ryan Bishop. On behalf of…" Teddy's chuckle interrupted Ryan's introduction.

"I'm sorry," Teddy said, laughing fully now, "You got a whole little speech and I'm about to bust it up." He hugged the taller Ryan. "I know who you are, boy. I know your whole family. Hell, doesn't everybody? I know big head Cliff and Tiny. That's Tina, or momma, to you."

Ryan was thrown by Teddy's use of nicknames to refer to his parents. And although California was definitely new to him, this is the first time he had felt this disoriented.

This man seems to know my family intimately, he thought.

"We will get back to all that," Teddy continued. "Sit down over there. I'm making ginseng tea. Have some?"

"Sure," Ryan replied. "Thank you." Ryan took a seat on a sectional couch facing a wall full of monitors. He saw familiar sites from Los Angeles. He noticed the Golden Gate Bridge. He saw the Mexico border. "These cameras are from all over the state?" he asked.

"Yep. That's how I am able to see what's going on all over. And I can switch them to different cameras. It's also how I do conference calls with the area heads."

"Speaking of area heads," Ryan remarked, "I met Ms. Scott and she was kind of stand-offish. I asked her questions but she didn't really want to answer."

"Yeah," Teddy said, bringing over the tea. "That's my fault. I told her that I wanted to tell you about most things. I made it a bit hard for her to speak freely. I apologize for any friction."

"I want to talk about my family's plans," Ryan interjected. "But I am really curious to know how you know my folks. There is a picture on the I swear I have seen before, back home."

"Well," Teddy said with a smile, "I guess I have a bit of a story to tell."

Kansas

There was a chill in the morning air. Frost laced fields of grass and treetops. The bright morning sun made the day seem deceptively warmer than the actual temperature. Brandon was really angry about being up so early. After traveling all night, it felt like he had just fallen asleep. Yet, he and his dad now sat at breakfast in an old elementary school cafeteria in Wichita, Kansas. Along with elders from several African American communities, this meeting also included members of the Pottawatomie, Sioux, Cherokee, Peoria, Fox, and Kakapo Tribes. The time had come to share information gathered from the recon missions in Oklahoma, Missouri, Illinois, Texas, Tennessee, Northern Texas and Kansas. Brandon felt a hard elbow jab his ribcage. "Wake up boy," Marquis said, noticing Brandon dozing off. "Pay attention."

As soon as Marquis stood, the voices in the room quieted and were replaced with applause. Ever since the son of Clifford Bishop came to the area, unity between the Native American tribes and the Black towns reached an all time high. And everyone appreciated it. After raising his hands to quiet the clapping Marquis spoke. "You all almost embarrassed me with your applause." he began. "It is I who applaud you." He stated as he began clapping alone. Marquis felt much more comfortable speaking. After months spent breaking bread with the people of the Midwest, he now found himself at home in front of the crowds. In front of their leaders. He knew these people. He understood their wants and desires. And it gave him confidence that they understood, respected, and honored his mission.

"It is you all and your people who have organized and worked hard, risking danger and death to map our paths and routes. I won't talk a lot. We have to hear from several of you today. Have your pens and pencils ready to take notes. When the time comes it's most important that we are all on the same page. We will start with Brother Charles and Chief Windtalker and work our way around." As Marquis sat, he glanced over at his son. Brandon's head was down and his ears were open. He had already began feverishly taking notes. The sight made Marquis smile with pride.

Over the next few hours, tribal chiefs and community leaders detailed their findings. They used colorful stick pins to mark a map with locations of Caucasian communities. They used Black sharpies to circle and identify the perimeter in which those communities were patrolled. And they used red sharpies to mark their recommended routes to different waterways that would eventually meet with the Mississippi River. Almost all of the plans included the best times of day, or night for travel and the locations of dozens of safe houses along the way. *Over the past five months, this organization had definitely been busy*, Marquis thought. By the time they finished, the plan covered five states. Not every state in the mid-west had large Black populations so those people would have to make their way into the network. The key aspect needing work was making the connections with California and through the mountains. Trackers were already out that way but it was a tough route to map out for the safety of the common folk who would have to travel it. Before the debate on California escalated too far, Marquis spoke up. "I will talk to my brother who is out west. I have a feeling that it is best to find out if they are mapping routes. We will have to work together to make this Western, Mid-west connection."

Leaving the meeting, the aroma of grilled meats and vegetable filled the air. As a natural tendency, the men followed the smoke, and their noses. They walked across the fallen leaves and toward the smells. Men, women and children waited patiently for their leaders to emerge from the day long talks. When they appeared a cue was given to the musicians. The drummers began by setting an enchanting rhythm. The people cheered as the children danced in unison around the fire.

Brandon's eyes were wide with amazement. He marveled at the sight of the boys, and especially the girls, as they ran, played, and sang. He longed to join. But because of his status as son to the son he did not even bother to give it a second thought. Then out of nowhere, as if reading his young girls around Brandon's age left the dance and grabbed

Brandon's arms, begging him to jam. Brandon was reluctant and he looked back at his father. Utilizing a slight head nod, Marquis expressed his approval and Brandon joyfully joined the dance.

As Marquis and the other community leaders walked toward the tables prepared for them, one of the men leaned to Marquis, "Not often does a boy your son's age get to enjoy being young."

"Indeed," Marquis responded. "We're going to send him to manhood training though. That's something we didn't do back home. He wants to play a bigger role in all this. I think it will be real good for him. He better enjoy the night. Soon the sun will rise on his manhood rites and afterward he has to put away childish things…"

San Diego

"There is no way to sugarcoat this, so I will just come out and say it: Son, I am your mom's oldest brother. Your uncle," Teddy told Ryan.

The confusion was visible in Ryan's eyes and the wrinkles in his forehead. He didn't feel compelled to speak. He just wanted Teddy to keep going. He put his glass on the nearby table and sat attentively at the edge of his seat.

"I am thirteen years older than her. By the time she was going to kindergarten I was off to the Marines. And that's really when we lost touch. Sometimes, I would get her to come stay with me for a week or two in the summer when I was stationed in Georgia or Virginia. Most of the time, I was out of the country or out here. I had a falling out with your grandparents because they wanted me to get out of the military and move back to Virginia. I had been taking college courses and was about to become an officer. At the time, I was sending money home and figured that was good enough. Since they weren't seeing it my way, I made a trip home. That's when I met your daddy. He was eighteen and your mom was sixteen. She told me about him. She was already in love with him!"

"Yeah," Ryan said, "she said they met as teenagers and got married when she was nineteen."

"That's right," Teddy continued. "That was the beginning of their story. It's also when we took that picture in the stairway. It was also the end of the story as far as me and the family was concerned." Teddy stood and walked over to the monitors, concentrating on two in particular. He sat in his big leather office chair, wheeled it around toward Ryan and continued. "Your granddad and I almost got into a fistfight. Your grandmother broke it up. All because they wanted me home. Your granddad was a lot like Cliff. Actually, he became my replacement as a son. Daddy was very nervous about the coming financial downturn and he wanted to keep the family close. He also wanted my military experience to use for the family's benefit. He couldn't see his selfishness. We all have our own paths to walk. Like I said, though, Cliff became his student. His soldier. Which worked out well for Cliff. Daddy molded him into who he is today.

"After that, me and the family didn't have any contact until after my term as President. I went to momma and daddy's funerals but I stayed in the distance and laid flowers on their graves after everybody had gone. Tina saw me at momma's funeral and her and Cliff came over and gave me a hug. All we said to each other was 'I love you' and we went our separate ways.

"I actually saw Cliff and Tina in the crowd at my inauguration. I was so excited to see them but at that point I couldn't associate with them. I was able to get elected without anyone finding out about Cliff's associations. See, by that time he and your mom were heavily involved with the MMMA though they were low on the totem pole. I still had to keep my distance. I kept track of them through my Office. I really wanted to work with them, and I did what I could from the Oval. As you may know, when I left office the public was saying that I was 'too Black' for the office because of the things I was trying to get passed. I have been laying low from the public eye since then. I did get back in touch with my sister and Cliff. They know what I been up to out here. I know what they been up to across the country. They also respect my desire to stay incognito.

"I will say it's so good to see a family member," Teddy said with a warm smile. "I haven't seen any of you all in so long. Of course, I've seen photos and video clips. I been watching y'all grow up. I wanted to play with you as kids. My little niece and nephews." Teddy looked into space in a moment of reflection. "Yeah, my little niece and nephews."

Ryan was speechless. What do you say when you find out that the third Black President of the United States is your uncle? He was dumbfounded!

"I know it's a lot to swallow," Teddy said softly. "I will be back. Just going to the restroom. You need anything?"

"Some air," Ryan replied, sounding exasperated.

"Sure, you can go out that door to the left. It leads to the back yard. Take all the time you need."

Ryan got up and took a real good look at his uncle before he headed to the door. He could see his mother's features. He could also see a lot of Marquis in his uncle's face. Ryan didn't doubt that this man was kin. Still, it was not part of the conversation he was expecting to have. He turned and headed out the basement door.

Teddy eventually joined Ryan in the back yard. They stood for a while in silence, listening to the waves and birds in the distance. "You all right?" Teddy finally asked.

"Yeah," Ryan responded. "I'm fine. I am shocked, no doubt. I am sure that all of this has been harder on you and my folks than it is on me right now. I'm grown. I won't trip. It is what it is. I'm glad to know you now." Ryan gave a genuine smile and the two men embraced. "Your Presidency was dope! It would have been nice to have you around though, Mr. Uncle President," Ryan halfway joked.

"I know, I know," Teddy admitted. "Its real messed up. But we have made progress on several fronts. Just so happens that our lives are not ours. We are servants of a larger mission. Gotta do what we gotta do."

"Indeed," Ryan said in agreement.

"You ready to go back inside?" Teddy asked. "I have more news to give you and I think you should be sitting down."

"Damn, what else Uncle Teddy?" Ryan asked.

It made Teddy feel good to be referred to and accepted as uncle. "It's time to talk about the move now." He put his arm around his nephew and guided him back to the basement.

***

Renée smiled as she listened to Brandon tell stories of his travels and adventures. She smiled not because the tales were so fantastic. Her joy came from the changes she noticed in her oldest son. Brandon had grown about six inches, and his voice cracked as it struggled to find new depth. Justin ran through the kitchen, smacking Brandon in the head as he passed. "You little…" Brandon took off after him and Renée simply continued washing the turnip greens she would cook later for dinner.

"Ya'll play hard, but don't hurt each other." She yelled.

Moments later Justin dashed back into the kitchen. "Momma, momma," he squealed as he grabbed her leg.

"I'm gonna kill you!" yelled Brandon as he walked into the room, red whelps on his chest. Apparently, Justin had won phase one of the war. Renée knew that Brandon would have his revenge, but not right now. She decided to save her baby.

"Ya'll cool it for now. Justin, go and sit your butt down. Brandon, get the big pot for these greens." Brandon grimaced and shook a fist at his little brother. Justin licked out his tongue.

"Mom", Justin said, "Brandon think he is grown just because he grew some and his voice sound like a frog. I told him ain't no man here 'cept for daddy."

"He is getting there," Renée said as she watched Brandon from the corner of her eye. She caught him licking his tongue out at Justin. "Your voice is getting deep now. Soon you will have a full beard."

"Stop playing, Ma!" Brandon said as he felt his chin for any sign of new grown stubble.

Marquis had slept all day. For him dinner would be breakfast. This was in no way uncommon. Renée knew that when Marquis slept all day he had a long night ahead. Aroused by the smell of food, Marquis casually moved his way to his family, already seated at the dinner table.

His plate was already fixed and in place. "Come on, baby" Renée chided. "Bless the food already. We been waiting on you."

"Brandon, why don't you bless the food?" Marquis suggested. Thinking only of his hungry belly, Brandon quickly jumped in and said a hurried blessing even before Marquis could be seated. "No son, that ain't gonna work." Marquis said as he took his seat. He reached out to hold hands with his wife and youngest son. They then took Brandon's hand. "Now son, bless the table."

Richmond

"Why are we talking like this, brothers and sisters?" Jonathan Hall said. "We know the Bishops are alive and well. And we know that they are working hard to make things better for all of us."

Jerico Kee interrupted, "How can we be so sure, brotha?" Who's to say that they didn't just cross on into Canada to get away from all of this?"

"Don't be absurd!" Mother Nesbitt interjected. "Not only are the Bishops too good of peoples for that, but they chilens spread across the country! Now they ain't never done a thang that steered us wrong. And they ain't did a thang to have us turning our back on them now!"

"Why thank you, Mother Nesbitt. That is so good to hear." Tina entered the room with a smile. Clifford was close behind but he did not share his wife's glee. They took off their coats, sat and joined the conversation.

"I never expected to come back to such a warm welcome," he stated sarcastically.

"We apologize, brother." Deacon Mayberry quickly said. "We have just been eager to hear how the conversation with the President went."

"We haven't been to see him yet."

"You haven't?"

"Sure haven't. We can hear his double-talk anytime." Tina added. "OUR people are our priority."

"Do you think that's wise, though?" asked Mayberry. "Blowing off the most important man in America?"

"A lot of people believe my husband is the most important man in America." Tina said with pride.

"Deacon Mayberry," Cliff interrupted while trying to maintain his cool. "You told me that President Reynolds does not want the move to happen, right? And that he has a plan to protect our cities?" Mayberry nodded. "That tells me that he has no plan to protect us unless we agree not to move. It also says that if he wanted to, or if he could, he would already have given us protection. Therefore, first of all, he ain't got no damn plan. Not one that would work long term anyway. And, two, it don't matter what he has to say. All he wants to do is snoop around, see what he can find out, and maybe even take me and my wife hostage. Deeming us Homeland Security threats or something.

"To put your minds at ease, we are going back to New York in a couple of months to finalize some things with the Children of the Farm and we are going to stop in DC on the way up. Now, if you don't mind, Tina will update y'all on everything that happened with us and our children over the last five months...

CHAPTER 13

Marquis always lay in bed with Renée for at least a half hour before going out for boys' nights. As they lay in the quiet of the quaint cottage the atmosphere was mellow and relaxed. Only the crackling of embers in the fireplace could be heard over Marquis and Renée's breathing. The chaos of the mission ahead had no place in this room. It was home. However, Marquis knew he would have to bring the moment back to reality. He turned to meet Renée's. "I gotta tell you something."

"What is it?" Renée asked.

"We are taking Brandon off tonight."

"Taking him off where?"

"Manhood passage rituals. It's time."

"What do you mean time? That's their culture, not ours. He don't have to go through that."

"He is," declared Marquis. "He is, and he leaves tonight. I will be part of the training, but I will be back."

"Ya'll are about to go and change him for good aren't you? Brandon's not going to be my baby anymore," Renée said sadly.

"You are right," agreed Marquis. "He will be different. Everything is about to be different anyway. Hell, everything is different already! Living here around cornfields."

"That's not what I'm talking about Marquis."

"I know that's not what you are talking about. What do you suggest? Suppressing our young men into little boys? I wish I had something like this to go through. And it will change him…We have a few hours before we leave. I'm sorry I broke our silent groove. Can we go back to that place?" Marquis reached to squeeze his wife.

"We can not." Renée said, pushing Marquis away. "You got me all worked up telling me your taking my first born off in the bush somewhere to do who knows what? In this weather? They couldn't do this in the summer? This ain't right. And then you want to cuddle all up on me? Goodnight. You, go over there."

Dejected, Marquis sat up. "Oh, it's like that?"

"Whatever, Marquis. You been knowing about this and you just gonna spring it on me tonight? You better go on. I'm mad at you. Get out the bed, go on and get ready for work, get away from me."

Marquis picked his face up off the floor and hung his head as he left the bedroom, looking back once more at his wife. *I guess I could'a handled that one better,* He thought.

***

It was a crisp winter evening back on the northwestern side of Florida and Lamar went for a walk. It was 11pm, well past the safety-imposed curfew. Lamar only walked a short distance outside of his domicile. As he kicked at the dirt he was pulled from his thoughts by the sound of a motorcycle revving to life. "What the hell?" he muttered. The bike stopped momentarily at the guard shack then sped away. Lamar sprinted to the shack to question the guard. The young twenty-something guard stood paralyzed because he figured he must've done something wrong.

"Who was that on the bike?" Lamar barked. "And why did you let him leave?"

"Sir, it was Mr. Luster," the guard quickly answered. "He said he had an errand to run under your orders. Even had papers signed by you, sir."

Lamar's eyes narrowed and he frowned. Already he was thinking the worse. "What else did he say?"

"Just to keep my mouth shut about him going out past curfew. Said he was supposed to run the errand hours ago."

Lamar was furious. Arnold was forging documents in his name and lying. Up to now, Arnold had done his duties well, for both Denise and Lamar. An original member of the expeditionary group that came from Richmond, all the Bishops saw him as a future leader for the Movement. At this moment, though, he became real suspect.

"Give me the key for that bike," Lamar demanded, pointing to another motorcycle parked outside the guard shack. The guard jumped to it, handing Lamar the key and a helmet. Lamar got on and shuttled off. Arnold had a huge lead, so Lamar just followed the tracks. The distance was good though. He wanted to see what Mr. Arnold Luster was up to, and it would do no good to be spotted.

Lamar could see Arnold's bike in the distance, speeding ahead. He knew Arnold couldn't see him because his headlights were off. Lamar knew that they were close to the state line and that Arnold would have to get past another couple of armed guards if his plan was to leave the state. And leave, he did. Arnold showed the two guards, who seemed to appear from nowhere, his ID and orders and they let him pass. Lamar knew the dangers of leaving the state alone so he had no plans to continue past the final checkpoint. He had seen enough unauthorized moves to know that Arnold needed to be detained and interrogated. After Arnold was well out of sight, Lamar cut his bike's lights on and went looking for the two guards that stayed in the bushes off the road. When they noticed who it was they snapped to attention and removed the flashlight beams from Lamar's face.

"Mr. Hargrove, sir," they both said while staring out into space.

"At ease boys," he told them. "Come here." The men approached and Lamar spoke softly, but authoritatively. "Gentlemen, Mr. Luster's actions are unauthorized. He should not be out right now and he is not running any mission for me. I want him detained as soon as he returns. I will be sending a truck with a few more guys to assist. If he returns before they get here I want him cuffed and anything he has in his pockets confiscated. If he refuses and tries to run, I authorize you to only wound him. It is imperative that we find out what he is doing. Understood?"

"Yes sir," they answered.

And with that, Lamar broke out. Speeding back to camp to prepare for an intense interrogation. He was both furious and embarrassed that it seems his most trusted confidant might be a traitor.

Arnold paced back and forth in the windowless room, weighing his options. He could tell every bit of information he knew and avoid the torture. He could hold out, and still end up talking after suffering a great deal. He could kill himself. Or he could tell them lies. He decided to go with the lies, but quickly jump to telling the truth if they didn't believe him. Arnold wasn't too much into pain and suffering.

The room had no two-way windows or mirrors. It was bugged so that Lamar could hear everything that went on. He didn't want to see because he didn't want to get softhearted. Lamar considered Arnold a friend and the actions required to make him talk…Lamar didn't want to see. He listened as the door opened and men entered. Because he had arranged the interrogation, Lamar knew there were three men.

"Listen guys," Arnold started, "I need to see Mr. Hargrove." There was an audible thud and a smack. Then painful sounding grunts and moans, obviously Arnold's.

"Mr. Hargrove doesn't want to see you," one of the heavy handed interrogators flatly stated. "All he wants is the truth."

"Look," Arnold said, sounding desperate, "all I been doing is brokering deals with the Mexicans and other Latinos. We want them to open up grocery stores and use our shit, right?"

"Liar. Later we will cut out your tongue. But let's start with some fingers. Gus, hold him."

Lamar grimaced as he listened to the struggle and the subsequent screams.

"Please...please. I will talk," Arnold cried out, weakly. "I mean I will tell you the truth." The room went quiet an all that could be heard was Arnold's out-of-breath panting and whining. Lamar heard the door of the interrogation room open and close. Seconds later, a burly man opened the office door, wiping blood from his hands. "He is ready for you, sir."

Lamar stood, readying to face Arnold. He wanted to look Arnold in the eye as he told of his doings. When Lamar entered, he just stood in the doorway for a second staring at his former right-hand man. Already light skinned, Arnold appeared even paler. He sat crying, bleeding from his nose and lip, and holding for dear life to the stump where his right pinky used to be. He hadn't even looked up, figuring the goons were back to deliver more punishment.

Lamar steeled his remorseful emotions, let the ice water flow freely through his veins and walked over to the chair opposite Arnold. "Talk, you piece of shit," he spat coldly at Arnold. Arnold's head jerked up in surprise when he heard Lamar's voice.

"Bruh..." Arnold stammered pathetically.

Lamar cut him off. "Start with the bullshit and I'm sending your friends back in. They said you were ready to talk truth. If not, we can keep subtracting fingers. Or maybe ears since you are not hearing us."

Arnold dropped his head and let out a long sigh. "OK, the truth."

Lamar asked, "Where the hell did you go?"

"I had a meeting with some militia guys. When we were back in Richmond some government dudes threatened me. They said they would kill all my folks in Tennessee. They said that as long as I cooperated they would be safe. And after this was all over they'd set us up wherever we wanted to be and we would be safe. They showed me pictures of my family out playing and bar-b-queuing. And they showed me pictures of different properties they would give us. And the kept saying that if I didn't go along with it my family would suffer. Especially my mom and grandmother. You know I couldn't let that happen! They been using me for information for a while now."

"What were you telling them last night?" Lamar demanded. "What have you been feeding them since we got here?"

"Everything!" Arnold confessed. "They been having me meet with some militia 'generals' and tell them everything I find out. Mostly about our security and manpower. Last night I was telling them how long we would be here, how many you have in your personal security detail, how our daytime and nighttime patrols rotate. That's about it."

"About it..." Lamar muttered to no one in particular. He couldn't believe what he was hearing. "And what did they tell you in return?"

"Not shit. Not even 'thank you'. They don't even look at me. They look through me."

"Why..."

Arnold cut Lamar off, "I'll tell you why. Because what we are doing is wrong and I will not sacrifice my family for it. Trying to live a separate life is wrong. We are here with all kinds of people trying to work and live together. Not apart. And we should be figuring out solutions together! How can our relationships ever get better if we don't all sit down at the same table and talk? That's why I do it. Because I am not for segregation. Brother, it will never work!"

Staring into Arnold's eyes, Lamar knew he believed every word he had said. And this was not the time to try to dissuade him. "Anything else?" he asked somberly.

"Nah man, that's it. They don't tell me nothing. All I do is tell them."

Lamar knew the goons would push for more information and he was cool with that. He had taken all he could take. Lamar had to send out scouts to make sure the state wasn't getting set up for an ambush. He stood to leave the room.

"I'm sorry, Mr. Hargrove," Arnold sobbed. "The Bishops got it all wrong, man! I didn't want to betray you."

Lamar just stared at him. "You did, brother. You did." As he turned his back to exit the room, Lamar blinked to keep tears from falling. He'd known Arnold for a while now. Had seen pictures of his family in Tennessee. His betrayal cut deep. Unfortunately this was not the time or place to be catching feelings. He had to undo any damage that had been done.

***

Somewhere deep in the woods of the Midwest…

They must have walked for miles. It was cold outside and Brandon had twisted his ankle at least twice on the branches and surfaced roots that he couldn't see. It's hard to keep your footing when you are forced to run through the woods with a burlap sack on your head; and while tied to sixteen other guys. The group finally stopped. In the darkness their sacks were removed but they were quickly blindfolded. Just when Brandon thought the nightmare was over he realized it wasn't. The boys were forced to the ground and Brandon could see signs of light as torches were lit. He heard whispers from some of his captured comrades followed swiftly by a lashing and a demand for silence. *The Klan invaded and captured us*, Brandon thought. The idea sent his mind whirling with thoughts of a slow and painful death. As he worked to process his fear something was dropped in front of him.

"Eat" a voice said. Brandon felt around to find a sandwich and a piece of fruit in front of him. He wolfed the food down hoping to sustain the strength to fight for his life.

Not long after they had sat the boys were yanked up as violently as they were pushed down. With bags once again placed over their heads the darkness was complete and the grueling midnight march continued. Quietly Brandon began to cry into his blindfold.

For two days the boys marched. One of the days brought a cold driving rain down on them. Yet, they continued. Brandon hoped he would end up in Florida so he wouldn't have to march home. By this time they knew they were in the hands of people who cared because they bandaged wounds and kept the boys fed. Still Brandon was not comforted. Too much of the unknown lie ahead.

The boys had not been allowed to sleep and on the third night, facing exhaustion and dehydration the group stopped. The boys were untied, placed in a line side by side and stripped naked. There they stood, still blind to the world around them and freezing cold, as torches were lit. The smell of kerosene and burning wood pungent in the air.

The sacks and blindfolds that had restrained these youngsters sight for the last few days was finally removed revealing to Brandon all familiar faces, though he had never seen his friends in the nude. Before the boys could fully adjust to the light a voice bellowed, "Attention". In front of them stood two men both about six foot three. One wore traditional African garb. The other, traditional Native American garb. The men spoke in unison, as if with one voice: "The Scriptures say 'when I was a child I spoke as a child, I understood as a child, I thought as a child; but when I became a man I put away childish things.' Over the next few days, weeks, months…as long as it takes, you will put away childish things. You will learn the ways of a man and you will return home a man. You must grow physically, mentally and spiritually. Rest tonight. The journey has only begun." The men went around extinguishing the torches. The boys remained silent until the men were gone. Once alone some of the boys started to speak.

"Silence!" a voice commanded, seeming to come from all around them. "Lay and rest!"

The boys obeyed, laying their tired, naked bodies on the ground and trying to get some sleep, which was hard to do in their naked and cold condition.

When they woke Brandon, he figured he had only been sleep for maybe an hour, being that it was still dark outside. Reality was, the boys had gotten a full eight hours rest. A six foot seven giant came through waving his torch and barking for the troupe to get their backsides up and get in line. They were marched to a makeshift dining area where they had their best meal in days. Though no one was really given a chance to enjoy it. Afterward the whole crew, still naked and unwashed, was marched a quarter mile to a cave entrance. From the mouth of the entrance you could smell rotting flesh and decaying corpses. Each boy was given a torch and commanded to enter. Not everyone could keep down his recently eaten breakfast. Brandon fought his body's urge to vomit. As they descended deeper and deeper the temperature rose. There was the sound of African and Indian chants deep within. The boys had no guide. All they had was the sound of the chants that progressively got louder. Finally after descending far enough for their ears to pop, the boys reached an open area. An underwater lake glimmered with the light of torches set all about. A wicked steam rose from the water. The combination of odor, heat and scenery make it seem to Brandon like they had entered the mouth of Hell. From an opening in the side of the cave came eight men all wearing dead animal skins and each carrying another dead animal. Foxes, goats, deer, and the like.

"Death is not a disappearance," one man spoke. "It's a transition from one state of being to another. You will soon transition from boy to manhood. Your bodies will be hardened through vigorous tests and exercises. Your minds will grow through teaching. Your spirits will expand through meditation. You will be trained in traditional and non-traditional forms of agriculture, mysticism, and combat. You will wear the skins of these animals, which represent your youth dying. When we conclude, you will discard these skins and emerge as men!" The men then began skinning the animals and throwing the remains onto a fire. With the smell of burning flesh and death filling the room Brandon finally gave up his morning meal. After the skinning was completed the boys were given pants to cover their lower body and thermal shirts for their torso.

"Kneel." A voice commanded. And the boys dropped to their knees. Each was draped with the fresh and bloody skin of a dead carcass which acted not only as symbolism but it would also protect them from the cold.

"Your transformation begins. Rise, leave this place and be taught! Now! Hurry! Be gone!"

The group was forced to run all the way out of the deep cave. Upon surfacing, the day's sun shone bright. A figure stood before the boys but they could not make it out. He stood nearly seven feet tall and had a wide frame. But it was not the man who had ordered the boys into the cave.

"I am your trainer, Master Uumah. Focus your minds, ready your body, and let us begin."

***

South Florida

"Mommy, the hot water went away."

A cold shower morning. *Great*, Denise thought. It always took a while to get such luxuries regulated when setting up new grids and systems. *I think I will just wash up this morning.* Dee decided. Not wanting the thrill of a chilling downpour so early in the day.

Zenobia walked out of the bathroom still wobbly and half asleep. "Morning, mommy."

"Hey baby," Dee said as she passed her and went into the bathroom. She pulled down her panties and raised her gown before taking a seat on the toilet. As she sat there, she reviewed her day's agenda. After she wiped and flushed she stood and removed her gown, readying to bathe. She lathered her washcloth in the cool water and began cleaning her shoulders, arms, and torso. Denise slowed as the cloth contoured the underside of her right breast. Dropping the washcloth into the sink, she ran her bare hand underneath her breast. She felt a knot about half the size of a golf ball. "Oh shit," she said in a half whisper. "If it ain't one thing, it's another."

As Mother Doctor examined her breast, Denise tried to keep her mind off the possibilities. She thought about the meetings she was supposed to be attending, but was now missing. She thought about how Mother Teacher had told her Zenobia's math skills were below par. And she thought about her husband. Thinking of Lamar brought her back to reality. *Oh my god*, she thought. *If something really is wrong how do I tell Lamar? When do I tell Lamar? I told him I would let him know if something serious came up.*

"Honey, is you listening?" Denise's thoughts were interrupted by the fact that Mother Doctor had been speaking to her for the last few minutes.

"I'm sorry, Mother. What did you say?"

112

"I said you need to get checked out better than I can do. You definitely have lumps."

"Wait a minute," Dee interrupted. "Lumps?"

"Yeah baby," Mother said in her best apologetic voice. "The one you felt on the right and two small ones on the left side. I'm sorry baby." As Denise started hanging her head Mother kept talking. She wanted to find a silver lining to give Denise some hope and keep her spirits up. "I see women all the time your age with things like this that don't amount to nothing," she continued. "We got to get you some more tests, though and we don't have the right equipment here."

Choking back tears, Denise asked, "Where do I have to go?"

"Biloxi. The township there has a hospital that's well staffed."

"And what if it's cancer? Can they operate there to remove it…if it's not too late?"

Mother hesitated. She knew they couldn't. They'd have to get Denise to Cuba for a mastectomy. Mother could only give so much bad news in one day. "I'm not sure, baby. Been a long time since I been there. They can do the radiation, though. Don't think the worse girl! It may be nothing."

"Prepare for the worse," Dee whispered. "Hope for the best…"

Oklahoma

Marquis was quiet lately. Brandon had been gone for weeks and he had only peeked in on him once. Brandon looked malnutrition and was depressed. Marquis learned that it was all part of the process to teach the boys independence. In the meantime Marquis worked hard securing routes and running emergency scenarios for the Florida excursion. Everyone was working with the same mantra in mind: Prepare for the worse, hope for the best. Within months it would commence, and there would be no looking back. Almost everything was in place and today Marquis awaited a call from his brother to get an update on the California measures.

"Thanks for a great breakfast, babe." Marquis told Renée as he got up from the table.

"You ready J?" Marquis had started keeping his youngest son, Justin, closer to him. Renée believed it was to fill the void left by Brandon's departure.

"Now when Brandon gets back you can't throw Justin off to the side," she whispered to her husband. "That would break his heart."

Justin loved the newfound attention he was getting. It made him feel older and more important. He finished off his grits and ran to grab his backpack where he carried a pad and pencil (he always took notes of his father's instructions) and snacks for their long days. "I'm ready, dad! Bye, mom!" Justin said as he hurried out the door.

"Boy, you know better," Renée scolded. Justin turned back and gave his mother a kiss.

"That's better." Since Justin had been hanging with his father he felt the kiss made him seem more like a child. These days he was in a hurry to grow up.

Once outside, Marquis told Justin, "That's twice this week your mother had to call you back like that. Don't let it happen again. One day, you will be missing your mom. I wish I could give your grandmother a kiss right now."

"Yes sir," Justin responded with his head down. "Where we headed, daddy?"

"To the square. We going to the phone. I'm expecting to hear from your uncle in about an hour."

Marquis stood holding the phone, smiling ear to ear. It had been months since the brothers talked. Though they knew their tasks were of the most importance Marquis and Ryan took a moment to catch up on each other's lives, and well-being. After a few minutes of laughter and grins, the men got serious.

"I got a shocker for you Mark," Ryan started. "The Cali side has decided not to do the trip."

"What the hell?" Marquis said in total disbelief. Justin's head snapped up to look at his dad. He didn't normally hear him curse.

"They feel it would be riskier to try it than it would be to hold down Cali. And people from Arizona, New Mexico, Washington, man all these states over here! They all coming to California! We are gonna hold down two states."

Marquis had never thought of such a possibility. His head was reeling. Instead of giving in, he decided to test his brother. "You couldn't sell it!"

"Huh?" a surprised Ryan responded.

"You couldn't sell the idea of the move. Couldn't show them the benefits."

"Man, they see the benefits" Ryan snapped back. "That's why the other states are moving here. Bro, you should see their operation. They got it tight out here! Weapons out the ass! Unity, organization ... remember when we used to read about the Panthers? It's like that, times one hundred, my brother! What they got going on here is on the level of what we want to do in Florida. Yeah, I guess they sold ME."

"When you gonna tell momma and daddy?"

"Already did. They cool with it. Matter of fact, we got an uncle out here running things."

Marquis caught himself before he spoke. "Justin, go play with the boys over there." Justin reluctantly jogged away, curious about what was going on with his father. "Ryan..." he stopped to take a deep breath. "What the fuck are you talking about?"

"I know man, I know. I was the same way! His name is Teddy Jones, the ex President. And he is momma's brother. He used to live in VA back in the day. Man, he got pictures of momma and our grandparents. I was mad at first, but you know, life happens."

Marquis was at a loss. With his jaw dropped, he stood there holding the phone. Ryan kept talking, "Since you have calmed down, check this out. We will be sending some soldiers your way. Added security for the move. They will be breaking out in about three weeks."

"And what about you?" Marquis asked.

Ryan paused. Just as he did when his mother had asked the same question. "Man, you know I am staying out here," he said with a little cockiness. Mainly to hide his sadness. "We gotta have some family presence out here."

"You just said we have an uncle out there!" Marquis' anger was starting to slip out. The news about his new uncle had him upset.

"Now we can build a team!" Ryan snapped back. The two men were silent. Faced with the prospect of never seeing each other again made it hard to find words. Neither wanted to leave their last conversation as an argument.

"I understand, Ry." Marquis finally said. "It's just ... it makes sense, man. Hey, what could be better than us having a strong presence on both coasts?" He tried to sound upbeat. "It's just that, you are my little brother. On the real, you are my best friend too.

And I miss you. Plus, this uncle news got me all twisted! This is a big pill to swallow, ya know?"

"I know big bruh. And I miss you too. I know this wasn't the plan when we went our separate ways. It wasn't in the dream, right? We ain't saying goodbye. Just 'see you later'. Now you have a reason to visit out west."

"Yeah," Marquis laughed. "Like that will be easy."

"All in due time, bruh."

***

Outside the city at the New York home of KoKo Lee, snow was falling. KoKo had invited the Bishops up to discuss the exodus. Clifford decided to stay in Richmond to keep things tight. He would meet Tina in DC to hear what President Reynolds had to say. When Tina entered she was greeted warmly by KoKo and led to a spa area equipped with a masseuse, and manicurist. Apparently KoKo had planned some pampering. "You didn't have to do all this KoKo," Tina remarked.

"Girl, this is just how I do. When I heard it was gonna be the ladies, I figured we would do what women do," KoKo replied with a big smile. Obviously the nation's tough times hardly affected the heiress.

As KoKo finished her sentence a toilet flushed behind a closed door. When the door opened out came Sonia Johnson of WMC, World Media

Conglomerates. She wore a long tan robe and slippers. "Lady Bishop, good to see you!" The two women hugged lightly.

"Same here," Tina said. "I had no idea this would be a girls day out!"

"I am sure you can use it." KoKo said as she handed Tina a bundle consisting of her robe and slippers.

"You are right, I can."

Sonia asked, "Do you have time? Are you on a tight schedule?"

"No," Tina said. "I'm free until tomorrow afternoon."

"Here is the plan, ladies," KoKo announced. "We will all trade off getting manicures, pedicures, and massages. I will have lunch ready in a few hours and we can discuss business after the meal. Agreed?"

"Agreed." The other two ladies said in unison.

Clifford worked from his home study. His face was tense. He was getting a mixture of good and bad news today. Former Staff Sergeant Leon Scruggs entered. Scruggs had been in charge of running reconnaissance missions to the south, finding the best routes to take and setting up safe house stops along the way. "We have had mixed results, sir," Scruggs reported. "The militias run active patrols that make them hard to predict. We have scouts out constantly. We will pick up a pattern that we can exploit. We have pinpointed eight Black towns that will work as rest stops. The leadership of the towns agreed to keep skeleton crews around after their populations start their haul. We also have about a dozen safe houses identified. These are mostly Latino homes but at least three are White families sympathetic to out situation."

"Make sure all of these houses are clean." Cliff expressed with concern. "We don't want any of our people walking into traps."

"Absolutely, sir."

"Anything else Leon?"

Leon continued, "We are also exploring the option of using waterways. Getting as many people as possible on ships and sailing to Florida may be the safest route. That's if we can get boats to make it happen."

117

Clifford's mood brightened a bit. "That is a good idea. Definitely pursue it and keep me updated. And get the word to Denise and Marquis to do the same."

"Without a doubt, sir," Leon said with a slight grin. "We will talk later."

As Leon left and the door swung open, Cliff saw Deacon Mayberry's assistant, Robbie waiting outside. "Come on in, Robbie."

"Good afternoon brother minister." Robbie said nervously. He was always nervous around authority figures. "Here are those population figures you wanted."

"Have a seat, young brother. I'm glad to see you." Robbie sat in a big leather chair right in front of the desk. He was even more nervous than before. Robbie planned to be in and out as quickly as possible. "I have been wanting to talk to you alone, young Taswell." Clifford continued his thought as Robbie sat. "I am meeting with the President in a couple of days and you were there with Mayberry. I never got your take on how it went or what was said. I want you to tell me about that day. Honestly, I am curious about Deacon Mayberry's demeanor…well, go ahead son."

Realizing that Bishop was waiting for him to start talking, Robbie cleared his throat and began, "Sir I was real excited to be in the White House. Too excited, I guess because the deacon scolded me and told me to chill. He was real cool about being there. Like it didn't faze him. So I cooled out too. When the President came in he put me out."

"Put you out?" Cliff asked.

"Yeah," Taswell continued. "He pretty much said that he wanted to talk to Deac alone. I didn't hear the conversation. All I know is that when Deacon Mayberry came out, he looked scared." Clifford frowned at the report. "His face was pale, his armpits were sweat stained, his hair was wet. He looked like he was in shock sir! When I asked him what was wrong he kinda snapped out of it. But he wouldn't talk about the meeting. He just rushed us outta there. I figured when he called you he would be saying that we were all in big trouble."

"Wow!" Clifford exclaimed. He sat back in his chair and took a deep breath.

"Thank you, really, thanks for being so candid. What have you noticed from him lately? Any strange actions? He been sneaking off from you or anything?"

"No, sir." Robbie said quickly. "He has been cool since then. What do you think? Should we be worried about anything?"

"I don't know about worried, Robbie. Always remain vigilant anyway. Ya know?"

"Yeah, you are right. Anything else, sir?"

"One more thing, when you pass by Leon Scruggs' place, tell him to meet me at Jimmy's Restaurant for some lunch.

Obadiah Holder

CHAPTER 14

Lamar's spies had kept watch over the True Mans Militia for several weeks now, making careful notes of their observations. By day, the group traveled, meeting up with smaller like-minded groups. Every time they left a meeting, the smaller group had joined the collective. There was no evidence of their plan yet, but their numbers were growing. Tonight the scouts would make a bold move. They planned to get in closer than they had before so they could finally have something worthwhile to report. And hopefully then, they could go home. The weather was a lot colder now and they couldn't make fires to keep warm without blowing their cover.

They moved into a range that increased their sound enhancer's effectiveness. As soon as the signal was clear one of the scouts hit record on a small digital recorder. Someone who appeared to be the group's leader stood and was already speaking when the recorder kicked in. He waved his hands amidst a huge bonfire.

"...and we are supposed to be the head, not the tail," the orator spat angrily. "That's why we have gathered, my brothers, to show the inferior race that we still wield the might of the sword!" The crowd roared and celebrated. The speaker calmed them so he could finish. "I am proud that our government has assigned us the task of being first to fight. The history books will count us as heroes!" Once again the camp erupted in praise. "Rest easy for now. We have a few more groups coming from the North and the West. In less than two days' time, we march. And on the third day, may God bless us as we cleanse our holy land!" This time when the men bellowed in celebration the leader didn't stop them. He joined the revelry as they drank and danced.

The scouts had already disabled their recorder and slowly receded from the camp, being careful to cover the footprints left in the snow. Once safely away they looked at each other with fear. It shouldn't take more than a day to get back, they thought. As soon as they were in radio range they would report back.

Every man, when they came to Florida, was made aware of the possibility of attack. It looked like the date was set. And the call to action was only days away. Finally the scouts made it back to their hidden motorbikes and high-tailed it home.

Early the next morning

"Hold on baby..." Lamar moved away from the phone and Denise could hear him yelling: "This radio battery is dead! I need a new one ASAP! And a backup too! Make sure the new arrivals check in before heading to the front. We may not need 'em up there." Lamar finished barking out a few more orders before coming back to the conversation.

"Lamar!" Denise said sternly.

"Yeah, I'm back."

"What the HELL is going on?"

"Recon sent back word that a militia group or two are gonna make a run at us. We're on the ready. Can this wait baby? I need to get back into this partial cluster-fuck we got going on."

"No you don't!" The fear leapt from Denise's voice. "You need to stay outta that!"

"Not like that baby. They got me in the rear but I am still doing shit. Let me call you back."

Denise hesitated for a brief second. "OK. Love you!"

"Love you too baby," he said. Then the phone went dead.

Denise just sat there in the silence of her home. Not really thinking anything. It was all too much for her right now knowing that her husband was in the middle of a worse ordeal than her.

New York

Lying on the lounge chairs in the sun room it felt to Tina like she wasn't even in America. Moments of peace and luxury were few and far between. And for most Americans these moments were non-existent. The women were silent as they sipped mimosas and chilled. Their luxurious afternoon had turned into a luxurious and tipsy evening. Business talk was put off until this morning.

Tina's solitude was disturbed by a sick feeling in her gut. She was familiar with the feeling. She had it when Ryan was a child, the day he broke his arm. It was a feeling that she came to associate with the coming of bad news. "Umf!" she grunted.

"You ok?" KoKo asked.

"No, not really," said Tina. "I have enjoyed your hospitality. Lord knows I needed it. Why don't y'all just tell me what you've been preparing me for. I know that neither my husband nor I will like it. Let's get it over with."

Sonia and KoKo looked at each other. They wondered how Tina knew. Tina swung her legs around and sat up. "Well?"

As talkative as KoKo had been all evening, she was suddenly unable to find words. Sonia spoke up first. "I can't move my operation. My board and I don't feel confident that your husband's venture can last long term. For us to pull up roots and possibly do it again in five to ten years would not be effective for us."

"And the same goes for you KoKo?" Tina asked.

"Yes, it does."

Tina readied her response. "First, let me express my disappointment. Sonia, my husband told you that just like you have a division here in New York you could begin with a division in Florida. You could expand from there. It's ok though. Just remember, we were talking about you having a monopoly on all media outlets. From print to film. I am sure we can make adjustments.

"And KoKo, you know that the fashion trends of urban America become the fashion trends of the world. For one, since we will be making the clothes we will definitely be wearing them. Second, what we wear, everyone else wants to wear. You are missing the boat, hun. Especially since your counterparts are signing on.

"Thanks for your honesty and hospitality today. I wish you both bright and safe futures. Now, if you will excuse me..." With a smile Tina stood and headed to the dressing room. In the dressing room she cried a little. Not because KoKo and Sonia backed out. But because she could foresee the fall of the businesses that their great grandparents had worked so hard to build.

***

Florida

The day's cloudy skies had given way to a clear and starry night. The temperature had dropped a good ten degrees. The adrenaline, excitement, and fear pumping through the camp kept everyone warm. "All personnel are in place sir," Staff Sergeant Gibbs reported to Lamar. "Claymores are set around the suggested perimeter with remote detonation. And troops are on the ready to deploy in any direction they are needed." Gibbs loved strategic planning. And he loved to fight. He was in the Marine Corps and fought in wars before he woke up to certain realities and punched his Captain in the mouth. He later fought in the Black Civil War. The battles that separated the Blacks and Niggas.

"Are there ample troops staying in the rear in case the initial surge is only a decoy?" Lamar asked.

"Affirmative, sir. We have reserves at the ready as a second tier of defense. We suspect that after we bust up their planned surprise they will either retreat or scatter down the outer loop perimeter, which we have completely covered."

"Very good," Lamar assured. "How are the men? I know the majority aren't trained military."

Gibbs let loose a sly grin. "The men are salivating, sir. Most of them want to fight more than they want to prep fields or build infrastructure."

Lamar nodded his approval. "I wanted to speak to…" He wasn't able to complete his thought. A series of Claymore detonations grabbed everyone's attention.

"Hmm, two quadrants," Gibbs said, pretty much talking to himself. "Their numbers may be greater than we anticipated.

He snapped himself out of his hypnosis long enough to get Lamar situated.

"Sir, we have to get you to the secure zone now." Lamar knew better than to object.

"Corporal, take Mr. Hargrove to the secure area. Lamar, I will make sure you have updates every hour at the most."

"Make it every thirty minutes at the most," Lamar retorted.

"Absolutely, sir. Now if you excuse me, I have to go lead this ass whipping." Both men grinned and shook hands. Staff Sergeant Gibbs broke into a brisk jog heading directly toward the commotion. Lamar, wanting to join the fight, but knowing his duty, went to be protected and guarded. As if he were Clifford Bishop himself.

Everything was quiet after the Claymore detonations. Gibbs and his men expected immediate retaliation. Judging by the number of bodies scattered in the distance maybe the militia took more casualties than anticipated. Gibbs' fighting forces walked the blast zone examining the dead for evidence and looking for survivors. When they came across the barely breathing and half dead, the soldiers made them all the way dead.

"Johnson," Staff Sergeant Gibbs called out.

Shortly after, Sergeant Johnson jogged up. "What you got for me Staff Sergeant?" he asked.

"Take a squad and walk the tree-line about 1000 to 1500 yards out. Make sure no one is out there trying for a delayed ambush."

"I'm on it chief," Johnson replied. "Golf Company, second platoon, fallout!" the deep voiced sergeant bellowed. Forty guys formed a straight line facing the trees. They cautiously entered the woods. The early morning sun was just starting to break through the branches.

Staff Sergeant Gibbs had turned to give directions to some of his other leaders when a barrage of small arms fire let loose. "Hit the deck!" he yelled as the hot lead cut through the limbs and leaves. "Take evasive action now! Corporal, get on the radio and tell the CO's to proceed as planned!"

The firing from the woods stopped, shortly followed by a deep, hollow sound. WOOSH! Then again…and again. "Mortars!" The soldiers were up and running. But not before the airborne grenades could create casualties.

The sun had risen more and now the mix of smoke and the low lying fog made for an eerie scene as the militia soldiers emerged from the darkness of the woods. First, all you could see was their cold breath making small clouds in front of them After revealing themselves fully, the militia troops split up into eight and sixteen man teams and they fell into better fighting positions. Once there, they began firing. From behind them, the mortars continued their barrage accompanied by fifty-caliber machine gun fire coming from several old military HumVee's.

Lamar's fighting forces did not panic. They remained calm, and in their fighting positions, patiently awaiting attack orders. Staff Sergeant Gibbs had taken over the radio. "Flanking units," he yelled over the receiver. With all the artillery exploding around them he could barely hear himself. "Are you at the ready? It's getting hot over here. Over!"

"Foxtrot Company in place on the right flank, over."

"Good," Gibbs exclaimed. "Stay on the ready. India Company what about you?"

"Two minutes sir."

"Make it one minute, and you have go orders right now! Go right into the attack India Company. Foxtrot, T-minus forty-five seconds. Then move!" After that Gibbs started barking to any and everyone in earshot. "Three minutes gents. Three minutes!" The command echoed to all of the pinned down soldiers. And they were all locked, loaded, and ready to rock.

Hot lead and the smell of gunpowder filled the air. The direction of the gunfire changed. The flanking freedom fighters advanced their positions and were taking the fight to the militiamen. In an unsuspected turn of events the battle for these proud Aryan men was now going north and south instead of east and west. Their leaders ordered them to split up to take on the two fronts, which soon became three fronts when the primary front line of Black fighters joined in the thumping. Being pressed from three sides, the pressure quickly became overwhelming. Fortunately, the militia was left an escape route: the route in which they had come. Staff Sergeant Gibbs knew he could have surrounded the mob and completely wiped them out. He was considerate of the Bishop name. Though it wasn't Gibbs's nature, he tried to have a bit of compassion, even within the throes of battle.

"All troops," Gibbs commanded, "on my mark overrun the enemy position. I want a few prisoners! OK, charge!"

From the north, the south, and the east, more than thirteen hundred brothers with guns merged toward a central point. All the men carefully kept their firing lanes. There would be no friendly fire deaths today.

As bravely as the White soldiers had been when the battle started, they were now scattered and running in fear for their lives. It seemed that the preparation for the battle lasted longer than the actual fight. Still, having to get to such a high level of alert was good. Who knows what the future may hold?

CHAPTER 15

Denise hadn't slept since her brief talk with Lamar. She wanted to call him but she knew he would call her when he could. She felt his life force reverberating strongly within her, so she didn't fear that he had died. She also wanted to know that he still had his arms, legs, fingers and toes.

Denise rode on a yacht that had been commandeered and reconditioned for solar power. Getting to Biloxi was much safer by water versus by land. She left Zenobia behind in order to keep her days as normal as possible and to keep the little one from worrying about her mother. Plus, there had been a pretty grueling six-hour drive to get to the shoreline. Denise was all alone on this one. And it felt like she were bearing the weight of the stress all by herself. Before she could lull herself into depression her phone rang. "Hey," she said nervously.

"Hey back at cha," Lamar replied, sounding tired. "So," he continued, "let's start with you. What's up?"

Denise began after taking a deep breath, "I'm on a boat headed to Biloxi, Mississippi to have some tests run."

"OK...go on."

She let out a short sigh. "I have lumps in my breasts and I have to find out if its cancer."

"Get the hell outta here!" Lamar said in surprise. "Are you kidding me?"

"I wish I were baby. I'm for real though. I have an appointment in a couple of hours. If it is cancer, hopefully I'm not too late catching it that I can't have surgery. I may have to lose my boobs, baby."

"Better your boobs than your life, love!" Lamar felt desperation and helplessness in his gut. Especially in moments like this, he hated being so far away and not being able to be there for his wife. "When will you be back to Orlando? I want to meet you there."

"Tomorrow. Pretty early in the day I'm sure. We will be heading back before daybreak."

"I should be there by tomorrow evening."

"Wait a minute," Denise interrupted, "what's going on there? If you don't need to be leaving, then I don't want you to. I want to see you, but not at the risk of the cause."

Lamar bit his lip. His first thought was, *Damn the cause!* Yet he didn't voice his frustration. He knew Denise would understand his emotions. But he knew she didn't need to hear the negativity.

"Everything is under control here baby. We had a flare up from some militia groups around the way. We pushed them back, real hard! And we don't expect them to retaliate. Even if they did I wouldn't be in the fight. They locked me away tight!"

"Hallelujah!" Denise said under her breath.

"I heard that," laughed Lamar. Denise laughed too.

"I will see you tomorrow?"

"Tomorrow baby. I will be there. If you need to, call me after your appointment."

"Nah", she said. "Handle your biz today and I will update you in person."

"I bet you will." Lamar replied with a sly grin. Yeah, they both knew what was up.

Early the next morning

As soon as she got back into the house Denise collapsed onto her bed, as tired as could be. Between the travels to and from, the poking and prodding she had been subjected to, all she wanted to do was stretch out for a while. She knew she needed to make her rounds, check on progress or lack thereof, and get her daughter. All before Lamar showed up, whenever that would be. "I will just close my eyes for five or ten minutes," she said to herself.

***

Back in Oklahoma

The children yelled, "Yaaay! Yaaaay!" as the young men walked toward Town Square, returning from manhood training. Brandon's eyes darted about, taking in the scenery. He felt he had been gone a lifetime. He and the others tried to walk taller and be smooth. They wanted to carry an air of manliness, and above all, they wanted to be respected.

Justin saw his brother and ran to him. Brandon's demeanor made Justin stop short of hugging and wrestling with him. "Hi, Brandon," Justin said. "I'm glad you're back." He stuck his hand out for his brother to shake.

"It's good to be back," Brandon said as he awkwardly shook hands with Justin. It seemed strange for them to act so formal.

"Do you want to go up to the house or you going to your new place first?" Justin asked.

"My new place?"

"Yeah. Momma and daddy said you will have a roommate," Justin explained. "One or two of the other new men."

Brandon had mixed feelings. He liked the idea of being on his own, among his peers, and able to do as he wanted. But he also was looking forward to sleeping in his own bed and eating mom's home cooking. "Let's go to my new house first," he decided. That was the manly thing to do.

At the small house, Brandon saw his dad alone on the roof doing repairs. As cold as the weather was, Marquis still worked hard. Brandon now understood that's what it means to be a man. Doing what you have to do, not what you want to do.

He also saw what must be his new roommates coming out of the dwelling. They were looking at Brandon like "Get your dad off our roof!" Brandon got the point. They needed to do their own repairs. He nodded to say that he would take care of it.

"We all got our own rooms," they told Brandon. "We're going to see our parents. We will see you later tonight."

"Ok fellas," he said to them. They all shook hands like grown ups.

Marquis watched as he made his way to the ladder. *They really need to loosen up*, he thought to himself.

He came down from the roof and hugged Brandon against his will. Brandon glanced around to see if his roommates could see it, which they couldn't. Marquis stepped back and looked at his son and smiled. "Good to have you back son."

"It's good to be back, Mark."

Marquis wiped the smile from his face and the tone of his voice changed. "If you ever refer to my by my first name again you will feel the wrath," he scolded. "Do you understand?"

"Yes sir," Brandon answered with shame. He knew better, but had to test the waters.

"Anyway," Marquis said to continue what he was planning to say, "I am almost done replacing a few of the shingles. And there's a little bit of stuff that needs to be done inside…"

"Me and the guys will get it," Brandon said coldly, looking to reclaim his position after being put in his place by his dad.

Marquis could see by the look in Brandon's eyes that there was no sense in going back and forth with it. "Fine," he said, "y'all get it then. Let me know if…"

"I am sure we will be fine," Brandon said, cutting his father off.

"Aiight," Marquis conceded. "I will get out of your way. Let you do your thing. Will your mother be seeing you later?"

"Yes sir," Brandon said out of habit. "I will be up soon." It took a lot for Brandon to hold back his excitement. He wanted to tell his father all that he had learned. He wanted to pick his little brother up and swing him around. He wanted to run to his mother's arms and squeeze her tight. He felt constrained by manhood.

Marquis struggled too. He wanted his son to still be his son. He had never dealt with a child going to "manhood training" before so he wasn't prepared for his first-born to come home and act like they are strangers.

And the whole thing confused Justin. He thought that an alien had returned. He wanted his brother back.

"I know you are a 'man' and all now, son," Marquis said before leaving. "Try to loosen up and take it easy on your mom. It will break her heart if you have to treat her like you are treating me." After the words came out of his mouth, Marquis realized he was being harsh. "I really hope you are able to chill out a bit. We are still family, son. I will give you your space." Marquis turned to walk away with Justin holding his hand.

"Dad," Brandon said. "Thanks."

With a smile Marquis said, "You're welcome, son. We will see you later, ok?"

"Alright, pop," Brandon said, smiling back.

***

Later that evening in Florida

The door slammed. Twice. Seconds later, before Denise could sit up, in ran Zenobia.

"Mommy, guess what? I have a surprise for you".

"What is it baby?" Dee said as she looked around for a clock. Trying to regain her bearings, she finally realized that she had slept the whole day away. Zenobia jumped from the bed and ran into the hallway. Denise could hear Zee's voice in a whisper.

"Come on!" she whispered "C'mon!" Denise focused on the doorway. She at least knew what she expected to see.

"Ok, little girl. Quit pushing me" the familiar masculine voice said in a hushed tone. Then Lamar appeared in the doorway. "Hi, baby." His strong brown shoulders and arms looked even more muscular than before. His powerful broad chest rose and fell with every breath. Lamar's smile and perfect white teeth beckoned Denise from the bed and toward him for a kiss.

"Hi back to ya" Dee said as she rose and approached her husband. A long and tight embrace followed.

Zenobia smiled and kept quiet. She knew it had been a long time since her parents had seen each other. It made her happy to see them together. Zenobia decided to join in, hugging her dad at the waist. "We miss you daddy".

"Yes" Denise said, as she raised her head from Lamar's shoulder to look him in the eyes.

"Yes, we do miss you, daddy". Staring at her husband Denise knew what questions he had. "A little later baby," she said and glanced down at Zenobia.

"That's cool" Lamar said, understanding that Dee didn't want to get into the conversation with Zenobia present.

"Let me go ahead and work on dinner".

Denise said as she reluctantly drew away from Lamar.

"What you cooking, baby?" Lamar asked.

"Your favorite," Denise replied, "Food!" they both cracked up laughing.

"You got me," Lamar said with a smile. Lamar was thinking how good it was to be back with his family.

Likewise, Denise was thinking how good it felt to hug, squeeze, smell and feel her man. They both knew that Lamar would probably have to leave come morning. *It is nice to breathe each other's air, if only for a night,* Denise thought, a smile slowly spread across her face.

Fresh corn, mustard greens, fried tomatoes, sweet potatoes. It was one of the most filling and tasty all vegetable meals Lamar had eaten in a while. He had just finished his second plate and sat back in his chair.

"Ok, big L, "Denise announced. "Let's go walk it off".

"Good idea, sweetie". The three of them put on hats and coats to head out in the cold. Though only a twilight stroll it seemed more like a presidential parade. Most of the people there had never met Denise's husband. Everyone wanted to say hi, find out what was happening up

North, or ask if he was there to stay. The night chill didn't keep anyone inside. And the love they were showing kept Lamar and Denise very warm. For the walk to be as short as it was it took Denise and Lamar an hour to complete. About halfway back Lamar had picked up Zenobia who was now fast asleep in his arms. Denise held the door open for Lamar when they got to the house and he headed to Zenobia's room to put her to bed.

Not since earlier in the evening did either Lamar or Denise even think about the reason Lamar was in town. Now, in the silence of the home, it was coming back to the both of them. Lamar entered the master bedroom and saw five handmade, scented candles lit and flickering their flames. Denise wasn't there. He saw a trail of clothes. Boots. Sweater. Coat. Socks. Panties. She was across the hallway in the bathroom. The door was cracked and Lamar could see candlelight coming from inside. He could take the hint. As he heard the shower water spattering like raindrops on hot pavement he entered and started removing his clothes. Sliding back the shower curtain just enough to ease in he joined his already soapy wife.

"Let me get that". He took the washcloth from Denise and washed her back and shoulders. "I like the natty fro babe," Lamar said as he ran his fingers into her hair and massaged her scalp.

Dee turned to let the water rinse her back and in turn, she washed Lamar's chest and shoulders. "Thanks", she said. She didn't think she would be so turned on by him pulling at her roots. She had to pull away from that for a minute…He moved closer, pressing his body against hers. She wrapped her arms around Lamar and partially washed his back and butt. Rising to her tiptoes, Denise and Lamar kissed, deeply and passionately. Turning sideways in the shower, the water ran between the two of them keeping them both warm and wet.

Lamar caressed the back of Denise's neck and pulled her ear close to his lips. "Show me," he said to her softly. He took his wife's hand to pirouette her around, turning her back to him. Denise understood. She took Lamar's hands and guided them over the surface of her breasts.

135

"Right there," she pointed out as she found the lump on the topside of her right breast. She guided Lamar's hand to the underside of her left breast. "And there's two under there. They're hard to feel."

Lamar felt one of them though. His eyes filled with tears as a brief thought of losing his wife crossed his mind. He laid his head on Denise's shoulder and squeezed her tightly. Sensing her mans tension Denise broke his grip so she could turn around. "They're not cancerous baby," she revealed. "I have to keep getting checked out every six months or so."

Lamar sighed heavily. "Thank God! Why you leave me hanging all day like that? You could'a told me earlier," he lightheartedly fussed at his wife. "And when you put my hand on them it scared the hell out of me. I don't want nothing happening to my baby."

"I know you don't," Dee said. "And I am glad you came down here for me. Sorry I didn't find a second to tell you earlier." Lamar kissed her eyelids. Softly, Denise said, "I don't want you to leave tomorrow."

"You know I have to."

"Then I want to go with you."

Lamar kissed her forehead. "Our time apart is ending soon, baby." He worked to console his wife.

"Yeah, but," Lamar stopped Denise's words by kissing her lips. She closed her eyes, released her thoughts and got lost in the moment. Running her hands down Lamar's back she stopped when she had handfuls of his ample butt. Dee squeezed and pulled him closer causing Lamar to lose balance. If it wasn't for the shower walls they would've fallen right onto the floor. After taking a brief second to laugh at themselves the two once again got wrapped up in each other. As the water turned cold the lovebirds got out of the shower and headed to the bedroom. Still dripping wet, they left puddle footprints in the hallway as they went toward the room to continue their "I Miss You's".

Zenobia listened quietly and giggled to herself.

CHAPTER 16

Washington, DC

Tina and Clifford casually strolled the National Mall. The architecture was still nice to admire. They decided to walk to their meeting at the White House, in the undisturbed snow. After giving it some thought, Tina figured the government would have listening devices or lip readers, or something monitoring them. So they conversed mentally, which was a huge benefit because they had much to consider.

"No sir," a FBI agent said into his communication unit. "They aren't talking. Just walking. Yes sir, I see them laughing, but our devices aren't picking anything up and I have not seen their mouths move. Copy that. I will move in for a better signal." The six agents assigned surveillance duty were frustrated. They saw facial expressions and heard laughter. Yet, no conversation. Only the sound of the falling snowflakes.

"It's a no-go with Lee and Johnson?" Cliff asked.

"No-go baby," Tina said. *"But last night I met with Sonia's senior staff in New York. I told them exactly what we offered Sonia and they want to manage the operation."*

"Sweet," Cliff said with a smile.

"What's up on your end, luv?" Tina asked. *"I see you brought Brother Leon with you."*

"Yeah," he said with a sigh. *"It's Mayberry. He is hiding something about his talk with Reynolds. Leon has been scoping out a northern escape route in case something happens in Richmond. If it does, I want to be able to make it back to New York."*

"Makes sense," Tina agreed. *"You had any dreams about this?"*

"No, but I met with Robbie Taswell. He said that Reynolds had Mayberry scared. Even though Mayberry made it sound like everything was fine and dandy."

"Is there any particular way you plan to handle this meeting today with the President?"

"Let's just try to see through the smoke screens and read between the lines. Listen more than we talk, ya know?"

"Gotcha," Tina said out loud.

"Got what? What the hell is she talking about? What did we miss?" The agents were agitated and confused. How could they miss a full conversation held right in their faces?

"They're headed inside now. Whatever was said, we missed it. Go back and check the tapes. Maybe they were doing sign language or something."

Inside the Oval Office, the Bishops were offered beverages and snacks. Cautious of being drugged, they refused everything and waited patiently as they removed their hats and coats. President Reynolds came in with his Homeland Security head, Bill McCregg.

"I am glad you could make time for us," Reynolds said while taking his seat. He didn't offer to shake Cliff or Tina's hand. "What took so long?"

"We've been busy," Cliff replied dryly. The tone had been set. This would be a very tense affair.

"Too busy for an invitation from your President?"

"Indeed. Matter of fact, so busy that we really need to get on with it."

Reynolds and McCregg looked at each other, shocked that this man had the nerve to rush them. Just who does he think he is? "OK," Reynolds said. "Why are you and all the minorities planning to move to Florida?"

"Why do you ask?" Cliff asked in return.

President Reynolds had to catch himself. He was about to say "I am asking the questions here!" He held off, instead answering, "Anytime a huge portion of the population wants to change the demographics of my country I need to know why. Apparently there are some concerns that need to be addressed."

Cliff quickly spat back, "And you know exactly what those concerns are."

I guess my husbands plans have changed, Tina thought. *Looks like he wants to challenge old Reynolds.*

"Why are you playing Mr. President?" Cliff continued. "Acting like you don't know what has been happening to my people, our homes, and our communities."

"I know there have been a few racial incidents, but that has always been the case," Reynolds rationalized.

"A few? There was an all out attack on Northern Florida. Complete with military grade weapons! Cut the crap Reynolds," Cliff bellowed vehemently. "Why do you have us here? What do you have to offer us? Because we are fed up and you ain't said a damn thing to ease our worries or change our minds."

President Reynolds' face was beet red. He exploded from his chair. "Listen ni…" Secretary McCregg touched Reynolds' arm to keep him from finishing his sentence.

Clifford stood up too. "Finish your thought, Mr. President," he said in a mocking manner. "What were you going to say? Go ahead and call me a nigger like you want to do. It's half-way out your mouth now!" The Oval Office went silent. The two powerful men just stood, glaring at each other. The only sound heard was the snowflakes hitting the window pane.

"Well," Tina said, breaking the silence, "this has been quite pleasant. I think we should be going now. Unless, Mr. President, you do have something you want to say to us?"

President Reynolds broke from his angry stare with Cliff. "No," he said as he sat down.

"I don't think there is anything for me to say."

"Me either," Cliff shot back.

"Stop it baby," Trina said to Cliff psychically. "You have done enough. Let's get out of here."

President Reynolds sat, staring into space. As long as he had been President no one had talked to him like that. Reynolds' pride had taken a major blow. "Alright Bill," he said finally. "I did my part. I met with the bastard. Now no one can say I didn't try. Anything that happens from here on out is on his ass.

"You know what to do. Once our people know, how long will it take for them to mobilize?"

"About a month sir," Bill replied.

"OK, hold off about three months then. That will give Mayberry a final shot at changing the Bishop's minds. And it will give us a little distance from the time of this meeting and the Florida operation."

"Understood," Bill replied.

"Do it Bill. Do it…I want this fucker's head," President Reynolds said in an almost sleepy tone. His anger had morphed into a deadly focus with only one vision in his sights: Clifford Bishop's demise.

***

Deacon Mayberry sat, alone, in the conference room. The Bishops had called ahead and requested his presence. They were still twenty minutes away, so Mayberry had plenty of time to wonder what was about to happen. Cliff and Tina finally walked in, soaking wet from a very cold and stormy evening. Mayberry stood to welcome the couple back. "I am glad y'all made it back safely. It's a mess out there," he remarked. The couple said nothing, stripped out of their wet outerwear and took their seats. "How did everything go?"

"As expected," Cliff replied. "The President had good things to say about you."

"Really?" Mayberry questioned.

"Yeah, he said you're his eyes and ears down here. How often do you talk to Reynolds?"

Mayberry was surprised. It seemed that the President had thrown him under the bus. "I don't talk to him. We haven't spoken since I was up there."

"And what exactly did he tell you then?" Tina asked.

Mayberry replied, "Just what I told y'all. That he wanted to end the violence and the move. And that he looked forward to talking to you. That's all."

"That was not his recollection," Tina responded. "He talked about you saying that not all the Council wanted the move. That a lot of them wanted to exile my family." Before the deacon could respond Tina continued. "And he said that's why we should reconsider. Not because he had some grand scheme to protect us."

Their plan was working. Deacon Mayberry was cracking. He could not believe he had been betrayed in such a way. "Brother and sister," Mayberry pleaded, "I have said no such thing about you or the Council."

"You need to tell us the truth. Reynolds may be trying to push a wedge between us, and it is working. We don't trust you anymore. Will we have to isolate you?"

The deacon contemplated his next move. Should he carry on the charade and play innocent, or should he come clean, at least as a way to expose the President's lies? It was time, he decided, for the truth. "Alright, y'all. Reynolds is lying, but so am I. He wanted to use me to get the Council to change their minds and vote you out. He told me to tell you that everything was cool, but he said that the move 'will not' happen and that if you didn't cooperate there would be 'hell to pay'."

Cliff got so angry listening to the deacon admit to his lies that he got up and stormed out, slamming the door behind him.

"Is there anything else, deacon?" Tina asked.

"He said if I told you about this, my throat would be cut. He said that I am not the only one up here passing along information. I haven't told him anything!" he quickly added.

"Did he give you any names?" she asked.

"No, and nobody has ever approached me either."

"Well, brother," Tina said softly, "Cliff is on his way back and he will tell you what we expect from here on out."

"Sister, I had no intentions of betraying y'all," Mayberry said, almost pleading. "I was put in a bad spot. I just had no idea what to do." Finally, he broke down into tears.

"Deac, you betrayed us when you kept this secret. How long have you known us?"

"I am sorry, sis…"

"How long deacon?"

"Nearly forty years."

"And what have we done in forty years of service to our people to deserve this?"

Mayberry hung his head. "Nothing, sister Bishop."

"We have made it through droughts, outbreaks, attacks, you name it. Look, I am gonna shut up. I'm about to get emotional. And you be quiet too. Let's just wait for Cliff."

Cliff stuck his head into the room and called Tina outside. He wanted an update on anything else the deacon had said. They walked back in together nearly twenty minutes later and Clifford spoke. "Go home deacon. I contemplated exiling you, house arrest, or cutting out your tongue. I want to know what they are up to. You spy for us now. If and when you hear from anyone, you let us know. And understand this: you are always being watched. Do not cross us again, old friend. You better bring us something useful out of all this. Alert the Council to meet at noon tomorrow and I will see you then."

CHAPTER 17

Ryan spotted the two brown boys coming to greet them. They must be very close to his brother's town. He grabbed his utility belt with two canteens attached, nudged the driver of the cargo truck, and pointed out their liaisons. Then he radioed the other trucks to stop. Ryan stepped from the truck Stephen walked toward him.

"Where they at?" Stephen asked. Again, Ryan pointed. "Ok," Steve said before speaking into a radio. "Send two bikes up here." The bikes quickly arrived. "Two o' clock," Stephen yelled to the drivers, and they took off into the dry, dead grass.

"Steve," Ryan said, "you or The General take the lead. I'm gonna fall back. I wanna surprise my brother. He's not expecting me."

Steve smiled. "Not a problem. I think that's kinda cool. He'll be surprised as hell!"

Minutes later, the motorcycles came back with a young Latino and a young Indian boy as passengers. Stephen greeted the boys and looked back to see Ryan's expression. But Ryan had disappeared into the ranks of the soldiers. It made sense to Steve. He made room for the guides in the front vehicles and the convoy moved on. Thirty-minute drive to town.

The convoy pulled in at dusk drawing the attention of everyone. Seeing the line of military vehicles roll into the town square caused the people to stop and stare. Then, seeing all these Black faces exit the vehicles put everyone at ease. Even though they knew the troops were coming, it still made everybody feel uneasy seeing those trucks.

As the troops dismounted and the townspeople continued bringing covered dishes for their dinner, Marquis and other leaders from the town walked over to greet the officer or officers in charge.

"Who is in charge here?" Marquis inquired.

"I guess that would be me," Stephen voiced. "My name is Stephen Andrews. And you are?"

"I am Marquis Bishop."

"Mr. Bishop," Stephen said with a grin. "I should've known. You and Ryan look a lot alike."

"You met my little brother?"

"Yeah," Steve replied. "We had a real good sparring session too. He put some hands on me a little bit."

"He gets it from his big brother," Marquis said with a smile. He went on giving Stephen a run-down of the night's plans. "We have shelter set up down the road along with a place to bathe. Y'all will have to take shifts though. If you want to get started, you can. The town is preparing dinner for you now. We should have everything prepared in an hour. Hour and a half at the most."

"Sounds good," Steve replied.

"Over dinner," Marquis continued, "we can talk about plans for deployment and departure. We have people that will be traveling this way from throughout the Midwest and it would be great if we can have troops in place to meet and escort them. At least some of the way."

"That makes sense," Steve said.

As Marquis and Stephen continued, Brandon walked amongst the troops watching them stage their backpacks, rifles, and other gear.

Looking at the soldiers faces he saw them smiling and laughing with each other. He also detected seriousness, a ferocity that he longed for. Sure he had completed manhood training and it had changed him, helped him grow up. Still he knew that his journey into adulthood was not yet complete.

He studied the men's faces. Then he noticed what he thought was a familiar face. His uncle leaned against the big truck's tire staring at his nephew and smiling. "Shhh!" he signaled. "What up nephew?" He fully expected Brandon to run up and hug him. Instead, he smiled, walked up to his uncle and extended his hand.

"Good to see you, uncle," he said with an elder's reserve.

Ryan grabbed his hand and pulled him close. "Boy, get over here!" He gave Brandon a big hug and Brandon didn't resist it. He missed his uncle. He missed the whole family, so it was great to see one piece come back together.

"What'cha doing here, uncle?" Brandon inquired. "I thought you were staying in California."

"I may go back," Ryan said. "But the family needs me. We are all in this together and I couldn't be sitting on my butt in Cali just hoping that y'all are ok."

Suddenly, all the men's heads snapped into the same direction as they heard a squeal,

"Uncle!" It was Justin. He saw Brandon and Ryan talking and ran over to them.

Marquis heard his son. "Uncle?" he said.

Stephen smiled. "I guess that's your son. Go see what's up with him. I'm gonna start the guys up the road to the quarters."

Marquis walked toward the direction of his excited son to see that both his children were huddled around his younger brother. "Ryan? What the hell?"

Ryan smiled at Marquis but didn't say a word. He just walked over and hugged him. Marquis returned the embrace and slowly the look of confusion left his face. He still had questions but what mattered the most was giving and receiving love from family.

"What are you doing here, little bro?" he asked.

"I just decided I needed to be here and working with y'all," he said. "We are seeing this thing through as a family and my place isn't sitting in the sun in California while my brother, sister, and parents do the heavy lifting. I'm here under your command. Let me know what you need from me, bro."

The brothers slapped hands and hugged again. "I can dig it," Marquis said. "We can work on details later. For now, go get cleaned up. Me and you are gonna have a long night. Boys, help your uncle get his stuff to the house. He won't be staying in the barracks. He can use Brandon's room." Marquis let another huge grin come across his face.

"Oh, it is on now! The brothers are in effect! We are gonna do this! Look out world!" His enthusiasm ignited Ryan, Brandon and Justin. They were all amp'd and the excitement was contagious.

Early spring in Richmond

Time passed and life was finally normal for Deacon Mayberry. He was elated to see a new season. It was a cold mid-March day and Mayberry headed to the back door to gather some kindling from his woodpile.

Right as the deacon was about to pick up some wood he heard a voice. "Psst, deacon." Looking around he spotted an unfamiliar face. Before he could question who the person was, the man thrust a cell phone in Mayberry's direction. The phone was on and a call active. Mayberry looked up again only to see the mysterious man leaving. He went back inside and put the phone to his ear.

"Hello?" he asked.

"President Reynolds said you have had plenty of time and he wants a progress report," a raspy voice on the other end said.

"The Council is nervous, but they won't turn against the Bishops," he told the voice.

The phone was silent as the person on the other end hesitated. "You might want to be out of town before sundown." The call ended.

146

Deacon Mayberry was momentarily perplexed because he knew he was being watched and if he went to the Bishops with this information he might be killed. In minutes, he realized what had to be done. As Deacon Mayberry said, he would never betray the Bishops again.

1:30pm

The Council quietly awaited word from the scouts that were sent out hours earlier. They all expected the worse: a mob being sent to sack the town. Everyone was on high alert. The townspeople were preparing to evacuate, and the security force was preparing to destroy all sensitive information, if necessary. Leon Scruggs was gathering historical data that the Bishops wanted. His phone rang. "Yeah," he said. The voice on the other end told him of a massive gathering of troops just west of the city. Just as he hung up he got another incoming call alerting him to troop movement coming down from the north. Leon immediately went to alert the Council.

3:45pm

The townspeople gathered in the park as instructed. They held all of their belongings they could carry. No one expected to ever return to his or her houses. The crowd was deathly quiet as they listened to Tina Bishop. "Our channels to the north and west are cut off and we expect the troops to swing to the south as well. We have our exit route to the east. There, we will board vessels set to take us south by way of water. The troops are only about an hour out, but we don't expect them to come at the town until after sundown. We will start boarding buses immediately. Just so you know, our destination is North Carolina. We have people expecting us. I know it is hard to say goodbye to our lovely town but we knew this day could come and we are prepared for it. Everyone keep track of those around you and we should be fine. Now let's move in an orderly fashion to the buses."

As they headed to the buses the people softly sang, "Can't let nobody turn us around." Many cried, for this was the only home they had ever known. The Bishops had prepared them all for change. It was inevitable.

Clifford pulled Tina to the side to talk to her. "Tina, baby, I have to get to New York."

"What?" she asked. "Why?"

"Because they are coming after me. And I can't keep the collective in so much danger. Not now. Don't worry baby. It's just a diversionary tactic. I will give a speech from there alerting the world of what has happened and assuring our safety. Then I will head down to you and stay low until the exodus."

"I don't like it one bit," Tina said. "But I am obedient. I understand what you need from me. I got cha babe."

The two of them hugged and kissed and Cliff walked Tina toward the buses before taking his leave with Leon Scruggs. He knew the trip to New York would be dangerous and that made him kind of nervous. "What will be shall be," he said to himself as he rushed off with Scruggs to make final preparations.

7:45pm

The first offensive line emerged, looking puzzled by the darkness of the town. It appeared that someone was tipped off. The forces broke into strike teams of six and they secured all the streets in and out of town. At first glance, the town looked deserted. On the other side of town the troops emerged from the north taking the same precautions and securing the streets.

Clifford Bishop, Leon Scruggs and four other young warriors watched the action on monitors inside their underground bunker. They were waiting for a couple of things: one was a signal on their handheld radio. That signal would come from their reconnaissance scout in the north. The second thing they were waiting for was to see the troops let down their guard and begin looting the city.

Two short beeps on the radio let Bishop and Scruggs know that all the northern troops were in the city, and the coast was clear to exit that way. "Great," Scruggs whispered into the handset. "Activate the trip wires, and then meet us at the rendezvous point."

Finally, an hour after entering the city, someone who appeared to be in charge barked at the troops. He took off his hat and waved it in the air. The men shouted in celebration and took off running in all directions.

"Ready the charges," Scruggs demanded.

Throughout the town men scrambled into the houses and buildings to pillage anything of value they could.

"Now," Clifford said coldly. Calvin pushed a six-button code on a mobile phone setting off explosives stashed in all the towns' buildings and several of the houses. Men ran from the buildings on fire and fell dead in the street. The panicked mob was taken totally off guard. Over half of their troops killed in an empty city by a ghost force. With buildings collapsing all around them, the captains tried to order a hasty retreat. All around the city, as they ran away, the soldiers found that they were in a mine field. The trip wires had been triggered when they entered the city.

The home of the Council of Medina was now a memory. Cliff and his contingent were already making their way north to the rendezvous point. With the sound of bombs going off behind him, Cliff shed a tear for the loss of his home and his way of life. *So many years, So many memories...*

Prologue

In a well-lit Brooklyn basement, Clifford Bishop sat quietly as a crew of two men and two women prepared their sound room for an audio transmission. Cliff was prepared to keep his weekly radio address and he looked forward to airing out all the madness that the government had authorized.

"We are all set, Mr. Bishop," one of the women told him.

"Great job. Twenty minutes ahead of schedule. Let's pray before the broadcast, if y'all don't mind." The small group held hands and Clifford led them in prayer. Then, they performed a final soundproofing check, making sure no sounds could give away their location. They were all set to broadcast.

"Good evening listeners," Cliff began. "I hope you all are in good health, and good spirits. First, let me say hello and 'I love you' to my wife, who is not here with me tonight. We have had to part ways, temporarily, for the safety of our friends and family from Richmond and the surrounding area. You may or may not know, but there were attacks on our efforts in Florida as well as attempt on my life, my wife's, and the whole township in Virginia. I have spoken to my son-in-law in Florida and they are ok down there. There were a half dozen casualties, which we never want to hear. Our prayers go out to their families. And their efforts will be honored.

"We were able to get everyone out of the Richmond area before approximately three hundred militia troops stormed the town. I saw them with my own eyes, y'all. They came in from multiple directions and they were very heavily armed. What they found was a ghost town. We had to leave our homes. We had to leave the place where the Council of Medina was formed, for our own safety. Simply because we are doing for self. I find it ridiculous! And it angers me that our government would allow, and probably sanction, such actions against their own citizens. Of course, with the treatment we've dealt with for centuries, I guess deep down I don't expect anything different. Still, I hope for a change. And still today, I hope for a change. But we will not sit around waiting for them to change. We must and will change. Change our way of thinking, which we have done successfully, and change what we do, which is what we are working on now. I have talked with our President. I've given him the chance to state his case, to offer solutions to the violence we face. His response is that racial violence has always happened. He expects us to simply accept it as being the way it always has been and the way it will always be. And we say 'no'. We have overcome the stress and strife of a recession and a depression. We have overcome the devastation of a fallen economy. We have overcome other countries turning their backs on the United States. And you think we will bow down and accept new abuses from within our own country? Oh, hell no! Absolutely not!

"All we want is peace. We just want to live and raise our families. And we want to help raise this country back to an acceptable status in the world. Not in the same vein that it used to be. No, that way was poisonous and it's why America is where it is now. We want to play our part in creating a new, prosperous, peaceful America, and I know we can do it. You all know we can do it! We have done it in our communities. And we will do it for the country. I love y'all and my family, as always, thanks you for your prayers. The next time we talk, loved ones, have your bags packed. Peace, power, and love."

***

President Reynolds shut off the transmission and waited. There was a knock on the door and the CIA head entered. "Anything?" the President asked.

"Nothing, sir. We could not get a trace. There was no ambient noise that gave us a clue as to where he is. He covered his tracks well, sir."

"Damn!" Reynolds pounded his desk. "We missed our shot. And I don't know if we will get another."

Book 3

Obadiah Holder

CHAPTER 18

Word on the street was that the President wanted to talk to Cliff. Cliff found it amusing that as powerful as the office of President is, they could not find him. He knew he would contact the commander-in-chief, but why not let him sweat a bit? After a few days Cliff was ready to call.

"There is a payphone on the block," he was told. "The phone is re-routed all over the place. It can't be traced back to here." Cliff walked to the corner, closed the door on the old fashioned phone booth, and made the call.

A secretary answered, "Oval Office?"

"Clifford Bishop calling for President Reynolds."

She didn't hesitate, as if she was expecting the call. "Hold please."

It didn't take long before President Reynolds picked up the line, "Mr. Bishop."

"Mr. President."

"I know our last interaction didn't go too peacefully," Reynolds began. "I don't expect to talk you out of anything today. I just want to know why you feel y'all need to do this? Do you realize how it makes the country look on the world stage? We are already the laughing stock of the United Nations."

"I get what you are saying, Mr. Reynolds," Cliff replied. "I don't know what to tell you, sir. You are right; you won't be changing my mind. Let me explain why." President Reynolds remained silent, and Cliff took a deep breath before continuing. "Man, really, it's simple. You know the history, and based on the history, we're trying something different. The thing is," he continued, "if what we do works, it's going to benefit everyone. You do realize that, right?"

"What it looks like to me," Reynolds returned, "is like you are only trying to benefit yourself and undermine the reputation of this country with your insurrection."

"Negative," Cliff said quickly. "We are just trying to live and survive without threat of bodily harm. Black people have lived too long with a weight on our chests and a sword to our throats." Cliff said no more. His father once told him to be mindful of arguing with power hungry White people. Everyone is a threat to their power, even when no one is even thinking about them.

Silence. "Is there anything else, Mr. President?"

"If this works, what is next? What's your end-game?" the President asked.

Cliff smiled, "One step at a time, sir." He hung up the phone and exited the booth to head back to his Brooklyn abode.

***

Once the line went dead an agent entered the Oval Office. "Sir, the call originated from the Eisenhower Building. We are en route as we speak."

"There is no way he is over there," Reynolds said with a smirk. "That guy is slick."

156

The agent received an update through his earpiece. "Sir, it appears they routed the call through the Vice President's office, somehow. We are doing a reverse trace from there."

"Fine," Reynolds said in disgust. He knew they wouldn't find anything. "Let me know what you find." The agent left and President Reynolds shook his head. "...too damn slick."

As he walked back to his residence, Cliff thought about his speech. The conversation he just had with the President didn't faze him. On the anniversary of the original Million Man March, he hoped to give the speech of his life, and he felt the pressure. Halfway home, his head started hurting. Then a sharp pain stabbed through his right side. It was there, then it was gone. Cliff kept moving, deciding to take some aspirin once he got settled.

***

Indianapolis

"All we are saying is that we can't leave our family behind just because they aren't Black enough for you." This conversation about the Exodus being for African Americans had been going for the last hour or so. The meeting at the Great Ebenezer Church was supposed to be about gathering the local leaders of the area and organizing for the upcoming mobilization. Brandon and Ryan had stumbled upon a greater pain point with the people. The Black man at the mic stood beside his White wife, who balanced one of their children on her hip, and she held the hand of another.

Ryan looked across the crowd. Blue-Black to redbone. Tan to extra pale. *Love doesn't have a color*, he thought. He'd figured the issue would arrive, eventually. The one big hole he felt that his mom and dad hadn't talked about or dealt with. The one thought had been, what if Whites wanted to come? And the answer from Cliff was in the vein of Malcolm X: "You can support us, but you can't join us. We can't have Black-White unity until we first have Black unity."

That idea is shot to shit, Ryan thought. *There's no way we can keep bi-racial people out. And how could we expect anyone to leave their spouse?* Brandon and

157

Ryan also learned that there were several mixed race communities where everyone equally shared the load.

Ryan thought he needed to consult with his dad before making a decisions either way. But how long might that take? He'd lose valuable time and if these people were willing to go through adversity, struggle, and risk their lives for their family, then the more the merrier. Even if Cliff would be pissed.

"Listen," Ryan said, taking control of the conversation, "your concerns are valid. And I believe if someone asked my parents to separate permanently they wouldn't do it. I totally appreciate your input. Your comments have expanded this movement from beyond just a Black/White thing. This has to be a love movement. A love for family, love for community and love for country.

"I will say it right now: we will not restrict spouses of any race from coming along. As long as you are willing to persevere through the trip and endure the hardships of creating a new home, we will all be in this together."

"What about other family members?" a White man holding a brown baby asked. "I have brothers and my mom is still here."

"No guarantees there, my friend," Ryan replied. "I have to run this by corporate," he said with a smile. "I am acting on my own right now." He was thinking, *I hope dad doesn't veto this whole thing. He may be pissed that I OK'd anything without his permission.*

Brandon thought his uncle Ryan soothed the disgruntled crowd quite well even though he didn't think his uncle was authorized to make such promises. It is easy to settle an angry mob by simply giving them what they want. He was eager to ask about his uncle taking things into his own hands but figured he would wait to ask when they were alone.

Right now they walked with a group of about fifteen people to a spot for dinner. Not only was someone constantly vying for Ryan's attention, but Brandon was also busy entertaining questions and holding conversations. Until recently the Bishop family had only been heard. Actually, Cliff and Tina were heard.

Not too many people had met the family. The fascination the public had with seeing, meeting, conversing with, or even touching a member of the family had Brandon mesmerized. He recalled the attention he and his dad got in Oklahoma, but he was just a kid then and all the attention he got was from other kids. Now the adults were sweating him, and the children just admired him from a distance.

Ryan could tell that his nephew enjoyed the star treatment, and he reminded himself to have a talk with Brandon later about remaining humble and keeping a level head. For now, though, his mind went back to the logistics of the mission. Ryan walked backward as he spoke with a group of mechanics who had been working to get as many vehicles as possible serviceable. They confirmed having a dozen buses, and just as many SUV's in good running condition. "Good job," Ryan told the mechanics. "We need more vehicles." He honestly didn't know how many people to expect. He also didn't know what the road ahead had to offer. They could get a couple hundred miles and run into a blocked road or a downed bridge. Then everyone would be walking.

***

Dallas

Marquis lay in bed periodically glancing at his watch. 3 a.m. 3:28. 4:15. His aching stomach wouldn't let him go back to sleep. *What was it?* he thought. Something he ate, maybe? It wasn't a hangover. Marquis had kept his head clear for a while now. Maybe it was nerves. He did a good job masking any fears he had related to the Exodus. He thought he had done a good job convincing himself that it was no big deal. Just a long trip with a lot of passengers. Nevertheless, the body has a way of revealing truths that we want to hide, even from ourselves.

He quietly eased from the bed, not wanting to wake Renée. In her pregnant state she already had enough trouble sleeping. Marquis put on some jogging pants, a White t shirt, and some old, beat up Air Jordan's and slipped out of the closet-like dorm room they occupied on the Southern Methodist University campus. Twenty-four hours from now, Marquis and his family would be leaving Cotton Bowl Stadium followed by thousands.

He was surprised to see that he wasn't the only one out in the quad so early in the morning. Seeking solitude, Marquis detoured toward what looked like a more isolated route. He wanted to be alone with his thoughts. He wasn't as optimistic as he had once been. With the news that Renée was with child, the last thing he wanted to do was have her traveling.

Marquis also missed his oldest son, Brandon. Now 15, he was considered a man, and had decided to join his uncle Ryan to aid with the Exodus from further north. Indeed, these days, Marquis had a lot on his mind.

He took a back entrance into the dormitory and when he got to the room Renée and Justin weren't there. "Must have gone to breakfast," Marquis figured. He wanted to join them, but he knew someone else would intrude, demanding his time and attention. Something about rations, or logistics, or security, or any other wide range of issues that had to be considered when moving with so many people in a dangerous and hostile environment. And he just wasn't ready for all that. Instead, he laid back and listened to his stomach growl.

Marquis jumped when he heard the door close. Renée walked in and kissed her husband, not aware of how much she had startled him.

"And where were you this morning?" she asked. "I made you a plate. It's in the kitchenette."

"I needed to lay down for a minute more," Marquis said. "I wasn't ready to jump into all the drama yet."

"Oh, I'm drama? Breakfast with your family is drama?" Renée chided.

"Not like that," Marquis said.

"Hi, daddy," Justin interrupted as he burst into the room.

"Hey, son. You wash your hands?"

"Yes, sir," the energetic boy replied.

"Good." Marquis turned back to Renée. "Anyway, babe, it's not like that."

She laughed. "Relax. I know what you mean. I'm just messing with you. You are getting sensitive in your old age," she said as she threw a pair of socks at her man.

"Whatever," Marquis said, finally cracking a smile.

"Go eat," Renée demanded. "Then you know you gotta get downstairs. Plus, I need you out of here so I can go back to bed."

"You are full of jokes this morning, huh?"

"I ain't joking," Renée replied. "And take your son with you. I need one or two more hours. Thank you! Goodbye!" she said as she forced Marquis from the bed.

"Aiight, woman, dang!" Marquis exclaimed.

"And don't forget Lil' B. Love you!"

"Of course you do, O' wife of mine…love you too."

Every detail had been hashed and rehashed to the point where Marquis could no longer focus. He was more than ready for this journey to be over and it hadn't even began.

"Brother Bishop?" Amy Lewis said for the third time, pulling Marquis from his daydream.

"I'm sorry, Amy," he said. "What was the question?"

"About the paramedic units and their placement among the ranks," she reminded.

"Haven't we discussed that a few times?" Marquis asked, sounding slightly irritated. "Matter of fact, haven't we discussed pretty much everything a few times?"

The room fell silent, seeing Marquis' agitation. "Look, I think we are over-planning here. We have a plan and it's a good one. Let's stick with it and quit looking for stuff to change. We will have steamboats, sailboats, and paddle boats, if necessary, meeting us at the Red River once we reach Shreveport, correct?" Everyone nodded. "Are we sure the boats will be there?"

"As far as we can say for now, yes," said one of the advisors. "But…"

"Good," Marquis said, cutting him off. "We are on the Red River to the Mississippi. The Mississippi to the Gulf. And the Gulf to Florida. Then we trek up from there. Am I missing anything? Any of the BASICS, that is."

"No, sir," they replied.

"Then that's that," Marquis said, as he stood. "We can't plan for absolutely every contingency. We have to expect the unexpected. We are prepared. Y'all have done a fine job at that. You gotta have faith too. Faith that the Creator will see us through. And that he won't put more on us than we can handle.

"At this point we need to take care of the next few days. I want to make sure the Cotton Bowl is secure, as well as the surrounding blocks. No IED's, snipers, nothing like that allowed to threaten us. Where do we stand on perimeter security for the stadium?"

With that, the meeting continued. Not with constant changes to existing plans, but with updates on security measures, updates on scheduled events, and an update on departure times and procedures. Marquis was much more content with this direction although he really longed to be back in Richmond preparing to go to his parent's house for Sunday dinner.

Renée stared at Marquis as he ate dinner. He hadn't said much all day, and hadn't shown Justin much attention. She knew he had a lot of pressure on him with everything going on, but, tonight he was more withdrawn than ever. Earlier in the day some of the organizing committee had contacted Renée and expressed a concern with what they called Marquis' "I don't really care" attitude. She assured them of his full engagement and attributed his attitude and agitation up to exhaustion and anxiety. She assured them that there was nothing to worry about. In reality, she wasn't completely sure where his mind was.

Marquis looked up from his plate and caught Renée's stare. "What up?" he asked.

"That's what I am wondering," she responded. "You seem kind'a out of it lately. What's wrong?"

"Other than a massive exodus leading thousands of Black folk I don't know across the country with my pregnant wife and child? With the constant fear and threat of attack by a militia or Klan group? Nothing is wrong," he replied sarcastically.

Renée didn't know what to say. She figured she would give Marquis room to vent if that's what he needed. "Speak what's on your heart, baby," she replied.

Marquis let out a long sigh and stared down at his plate. "I'm in over my head," he said without looking up. "This ain't my cup of tea. Not my bag. This is dad's thing. Denise, even. Not me. This whole leader of men thing? Babe, I just want to love my wife, and raise my kids. Being the oldest son of Clifford Bishop kind of dictates your mission in life, ya know? Your mission in life is his mission in life.

"I'm not as nonchalant as they may think. I know that's the perception. I'm just tired, already, and we haven't even left." Marquis looked Renée in the eye, the stress and fatigue written all over his face. She searched for the right words.

"Déjà vu," she said.

"What?"

"Déjà vu," she repeated. "You sound like my mom right now."

"Oh, so you clowning me?" Marquis asked, defensively.

"No," Renée retorted. "What was my dad's occupation?"

"Preacher," Marquis said cautiously, not sure where his wife was going.

"Which made my mom what?" she continued, rhetorically. "Exactly! A preacher's wife. She would talk about the pressure on her to act like this, talk like that, wear certain clothes. Not only did she feel pressure from the outside, but my daddy, rest his soul, used to tell her she needed to carry herself a particular way to properly represent the church. What he meant was to properly represent him! She hated it and they fussed and fought. She did everything she could to be a good wife. She often told daddy that he was called to preach, she wasn't. At the same time, she continued to represent herself and her husband, and our family, very well.

"When I got a little older, me and mom were having lunch and I brought up those old days. You know what she said to me? She said she decided that she was going to keep up the look, speak at the functions, and do everything she was asked, for God and for the faith of the flock. Because she too was a shepherd. Not a sheep. And she was ordained to lead. Not as a pastor, but simply as a humble vessel.

"You, too, are a vessel, baby, filled with leadership spirit. And when you lead these people you also lead your family. Justin watches your every move. And Brandon is out there right now, trying to be like you! Not like his granddaddy."

"And what about my wife?" Marquis asked.

"Your wife," Renée said, smiling, "will follow you to the ends of the earth. And she will help carry the load. You ain't alone! I walk beside you, not behind you."

The lukewarm shower pelted Marquis as he thought about his wife's words. She made a good point. The kids were watching him. He vowed, right there in the shower, to perk up, be more energetic, and get this move done. Once they got to Florida he could settle back into just being a loving and providing husband and father.

When he walked back into the room he saw Justin knocked out on his cot. Renée lay on the bed with her swollen feet elevated and nightgown pulled up, exposing her pregnant belly. She held up a jar of shea butter for her husband to see, and smiled.

"Of course I will," Marquis replied with a grin.

He sat beside Renée and she handed him the already opened jar. Spooning out a good amount, Marquis rubbed the cream into his palms then gently placed his hands on her belly. He moved his hands in a circular, massaging motion. He stopped when he saw a tiny footprint. Renée looked down and saw it too.

"She likes it," Renée said.

"She?"

"Why not?" she asked. "You have your boys. No harm in wishing for a girl now."

"True," Marquis conceded. He went back to massaging in the shea butter. "I hope you are a little girl too," he said, now talking directly to Renée's stomach. "Daddy is gonna love you regardless. Mommy and your big brothers too." He saw the footprint again and he leaned in to kiss it. "I love you already, little baby."

Renée stroked her husband's short locks. He looked up at her. "Thank you baby," she said. "Now come up here with me. Hold me."

Marquis turned off the lights, then he crawled into bed with his wife. Holding her gently, he, wife, and baby all fell asleep together.

***

The doctor frowned as he deflated the cuff around Clifford's arm. "Mr. Bishop, your blood pressure is dangerously high," he said. "And I figure it is all stress related. Your cholesterol and diet are fine. Any chance of you slowing down anytime soon?" Cliff stared at the doctor. "That's what I thought. Then, I am going to prescribe…"

"Stop right there," Cliff demanded. "I am not taking any drugs."

"You are going to keep these high stress levels and you aren't going to do a damn thing to keep your heart from exploding?" The doctor was perplexed. "Mr. Bishop, when you decide that you don't want medication, do you think about your wife? Your kids? The cause? It doesn't sound like it. It sounds like you are being selfish."

"Doc, I give of myself every day of my life!"

"And that is the glorious choice you have made! I admire you. I also want you to see this thing through to the end and keep on living afterward!" The doctor normally didn't yell at his patients and he took a deep, calming breath before he continued. "Brother," he said passionately, "I am sure that after all this is over you will be able to chill out a little," he said, knowing it was a lie. "As of today, you are high risk for a heart attack or stroke. You are the leader of a movement, and we need you. Just take this script, bruh. You can fill it down the hall. It won't make you jumpy or drowsy or cranky. None of that. Think about the cause. Think about your family."

Cliff hung his head, almost in defeat. "OK, doc," he resigned.

"We all appreciate it, Cliff, believe me. And remember, you can get them down the hall. Now, how much longer will you be in the area?"

"A couple more weeks."

"Fine. Come back by before you go, maybe in a week, and I will give you one final checkup. Deal?" the doctor stuck out his hand for a shake. Cliff responded to the shake.

"I'll see you in a week and a half, doc."

Cliff walked on the abandoned street, lost in thought, which was often the case. Suddenly a young girl came running around the corner.

"Mr. Bishop," she half whispered, as she caught her breath, "your wife is on the phone."

"Is everything ok?" Cliff asked.

"Yes, sir, as far as I know."

"Child, don't come running up like that. I thought something was wrong."

She apologized and led Cliff to the phone. "I'm sorry, again. I didn't mean to upset you."

"That is ok," Cliff said with a smile. "It's fine." He dismissed her and lifted the phone. "Hey, baby!"

"Hey, you," Tina replied happily. "How you be?"

"I be aiight," Cliff said playfully. "How you be?"

"I asked you first, and aiight ain't enough of an answer," Tina said. "Maybe I should rephrase the question: how does the doctor say you are?"

"He says I am stressed, which is not a news flash." Cliff tried to keep the tone light and playful.

"Boy, don't play with me," Tina said sternly.

Cliff felt like one of the children. "Ok, he said my pressure is high. He knows it isn't my diet so he figures it's stress. He wants me to take medicine for it because he knows I can't slow down right now. And yes, I am going to take the pills. Don't start tripping about that." Cliff stopped talking but Tina remained quiet, waiting to see if he had any more to say. "No, there is nothing else," Cliff finally said after he realized his wife's tactic.

"You sure?" she asked.

"Yup! That's it."

"Can't you put someone else in charge so you can chill some?" she asked with concern.

"I already have," Cliff explained. "Nobody else can give my speech for me. They can't talk to the President for me. They can't worry about my family for me. "And speaking of stressed, what about you?" Cliff said, turning the attention to his wife. "I know you are stressed too. What are you doing about it?"

"I'm going to an herbalist/natural healer. He is the best on Guhula and he has me doing meditation exercises, drinking herbal teas, and other naturally de-stressing activities. It's cool because down here I am really out of the loop, anyway. I am trying to get a regular regiment that I can keep up once I get with Denise in Florida. I know my vacation will be ending soon."

"And how is everyone else doing?"

"They're fine now, for the most part. We all have our times when we miss home, even though we knew we were going to leave anyway. No one wanted to leave the way we did. Also, we miss you," Tina added. "We've never been away from each other this long."

"I know, and I miss you too," Cliff said. "Think, when we see each other again, it will be a whole different lifestyle. We will be setting up government, business, life for a whole state; not just a community."

"No, dear," Tina said emotionally. "I am not talking about the big picture right now. I am feeling selfish, and I miss YOU. I know that all this is bigger than me and you, and I don't want to stress you out. Just know that I miss my husband, my man."

A tear ran down Cliff's cheek. His high blood pressure and headaches made him want Tina by his side even more. "I miss you too baby. I really do."

CHAPTER 19

The Brooklyn arena was not full to capacity, but the bottom bowl was. Every borough represented, plus New York state, New Jersey, Delaware, Massachusetts and Connecticut. The Bishop's plan was no longer a secret. Most people were just waiting to hear the official word, and the time was now. All over the nation, wherever the Bishops were speaking, people brought their families and their belongings, fully expecting to begin a journey to a new life.

***

The Bishops scanned their audiences and connected with several faces. Mixed emotions filled their eyes, from anticipation, to fear, to fatigue. Many had taken considerable journeys to get to the gatherings and they already knew the stress the travels ahead of them would bring.

The family spoke individually, yet collectively, with one voice and one message. "This country belongs to us just as much as it belongs to anyone else," they began. "And not only because we have been here since 1619. And not because our ancestors bled and died as slaves. Our people have been fighting for freedom since the American Revolution! Peter Salem, at the Battle of Bunker Hill; James Armistead worked as a double agent. Oliver Cromwell and Prince Whiffle served with George Washington! We have always heard about Paul Revere's ride, you know, 'The British are coming'? There was a brotha, Robert Chessel, riding in the other direction doing the same thing! We fought and we have just as much right to live in peace.

"When the early Americans felt like they were getting a raw deal from the British, they declared their independence. And that is what we are here to do today, in our own way. We declare our independence as a people, as hue-mans; men and women of color.

"Being that we have fought and died for THIS land, we don't seek to leave, no. This is our home. We ain't leaving. We want to help reinvent America and in order to do this, we must survive. Divided across this country, we're picked off one by one. United, we will stand tall, as evidenced by the strength of our great communities. The time is now that we draw those communities together to re-create cities and to form a strong and productive state!"

Those gathered in the different areas where the Bishops spoke, shouted and yelled their approval. Black families congregating by their radios and computers voiced their "big ups".

"Speak, brotha!"

"I know that's right!"

The President scowled and his cabinet, they were afraid to take a breath. Whites, Latinos, Asians, and "others" scattered throughout the states didn't know what to think.

"Be ready, my children. Be prayed up and be ready. The time for tests is over. This is not a test. I repeat, this is not a test. This is the exam, folks." There was a pause, and the arena was silent. Cliff felt a slight tug in his chest, then in his arm. He was sure that the crowd didn't notice his discomfort. "And my people," he concluded, "I will see you on the other side."

As the audience shouted, sang, and praised, Cliff made his way from the stage. He motioned for an aide to come over. "Yes sir?"

"Brotha, I want you to get my kids on the phone and I want all of our leaders here gathered as soon as you can set up the conference call," he instructed.

The aide could see that Cliff was in pain. "Brother, are you ok?" he asked.

"No I'm not," Cliff admitted. "Just do what I asked."

The aide followed his orders, but on his way out he asked the doctor to examine Cliff.

When the doctor reached Cliff, he had made it into the back offices of the arena. "Doc, glad to see you," he said. Dr. Jones immediately knew things must be bad. "I just have one piece of business I need to attend to," Cliff continued, hoping to keep the good doctor from talking. Jones took the que and remained silent.

As Cliff turned away from Dr. Jones, a lightning bolt of pain flashed in his head. "Everyone, give me and doc a minute," Cliff said, with noticeably slurred speech.

Everyone looked at Dr. Jones. It was obvious that something was wrong with Brother Bishop. "Is it ok if Marshelle stay?" Dr. Jones asked. Cliff nodded, never raising his gaze from the floor.

Marshelle slowly guided Cliff to a seat on an old couch. Dr. Jones closed the door behind the last person and hustled over to Cliff.

He got on one knee in front of the now sitting Bishop. "Cliff, look at me. Cliff? Mr. Bishop, look up here. Look at me Cliff," the doctor said repeatedly. Cliff was stuck in a distant stare at the ground.

After the fourth time the doctor called Cliff's name, his eye twitched. Then he actually started hearing Dr. Jones' words. Slowly, his eyes focused and he raised his head to meet Jones' wide eyed gaze. "Hey, doc," he said with hardly any slur.

"Marshelle," doc called, "hand me that water and my bag." He retrieved a couple of aspirin and gave them to Cliff. He then proceeded with checking his vitals. It didn't look good.

Just then, Jake Talbot walked in. "Doc, what's wrong?"

"I just got a little dizzy," Cliff interrupted. "What's up Jake?"

He is good at that, the doctor thought. *Over talking someone and moving right into the next subject...*

Jake looked at Cliff, a bit surprised, then he continued. "The organizers are present and gathered. And we have your kids, son in law, and wife on speaker phone, along with the other national organizers."

"Great," Cliff said as he started to get up from his seat, but Dr. Jones objected.

"Oh, hell no. Cliff, you just had a stroke," Doc whispered into Cliff's ear. "You are not in shape for meetings and conference calls right now."

"Hold up," Jake said, "a stroke?" He had overheard even though Dr. Jones tried to keep it private.

Doc looked at Cliff, and Cliff nodded his ok. "He is showing several signs of a stroke, yes," he said. "It just happened ten minutes ago and I can only do so much testing here. We have to get him to the infirmary."

"You will do no such thing," Cliff said as he rose from his chair. His voice sounded as articulate and strong as it did before. "Doc, give me thirty minutes and I am all yours. I told you I had one other thing to do."

"We don't know what thirty minutes will do to you! We..."

"I am done talking about it doc," Cliff said calmly, but sternly. "You can stay nearby, but out of the way.

"Jake, where is everyone?"

"Right down the hall."

"Lead the way, my man," Cliff said in an excited voice, as if nothing was wrong. "And not a word about what was talked about in here, understand? You weren't supposed to hear all that anyway."

The room was buzzing just moments before Clifford walked in. It went dead silent once he entered. The noisy silence made Cliff laugh out loud. "Thanks for the respect and being quiet so y'all can hear me," he said. "But, damn!" Everyone laughed. They all had felt the elevated stress created by the silence and it was a relief when Cliff cut through the tension.

"First of all," Cliff began, "where is my wife?"

"I am here, baby," her voice resonated from the mobile phone that was acting as the speaker phone.

"Aww," said some people in the room, in a teasing manner.

"Whatever," Cliff smirked. "Denise? Ryan? Marquis? Lamar?"

"Here, Daddy," each of them said.

"Hi, kids," Cliff said. He was getting a bit choked up. Cliff missed his children. "I hope you all can excuse me. It has been a while since I spoke to my kids and even longer since I have seen them."

He felt pain all over his body, Cliff sat in his reserved seat at the head of the table. "Any more of a reunion will have to wait though," he said as he started talking about the business at hand. "I know some of you are about to get on the move in the next day or so. And the rest of you aren't going to be far behind. I need you all to be able to show restraint for the sake of the Movement."

"What do you mean, Pop?" Ryan asked.

"What I mean is that I want our military elements to stand down," Cliff explained. There was a bit of rumbling in the room. A quiet discomfort filled the air. "I have been praying about this," Cliff continued. "And the Creator wants us to trust in his protection. Not only is this movement about making a new life, but it is also a test of our faith and our resolve." Cliff paused for a second to let that sink in before he continued. "Another part of it is that I don't want a Civil War started out there. We don't need to give the U.S. Military more reason to take aim at us."

"That is liable to happen anyway," someone on the conference call commented.

"And God," Cliff responded, "will protect us. That is, if we can refrain from taking matters into our own hands."

"With all due respect," someone else on the phone lines said, "what was the sense in building up our arsenal if it wasn't to protect us on this journey? And what do we do when we encounter hostiles? Please note, I did not say 'If', I said 'WHEN'".

"Holster your weapons against people," Cliff declared. "In the event that you are attacked by wild animals, protect yourselves. If you need to hunt, then hunt." Cliff paused, then said, "Woe be onto those that get into gunfights with your attackers! The grace and mercy of the Creator is our protection. Do not render that protection null and void because of a lack of faith. We have too many lives at stake." Cliff paused again. He knew he hadn't answered the question directly so he figured someone may follow up with a "but". No one did, though.

He took a deep breath, preparing his next words of explanation. A sharp pain in his chest completely overcame him. If he would've been standing he most definitely wouldn't have been after the pain. *Time to cut this short,* he thought. "This is the last time most of us will speak until after this is all over. I just want you all to know how proud, excited, scared, and nervous I am. That is right. I can admit to being nervous. I think it is more of a nervous energy for us all to get where we are going. I know this will be hard, and not everyone will make it," he glanced over at the doctor. "I ask that you all remain faithful and prayerful. That is all."

Too weak and in pained stand, Cliff requested everyone clear the room. Once the room was empty, Cliff relaxed his fake smile, clutched his chest, and went limp in his seat. "Doc," he cried out, weakly.

CHAPTER 20

Just across the Arkansas border on the west side of the Mississippi, another meeting was beginning. This conclave had convened from Alabama, Mississippi, Tennessee and some from Georgia. The headcount was minimal, especially compared to the Bishop's meeting. Those in attendance represented much larger numbers and they would take their decisions back to their respective communities. They met in the dining hall of the First Community Church of Christ. The folding chairs were lined up like pews. The Bishop's broadcast had been a few days prior and everyone in attendance had either heard it live, or heard about it. Which is what brought about this emergency meeting now.

"Y'all, we need to decide as a group how we feel about this, and what, if anything, we are gonna do about it." Jebadiah was a tall, slim White man in his early forties. His family maintained a farm and remained fairly self sufficient. Though life was seeming to get tougher day by day. He didn't have any personal experiences that made him racist. His racism came from his father and grandfather's teaching. They taught that Blacks were lazy, violent hustlers that you shouldn't trust.

Jeb didn't consider himself a leader in the least, but he was one of the deacons of the church. The lead deacon stuttered, so he didn't want to speak. The pastor felt that it wasn't his place to lead this type of meeting. That left Jeb, calmly and confidently standing before the condensed, all male congregation.

"Personally," Grady Smith began, "I don't care what they do. Long as I don't see 'em. If I do see anybody cutting cross my property, they gonna eat buckshot!"

"I for one do care what they do," it was Edward McGrath. He lived in a neighboring city. Edward really wanted to help get things back together, and he was jealous and curious about the technology in the African American community. Edward stood and walked toward the front of the room as he spoke.

"Thing is," he continued, "They got a lot of stuff we don't have." He tried to keep his language simple so everyone would understand. "Like how they use solar power, how they power cars, and who knows what else. Now, I been trying to come up with some of this stuff myself, but it will be a whole lot easier if we can just get it from them. Hell, they should be sharing with us anyways!"

"Ingrates," someone mumbled from the rear of the room.

"Let them go?" Edward asked the hypothetical question to no one in particular. "I could care less. I say we send their asses to wherever it is they want to go, empty handed! No cars, no guns, no seeds for crops, nothing. And if they don't give it, we take it. Even if it means taking their meaningless lives. Whatdoyasay?" Edward didn't get the immediate jovial explosion he expected. Instead, most of the room began to talk amongst themselves. Not everyone lived in areas that gave them the numbers to compete in armed conflict.

Sensing the hesitation to his emotional plea, Edward spoke again. "My friends, our forefathers brought the Africans here to serve. The Bible mandates that they serve. And we once built a great nation with the power of our minds and their muscle. Do you really think they have the brains to bring America back to greatness?" He didn't wait for an answer. "Sure, they came up with a couple of useful gadgets. They have done that in the past. Those gadgets were never maximized until they were in our hands. The good book says not to cast pearls before swine, and…"

"Not all of us have an Army to send out and fight," someone interrupted.

"It's just not worth the risks," another voice said.

"The hell it ain't!" an angry voice rang out. The room was divided.

Edward was waiting for someone to champion his cause so he could jump back in. "Exactly! We have nothing to lose, and everything to gain."

"Look," Jeb interrupted, trying to get a handle on the meeting, "we are going around in circles. Seems like we are arguing over two options: either don't bother the darkies, or bust their F'ing heads." He paused, then he went to the corner and wheeled out an old dry erase board. He wrote down the two options he had just mentioned.

"Now let us think and see if there are any other options. Thank you, brother Edward," he said, encouraging Edward to take a seat even though he wasn't really ready.

Jeb continued, "from what we heard it seems this move could start any day. Hell, it may have started already. We need to do some deciding tonight so we can be spreading the news tomorrow. Agreed?"

CHAPTER 21

Brandon and Ryan watched from their hotel window as the masses gathered at the old arena. It was 4AM. By five, the number of people who had entered the arena and the number of people still outside waiting to get in, was staggering. *Thousands of lives in my hands*, Ryan thought. *I know not everyone will make it, but still, this could go real good....or real bad.*

Brandon was counting the buses as they lined up. "I got 30 buses here, Unc."

"That's what they said they could get us," Ryan replied.

Brandon was doing the math. By his calculations, the buses should accommodate around sixteen-hundred. Though at the rate people were piling into the arena there were liable to be sixteen-thousand or more traveling. Of course, there were still the SUV's and people with their personal vehicles, but reality was, most people would be walking. And even with all the vehicles, this caravan would move at a snail's pace.

"Alright, nephew," he said, "get the rest of your stuff together and meet me in the lobby. Time to get this show on the road!"

***

The convoy lined up on South Pennsylvania Street. Brandon was at the beginning and Ryan in the middle. "This is exodus one," Ryan said into the radio. "Report. It's time to get this thing moving." The late morning sun was getting hotter and the temperature rising.

"Exodus six, all ready."

"Exodus three, all ready."

And so it went until everyone signaled their readiness to move out.

"Exodus two," Ryan signaled to Brandon, "let's move!"

"Move 'em!" Brandon yelled excitedly as he took the first steps in the long journey south.

Leaving the arena they headed down South Pennsylvania and turned on East South Street. It was like a parade. People of all backgrounds lined the street to watch and send off the brave travelers. Though, unlike a parade, there wasn't a lot of cheering. As they got outside of the city, the mostly White onlookers turned up their noses in disgust when the caravan passed them by.

"Uppity niggers."

"Good riddance."

"They ain't gonna make it."

The group marched on, paying little attention to those on the sidelines. As the first part of the group passed South College Avenue and approached the entrance to Interstate 65 South, the end of the group was still on South Pennsylvania St. The onlookers were in awe of the sheer numbers, though they wouldn't admit it. Obviously the travelers were not just Indianapolis residents.

"Where the hell did all these niggers come from?" one older White woman asked her husband.

"Don't know," he said, "and I don't really care. I wish them the best luck though. This country needs something to get it back on track. Positive, or negative, I hope this is it."

***

Marquis opened his eyes, rolled over and looked at the ceiling. "A journey of a thousand miles starts with the first step," he said aloud, but soft enough as to not awaken anyone. "We take that first step today. Lord, protect us."

He got out of bed, dropped to the floor, and knocked out fifty push-ups. His energy was good today, and he was ready! Everything his family owned, everything they were taking with them was packed in three old military "C" bags sitting by the door. He would come back for those in a few. For now, Marquis gathered his wife and son and went together downstairs for what would probably be their last good breakfast for a while.

They entered the cafeteria to a startling ovation. It made Marquis laugh. It made Renée nervous. Marquis held up his hand to cease the clapping. He repeated the line he said to himself that morning. "People, a journey of a thousand miles starts with the first step. We take those first steps today. And we have a long way to go. Thanks for the love, but we haven't done anything yet. We are doing this as a collective! I should be applauding YOU." He started clapping and Renée followed. Then the whole room was clapping again. Justin tugged at his dad's shirt, ready to eat.

Overnight the campus had filled with people camping out and prepared to begin their journey. Black and White, young and old faces sat patiently waiting. When Marquis and family emerged from the dormitory doors the people outside stood. It looked like a tidal wave as they all got to their feet. *I guess the Exodus starts now,* Marquis thought. He smiled and waved at the people. They shouted, hooped and hollered back.

"Let's do this!" "We are with you!" "Halleluiah!" "Yes, Lord!"

Renée pulled Marquis close to whisper in his ear. "I am so scared," she admitted.

"What happened to all the bravery you were showing me the other night?" Marquis whispered back.

"That was just some bullshit to gas you up," she said with a grin.

"Yeah, right." Marquis grabbed Renée's hand and held it tightly. "I'm your rock," he said, "and you are my inspiration. Feed off my strength and we can be brave and strong together. OK?"

"OK baby," she said, smiling up at her hubby.

They headed down the stairs to a waiting bus. Marquis led his wife and son onto the bus. "My march starts here, baby, with the people walking to the stadium. I'll see you there." Renée wanted to object, but held her tongue.

When the crowd realized Marquis was about to walk with them, they erupted again with shouts and clapping.

Marquis arrived backstage and listened to the minister on stage delivering a very spirited speech. "Brother Bishop, we have a seat onstage ready for you," one of the aides said.

"No," Marquis said politely. "I'll watch from here." He had already decided to abandon his proposed speech and just "wing it." He was able to enjoy the minister's moving and motivational words.

Renée hugged and kissed him. "Knock em dead, honey."

"Don't worry," he said. "This won't take long." Marquis walked up the five stairs leading onstage and he waved to the roaring crowd as he reached the podium. He stood there silently for a bit to allow the crowd to share its adulation. Then he held up his hands, gesturing for silence, and the crowd obliged.

"Please, remain standing, though," he requested. And they did. "So," he began, "are y'all ready to do this?"

Everyone roared their deafening, "yes".

"Y'all ready to get started? Ready to go?" he practically shouted the question.

The crowd shouted back, "YES" and they clapped and roared.

"Well," he said. Then he paused and looked over the faces in the crowd. Elders and children. Black, White, and mixed. "Family, lets go!" and he walked off the stage, heading outside and ready to shove off.

Some members of the audience were disappointed, expecting more. Most appreciated the directness. It was time to handle business. And this was such an extended mission, why waste energy? Time to get to it!

CHAPTER 22

The sun rose as Jeb walked home. Its heat burned the back of his neck. His mind replayed last night's meeting. As Jeb walked up his gravel driveway and headed to the side door, he didn't even notice his Grandma Agnes sitting on the porch.

She coughed, most likely to get his attention, and it worked. Jeb snapped his focus toward the row of three rocking chairs on the porch. Agnes sat in the middle one. "Oh, good morning grandma!"

"Come over here. Sit a spell," she said without even saying hi. Jeb, as tired as he was, went to sit with his ninety-two year old elder. "Jackie and the kids didn't think you'd be gone all night," she said. "Must'a been some meeting!"

"Yes, ma'am, it was," he replied, rocking backward in the chair and rubbing his tired eyes.

"Well?" Agnes prodded.

Jeb knew what she wanted, but the last thing he wanted to do was get back into the whole discussion now. He just wanted to lay down, sleep, and forget it all for a few hours. "Aww, grandma," Jeb whined, "not now. I'm beat. I gotta call a gathering for later and I'll be telling everybody then."

"I'm not 'everybody'," she said. "And you know I will not be going nowhere outside of this yard. Just give me the short and skinny version. I won't keep you long, promise."

Jeb let out a long sigh, rocked forward and rested his head in his hands. "Grandma," he said, "the short and skinny is that we will recruit as many bodies that we can get to volunteer and we will at least disrupt this move. Hopefully all the other Blacks will hear about the trouble they are in for and decide to go back where they came from."

Grandma Agnes shook her head the way older people do when they are disappointed.

"What Grandma?"

"Y'all should let them people be," she said. "That's all. Our people been stirring up shit for niggers for so long that it's biting us in the ass right now. If we keep it up, our doings are liable to be the death of us all. And I don't mean the death of me and you. I mean the death of all. God's already let us get away with a lot. From the Injuns to the niggers, to Muslims and Mexicans. One day he is gonna bring down his wrath on us."

"You don't think we're already living under his wrath?" Jeb asked. "I mean, how we are living now?"

"No, baby," Agnes said. "This is just a test." She paused for a while before finishing. "I'm afraid we about to fail though."

Jeb said as he stood to go in the house, "That's the plan. Who am I to stop it? I am sure the good Lord will protect us," he said as the screen door closed behind him.

"Um hum," Agnes said softly to herself. "I am sure he will."

***

President Reynolds was tired of Oval Office meetings. The stale air. The boredom. The loneliness. It felt more like a tomb instead of the office of, what used to be, the most important leader in the world. Instead Reynolds sat in a small library in the East Wing. He stared into space, thinking about his tarnished legacy, as he waited for the National Defense team. The four men were surprised to get there and see the President already waiting. The sight prompted them to check their watches. "No one is late," Reynolds said. "Get in here."

Once they were seated, Reynolds was briefed. He learned that the Bishops weren't limiting this exodus to Blacks only. That bit of news frustrated the President. He always felt that it would be easier on his conscience if he ordered military action, if he wasn't ordering any actions against White people. "No matter," he concluded. "Traitors come in all shapes and sizes. What about the agents down south?" he asked, searching for some good news.

"Yes, sir, we had a couple agents who attended the Arkansas meeting. The militias decided to encourage disruption of the travels, and they plan for physical confrontation."

"That's more like it," Reynolds said softly.

"We have more undercovers headed south to infiltrate the groups, provide leadership, and point them to weapons reserves, if needed. Believe me, Mr. President, we will throw fuel on the fire."

"Does the fire need fuel?" Reynolds asked.

"In some cases, yes, sir. Not everyone is enthused. We expect when they go home and look to rally support, there may be some detractors. But we will have the propaganda machine in full effect."

"Let us hope so. And make sure they try to acquire the technology so we can replicate it," Reynolds added. "That is all." The President hadn't had a reason to smile in days. Now he let loose a small, sly grin. Still, he subdued his happiness. There were too many variables and too many unknowns to get over-excited at this point.

***

Jack could see a footprint on his girlfriend's pregnant belly; his son, or daughter, inside, stretching for space. Jack never thought having a child would change his sensibilities so much. The greater part of his life had been spent growing tobacco, slaughtering hogs, and cracking a Black person in the head every now and again. Jack applauded the attacks up north. He was a devout racist, and proud of it.

The baby didn't make Jack want to change his redneck ways, but it did make him consider staying around the house more. The call went out for all able-bodied White men to join the fight, and all of Jack's running buddies were ready, willing and able. So was Jack, but his girlfriend didn't want him to go. Something inside Jack told him he shouldn't get involved either. As he lay there rubbing his woman's belly he heard a knock at the door, and Jack had to make a decision. Jack looked out the window of his mobile home and saw six of his buddies, all with shaven heads like himself. "You are staying here, right?" his girlfriend asked.

"Let me talk to the guys for a second and see what is going on," Jack replied. He went to the door and stepped outside. The guys were antsy and impatient, crackling with restless energy.

"Ready to go?" one tobacco spitting youngster asked.

"I don't know just yet," Jack said. "My girl is preggos and she is nagging me to stay put."

"Aww! You hen-pecked now?" Ralph asked. He and Jack had been friends since they were toddlers.

"You know better than that," Jack shot back. "It's just that I'm not a kid anymore and I got new responsibilities."

"And this ain't kid shit," Ralph said. "Maybe we been doing kid shit in the past, but it don't get much realer than this. I hear this military guy is joining us and he's got all kinds of weapons and connections. I don't think we will be gone any longer than two days, three, tops! You can't give three days to the cause, Jack? Man, you sure have changed." It was easy to make Jack's blood boil and Ralph knew exactly what buttons to push. It was a shoe in that Jack would come now.

"Maybe I have changed, but I'll still crack your skull, Ralph!" Jack lashed out angrily. "And I can crack more nigger skulls than any of you fucks!"

"That is all just talk unless you are coming with us," Ralph said.

Jack paused for a moment. "Hold on, let me grab my bag!" He stormed into the house, ready to tell his girl that he'd only be gone two days.

After he disappeared into the house Ralph turned to the rest of the guys. "Told you I would get him," he said with a toothless grin.

CHAPTER 23

We have to keep this quiiiii-yeeeeet," Cliff slurred to the doctor. Cliff's facial expression had changed as he slowly lost control of the left side of his body. His eye and lip drooped.

"Clifford," the doctor said calmly, "you are having a stroke, my friend. We have to get you to treatment or the damage could be irreparable."

With his right hand, Cliff pointed to the floor. "Here," he said.

"No, not here. We can't." The doctor walked to the door and eased into the hallway. He found Cliff's assistant and called her over. "I need one other person," he said. The assistant motioned over a young man in his early twenties. "What's up doc?" she asked.

"The car is already outside waiting, right?"

"Yes," she nodded.

"Ok," he continued. "You find me a wheelchair," he said to the young man. "Look for a coat check area near the box office. That's where places like this usually keep a wheelchair. Go now."

Then Doc turned to the assistant. "Mr. Bishop is having a stroke. We need to get him to my house ASAP. I have medicine to break up blood clotting, but time is of the essence. There is only so much I can do, and I can't do it here." The assistant was about to run off but Doc grabbed her arm. "Bishop wants this kept quiet! Clear the hallways and pathway to the vehicle. Only essential parties need to be in the know right now, understand?" he stressed.

"Yes sir, I understand," she said.

"Alright," Doc replied, and he let her go. The Doc dipped back into the room only to find that Clifford had fallen out of his chair unconscious.

"Shit!" Doc said. "No Bishop! Not today! Not on my watch!"

Cliff lay motionless in Dr. Jones guest room, hooked up to an IV, heart rate monitors, oxygen, and other bags of liquid feeding fluids into his arm. No one was allowed into the room except for Dr. Jones' trusted nurse, and wife, Delana. They both stood over Cliff holding hands and praying. As their prayer ended, Delana asked, "Is there anything else we can do for him?"

"Not right now," Dr. Jones replied. "The TPA has to do its work since we don't have the facilities to deliver meds directly to the brain or go in there and remove the clot. The meds should be in his system in an hour or so."

"Which leads to the possible arterial blockage," she said.

"Yup!" Dr. Jones answered. "Once the clotting breaks up it could enter his blood stream, clog an artery and cause a heart attack."

"Oh dear," Delana moaned.

"This is a bad time," Dr. Jones admitted. "Clotting, brain swelling, fluid pressure…"

"What chance do you give him of making it?" she asked.

"Between us, twenty percent; thirty, at best. If he gets through the next twenty-four hours those chances will start to increase. You hear me Cliff?" Dr. Jones said loudly and directly to the still figure. "You thought you had to fight for your life before? This is the real fight, my friend. You have to fight. People are depending on you. They are moving on your word and they want to see you there. Your wife..." he trailed off, but finally finished his sentence. "Your wife and kids want to see you there."

Dr. Jones then took Delana's hand and led her out of the room. "Has anyone been in touch with Mrs. Bishop?" he asked.

Delana thought for a second, "I don't know who would have," she said. "We have been keeping everything so quiet. Only a handful of people even know."

"Lord," Doc said. "Can you get his assistant for me? We need to contact Mrs. Bishop and make her aware."

"Sure baby." Delana headed to the front door. She knew Cliff's assistant, and a select few, were right outside awaiting word themselves.

***

Tina stood holding the phone. Tears rolled down her cheeks. "How long has it been? Is he in a coma? I'll make my way up north. No, I won't promise that." As she talked to Dr. Jones, Tina paced the room and those in the room with her watched on nervously as they heard one side of a two sided conversation.

"I need a direct phone number," Tina continued. Finding a pen, she wrote a phone number in her palm. "And when will you know more?" She listened silently for a while, then she dropped the phone and gave in to her tears and her sadness. The women in the room with her kept her from collapsing into the floor, and they led her to a chair. As one of the others consoled Tina, another elder picked up the phone to get more information from the doctor.

After the call ended and Tina got herself together enough to tell the ladies what had happened, they all went into prayer. Tina continued crying with her head down. "What can we do to help, sister?" one of the ladies asked. "Get you north? Get him south?"

"He says there is nothing I can do up there right now," Tina said. "And that I need to think of the Movement."

"Bullshit!" the elder exclaimed, asking for no excuse for her language. "The power of two connected souls is a force stronger than medicine. I think you should go to your husband, get him stable and out of trouble,

191

then bring him back here. We will prepare for rehabilitation." The elder's gray hair was in matted plaits. She wore a purple house dress and slippers. Her wrinkled face, now more animated with worry from the news they just received.

With her head still down, Tina eventually nodded in agreement.

"Fine," said the elder. "Let's make it so. You," she pointed to a younger woman wearing a t-shirt, sweat pants, and sneakers, "tell the captain to ready the fastest small boat for a trip up north. Inform him to tell no one he don't need to tell. And do not tell him who his passenger is."

"I will go to the Gullah medicine workers. The doctor wouldn't tell me much, but I know strokes involve blood clots. I am sure our people can come up with something for you to take to him, Tina." She went over and kneeled in front of Tina, lifted her head and took her face in both hands while gently wiping the tears away. "My dear," she said, "all will be OK. My Spirit tells me so. Nothing will be the same as it was, and this will be a tough process, I admit. In the end, it will be OK, my child. It is fine to cry. Get it out! But do not cry as if in mourning. There is nothing to mourn. The Creator is with you, your husband, and this mission."

Tina looked up and wiped her own tears. "Yes ma'am," she said, "you are right. I feel it too."

CHAPTER 24

A couple of hours into their travels Ryan commandeered a motorcycle from one of the patrolmen and rode to the end of the caravan to see how everyone fared. There were significant breaks in the formation. People were falling behind. Ryan knew it was bound to happen, but he wanted to keep ranks as tight as possible. He radioed ahead for a short cessation, allowing the others to catch back up and fill the gap. "This will just be a small break," he announced to his crew leaders. "Fifteen minutes, then we are back at it." Ryan dismounted the motorcycle, passed it to another patrolman, and mingled with the group at the later part of the convoy.

Further up, Brandon studied a map with a group of guys. The convoy hadn't progressed very far at all. That's when Brandon really realized how long this would take, barring any serious incidents.

"Man, we gon be walking for like six months!" one man said.

"It won't take that long," Brandon assured.

"How long you think, then?"

"It will be easier to judge after a full day's travel, to see how far we get today," he replied. "If I had to guess, I'd say a couple of months," speaking wisdom beyond his years. He sensed some grumblings about to begin so he kept talking. "Which, in the grand scheme of things, isn't a long time."

"A long time to be walking," someone replied.

"Not when you are walking to get to something greater," someone else said.

"That's right," Brandon said, glad to have a supporter. He was just about to get on his soapbox and start preaching when the word came for them to rise and get moving again.

As the sun set, the group exited the highway. Brandon and Ryan ordered the buses parked in square formations as a security measure. With seven squares formed, camp was set up inside each perimeter. People started camp fires and warmed canned goods and such. Food, water and supplies filled the storage areas underneath each bus, and Ryan could only pray that it would be enough.

Brandon and Ryan sat in the solitude of one of the buses. They both looked out the window at the tent city. "Unc," Brandon said, "What do you think about 'day one?'"

"I think we need to cover more ground than we did today," Ryan replied. His eyes never left the window. "I just wanted us to get out of the city and on our way today. Starting tomorrow, we are gonna put in more miles."

"Have you talked to my dad, granddad, or anyone, for that matter? How are they doing?" Brandon asked.

"Nope. Haven't even tried," Ryan said. "I'll try after we gain momentum and can actually say something more than 'we are on our way,' ya know?"

"I get it," Brandon replied. He missed his brother and parents and hoped he hadn't seen them for the last time.

"C'mon," Ryan, his back cracking, said as he stood, "let's go mingle and talk to our people."

They talked to a family of four. Two of their young relatives had been found tortured and lynched. They feared for the safety of their teenage daughter and pre-teen son.

Another grandmother traveled with her three grandchildren. Their parents had been missing for more than nine months.

Sprinkled among the families were single travelers, antsy and reserved among so many strangers. Ryan prodded them to assist the families and children. And he also asked the families to "adopt" one or two of the single travelers. He wanted to foster an idea of comradery, a sense of community beyond blood ties. Something within Ryan told him that they'd need it.

Ryan told Brandon to get some sleep around 11pm. Ryan kept visiting with families and talking to his security team until well after 2am. By 4am, the call was going around to awaken and pack up. The plan was to be back on the road by 5.

***

Dallas area

Originally, Highway 20 East was a mess. Abandoned automobiles littered the street. They were gas powered in a nation devoid of gas. It took months to clear the stretch of highway needed to make it to Shreveport.

As they made their way west, people broke ranks to forage for supplies. They weren't the first to have the idea. The most anyone found was a couple of flares. Eventually everyone stopped wasting energy on the fruitless pursuit.

Justin was determined to walk with his father instead of riding the lead bus with his mother. And he did a good job keeping up and not complaining. Marquis wanted to work the crowd and see what kind of people were traveling with him. He knew Stephen's crew or warriors from California, and some of the nurses, as well. Many had joined the ranks at the Cotton Bowl and many converged on the route when they departed. Now they didn't have a good headcount. They definitely didn't know everyone and their skill set. "J, I need you to ride with mommy for a while," Marquis told his son.

"Why, Daddy?"

"Because I said so, son. Don't worry we have a long way to go. You will get tired of walking with me."

"Ok, Daddy. Ill go make sure Momma is ok."

Marquis and Justin raced to the lead bus. Justin won. The busses moved along at a snails pace. Marquis opened the door and lifted Justin onto the steps while the bus continued. With Justin secured, Marquis blew a kiss to his wife, then walked to the side of the road. He motioned toward the walking masses and a dozen men broke ranks and ran to him. "Gents, I need some census work done," he said. He handed each of them a pencil and paper from his backpack. "We need to find out what skill sets we have among us. Doctors, nurses, engineers, people whose expertise may come in handy if..." He trailed off as the men's eyes left him. Everyone stared behind him. When he turned, he saw a young pre-teen White girl. She had come out of the woods. Eleven years old and quite dirty, she wore a night gown and no shoes. She stared at them without speaking. Marquis attempted to make nice, and waved, but she didn't wave back. She just stood there staring, as if in shock.

"We got it, Mr. Bishop," one of the security officers said, breaking the uncomfortable silence. He touched Marquis' shoulder to draw his attention from the girl and move him along.

"Ok," Marquis said, breaking out of the his trance.

"Your day will come," the little girl said, drawing Marquis' attention, once again. "The day of the serpent is near. Live or die...live or die." She stared directly at Marquis and he stared right back at her. Then she turned and walked back into the woods.

Her words spooked Marquis and alarmed the security detail. "High alert," one of them said into the radio. "We have a credible threat."

"From an eleven year old?" Marquis questioned.

"Yes, sir, from an eleven year old," the guard replied. "She gave an obvious warning. Of what, we don't know."

"Yeah, I heard her," Marquis said, trying not to let his irritation show. He decided to let it go and let security secure. "Y'all do what you need to do," he said. "Just keep your guns holstered."

CHAPTER 25

Having military veterans aboard comforted Jeb. Neither he nor his younger brother, Micah, had the skills to organize militia, arrange reconnaissance, or prepare attacks. Like most men of his generation, he was all too happy to hand over the reins and take a seat in the audience.

Former Marine, Master Sergeant Runyon took over. Runyon looked like a prototypical jarhead, tall and strong, clean shaven with a sandy brown buzz cut. Jeb admired that the Master Sergeant didn't hesitate. He was forthright. The man had purpose. He had already split the group of fifty men into units for various activities like formation training and target practice. A select, experienced few did recon, planning the units initial ambushes.

Jeb didn't want to kill anyone. He hoped they could just scare any travelers back home. If he had to shoot someone, he would. Or at least that's what he told himself. *I'm just protecting my land, family, rights, and my way of life,* he would tell himself. Lost in thought, Jeb missed his call for target practice.

"J.B.," Runyon's stern voice yelled. "Are you with us today or should we send you to cook with the girls?"

"I'm here, Master Sergeant," Jeb yelled.

"Step up here, lock and load, and show me something."

Still targets were nothing for Jeb. Nor moving targets. Normally, he was shooting at pesky rabbits or foxes with a shotgun or a .22 rifle. The AR-15 he now held intimidated Jeb at first. He quickly adjusted and knocked down makeshift targets fifty yards away.

Jeb wondered where the crates of guns and ammo came from, though he had his ideas. He had no intentions of asking any questions. He looked over at his brother. Micah was really into it. He released his last few rounds and raised up with a huge smile plastered on his face. "I can't wait to shoot some flesh," Micah said.

"That's what I like to hear," Master Sergeant said. "Blood makes the grass grow."

"Micah," Jeb said as they walked to afternoon chow, "you are real gung ho, huh?"

"What 'cha mean?" Micah asked.

"You seem real excited about shooting people."

"Well," Micah said as he organized his thoughts, "guess I'm not too much against it. As I see it, for one, they are trying to show us up. I can't stand by and watch that happen. And, for two, they got stuff that we could use. I'm not so dumb that I don't know that this country was pretty much built on us taking what we want and need. I'm just being a patriot," he concluded with a smile.

"You need help," Jeb said with a smile.

"It sounds like you're against it."

"Man," Jeb answered, "I'm just going with the flow."

***

The first week's travel was uneventful. No one decided they didn't want to march anymore. No one felt threatened by other members. Food and water were plentiful. They were traveling from just before sun-up to shortly after sundown. And they had finally got outside of the Indiana state line.

The weather, warm and rainy had umbrellas up. People were quiet. Too quiet. Ryan could sense their weariness. It wasn't like they were sleeping in beds nightly, taking hot showers and putting on clean clothes. On the contrary, everyone was funky. Backs were sore and moods cloudier than the weather from sleeping on cots, or the ground. With the conditions taking a turn for the worse there was a good chance people would get sick.

Brandon walked with the front of the pack, and Ryan, not too far behind. It was just past noon, an hour before the scheduled break when Ryan got an alert on the walkie talkie.

"Exodus One, Exodus One, this is Exodus Five. Over."

"This is Exodus One," Ryan replied.

The voice on the other end continued, "We have a situation back here. I think this woman is having a seizure."

In his conversations with the people Ryan had located doctors, nurses, and EMT personnel, and he knew who to grab. "I'll be back in a second," he replied. "Brandon," he said to his nephew, "Code yellow. Locate Ms. Jackson and Dr. Phillips." Brandon went to it. Meanwhile, Ryan was back on the radio. "Get me an SUV to the front immediately."

Brandon ran past Ryan yelling, trying to locate the nurse and the doctor. Shortly after he passed, a Black Tahoe zoomed up the other side of the formation, made a U-turn in the front, and sped down the other side to pick up Ryan. Ryan opened the driver's side door, told the driver to fall into the ranks of the marchers, and he took control of the vehicle. He picked up Brandon, Ms. Jackson, and Dr. Phillips shortly thereafter. Dr. Phillips took the passengers seat and the others jumped in back.

"What's up?" the doctor asked.

"I'm not sure," Ryan said. "I just got a call that someone is sick in the back. Sounds like a seizure."

It wasn't hard to spot the group of people circled around someone. Ryan stopped the truck and asked anyone who was not medically trained to continue walking. Once the crowd cleared a bit, he could see that the woman was already being attended to by a nurse.

"She has symptoms of a heat stroke, Brother Bishop," the nurse said. "And that sent her into a seizure."

As she was being held down, her violent thrashing subsided. Eventually she lay limp. As her senses came back to her and she was able to focus her vision she saw people looking down at her, including Ryan, and she started crying. The doctor started to kneel to her but Ryan stopped him.

"Let me," he said to the doctor. Ryan knelt beside the woman and took her hand in his left hand while he stroked her forehead with his right hand. "Hun, what's wrong? You are ok. You're going to be just fine."

"This is just so embarrassing," she said through her tears.

"Don't be embarrassed," Ryan said with a warm smile. You see these people around you? They are family. Ain't no reason to be embarrassed around family, understand?"

She didn't answer.

"When we got here," Ryan continued, "they were already taking care of you like the sister you are. There's no shame in getting sick. OK?"

"OK," she said this time, barely getting it out through her tears.

"Rest for a moment. Let the doctor check you out," he said as he kissed her hand and touched her forehead again. As he stood he said, "Doc, check her out the best you can then get her in the truck. Brandon can drive it back to the front if you want to get back where you were. I am going to hang back here for a while."

"Sure thing, Brother Bishop," Dr Phillips replied.

"Please," Ryan urged, "just call me Ryan. My dad is Brother Bishop," he added a wink and a smile, which Dr Phillips returned.

"Certainly, Ryan."

"Brandon, come here," he motioned to his nephew. "Hey, you stay with them until they are ready to head back to the front. And I want the sick lady to ride for a while, until we are sure she is straight."

"And what about you?" Brandon asked.

"I'm gonna walk back here. Probably for the rest of the day." Ryan really didn't want anyone to feel alienated, so he did his best to intermingle with everyone. Plus, he didn't have the greatest comfort level with being in charge. He always tried to blend in and be one of the people instead of the "leader" or the "Bishop's son". He wanted everyone to understand that he was going through this ordeal just like them. He fell into the ranks, took someone's baby from their arms to give them a break, and marched on.

After the rains, several travelers, including some small children, fell ill. Mostly with simple colds, but still, it made for miserable children, and miserable children made for miserable adults. The mood of the group took a turn for the worse. From time to time someone would try to strike up a motivational song like "can't nobody turn us round" but it wouldn't last long. After a verse or two the silence would return. Only footsteps, vehicles, and the occasional sneeze of cough were heard.

The night brought more of the same: quiet from adults and crying from various uncomfortable and sick kids. Chris Hill sat alone in his tent, unable to sleep because of the constant whimpers coming from nearby. Frustrated and tired, he reached a breaking point. "Can you shut that goddamn baby up?" he yelled angrily. "Some of us are trying to sleep."

No one answered, and the baby kept crying.

Chris rolled from his stomach to his back. The crying was like fingernails scraping down a chalk board. *This is some bullshit*, he thought. Getting up and exiting his tent, Chris went looking for the source of the noise. It wasn't too far away, just two tents over.

"Look," he said, speaking to the tent, "can you stick a titty in that baby's mouth or something? That little mother fucker is wrecking my nerves!"

Inside, the child's father's nerves were even more fried than Chris', and hearing Chris complain didn't help. It only gave the dad some place to direct his anger. He quickly handed the child to his wife, put on his shoes and got ready to confront Chris. As he got out of the tent Chris was standing right at the entrance. When he stood up straight, the two men were nose to nose.

"Look, bitch," he started saying to Chris, "don't worry about my wife or my baby. If you got an issue, move your ass somewhere else."

"I'm not the only one with an issue," Chris replied. "Your damn loud ass kid is keeping everybody awake. You can't control that little fucker?"

"He is sick!" the man yelled.

"So!" Chris yelled back.

Unable to reason with Chris, the man did the only other thing in his nature to do. He cocked back and hit Chris in the mouth.

Chris sensed the blow, and avoided the full impact with only a graze. Now he was really pissed. He readied to retaliate but more blows were coming. Wild haymakers that Chris easily checked. He took the child's father to the ground where they grappled, with no one landing a punch.

The weary travelers stood, shocked that the argument had escalated into a fistfight. The man's wife exited the tent, holding the now silent baby. Even the baby was mesmerized by the action.

A couple of men came over and interrupted the encounter. "Y'all break this shit up!" the men said as they separated the quarrel.

"This is some bullshit!" Chris yelled. "All of this!"

Ryan, in the next campsite over, heard Chris yelling. He stood from the campfire. "Would you all excuse me?" he said. "I may be needed elsewhere." Ryan broke into a light sprint as he headed to the altercation.

Between the initial yelling, the fight, and now the post-fight yelling, Chris had created quite a scene. Ryan saw people from the other campsites heading over to see what the ruckus was all about. When he entered the circled buses he couldn't see Chris because of the crowd. But he could hear him. Ryan pushed his way to the middle of the circle where Chris was holding court, stood and listened.

Chris ranted about everything. "Got us sleeping in tents every night. And for what?" he asked no one in particular. "When we get to Florida, if we ever get there, then what? Build our own houses? Hunt for food? Have no jobs? We would have been better off keeping our Black asses at home."

"That's some perspective," Ryan said, loud enough to be heard over Chris. Chris turned and looked at Ryan, surprised to see him standing there. He didn't utter a word. "You are Chris, right?" Ryan asked.

Chris nodded. He was dumbstruck that one of the Bishops even knew his name.

"Chris, can you take a walk with me?" Ryan asked. "I am sure these people would appreciate getting some rest."

Chris looked at Ryan suspiciously. He walked toward, and past Ryan and exited the circle formed around him. Ryan gave a warm smile, turned, and followed behind. As pissed as he was he was impressed by his diplomacy.

Ryan led them away from the campsites and back up to the road. Chris, still fired up from the fight, started in. "Look, before you even start preaching to me I'm letting you know…."

Ryan didn't want to hear it anymore. He had heard enough from Chris. "Shut the fuck up right goddam now!"

Chris' eyes widened and his mouth shut. Ryan continued.

"We have hit the road! Nigga, we gone! And we got a long way to go, but we damn sure too far out to go back. In essence we are heading home. Our new homes.

"Now, I understand tempers flaring and maybe a fight breaking out. But the poison you were talking is unacceptable! No one will fuck up this operation. It's like this: you are either with us, or you die," Ryan said as he pulled a pistol from his waistband. The guards were stunned, but they didn't let it show. They figured it was just an act. "We will simply tell the others that you decided to leave," Ryan continued. "The choice is yours. I ain't playing with you," he said as he raised the pistol and pointed it at Chris' face. "Either you are with us, or you're dead."

"Look, Mr. Bishop," Chris stuttered, "I didn't mean to…"

"Either you are WITH US or you are dead!" Ryan yelled as he cocked the pistol.

***

The week's travels went without incident as Marquis and his team passed Tyler. Of course they saw the occasional noose hanging from a tree, or an old torn confederate flag. This is Texas. Nothing new.

Renée missed her husband. He kept her on the bus while he refused to ride. At night she was awake because she slept all day and Marquis was knocked out. She watched him sleep, tracing his laugh lines with her fingers. Frowning at the beard he was growing and looking at the gray whiskers within. She smelled his souring locks. "Baby needs a bath," she thought.

A pain shot through her stomach. "Oh, lord," she said under her breath. "No, little baby," she whispered to her stomach. "It's not time. Keep cooking in there. You got a couple more months." She rubbed her belly, wishing Marquis was awake to do it for her. Then she rolled over and nuzzled close to her husband, still not sleeping. Just resting and feeling his warmth.

A day-and-a-half out of Shreveport, rations ran low. Marquis didn't know if it was that they'd underestimated the number of travelers or if they had been eating too much. That morning, people were mad and children were whining because breakfast portions were cut in half. It had to be done to ensure having lunch or dinner. It was a quiet day of travel. Except for a scuffle that broke out when one guy stepped on the back of another man's heels one time too many. They were both too weak and tired to do any real damage to each other and the fight was easily broken up. Yeah, tensions were a bit high.

As the sun set behind them, the travelers pushed on. And in the ensuing quiet people heard branches breaking in the tree line to the left. No one saw anything so they dismissed the sound as maybe a deer running through the woods. A couple of men who fancied hunting figured that some deer meat would make a great meal. They also saw it as a chance to provide for the collective. The two of them broke from the ranks and, with bow and arrows, quietly entering the woods. No one really knew what they were up to. Most thought they were just going to take a leak.

Twigs broke and leaves rustled as the men walked in the shallow tree line. Their prey stilled, throwing off the hunter's search. They went a little deeper into the bush, determined not to let a chance to feed the collective get away. Finally they heard the rustling again. Still, they saw nothing. One of the men heard puppies whining.

"You hear that?" he whispered. His partner nodded. Suddenly six growling streaks bee-lined toward them. "Wild dogs!" one of them yelled. It was too late. They turned to run but only made it ten feet before sharp canine teeth grasped their calves and thighs; before paws climbed their backs and shoulders; before jaws locked on their arms, legs and throats-pulling, tearing, gnashing madly.

The men's screams echoed, along with the dog's deadly growls. The walkers panicked. The security detail worked to manage the situation. "Keep calm everyone, keep calm!" It was too late. A couple of people took off running, and that's all it took. Everyone started running and screaming. Half of the security team pulled their weapons and lined the roadside facing the growls and screams. While the other half worked crowd control. Finally, well ahead of the buses, the running stopped, leaving three women and two children trampled and injured in the craziness. What had been an organized march quickly morphed into a panic stricken cluster-fuck.

People mumbled among themselves, asking what happened. No one really knew. People started running and then other people started running. That's how it goes.

Along the tree line stood ten armed men, looking around at each other and awaiting an order. After calming the masses, Marquis went back to the work of figuring out what had just happened. "Two guys went into the woods, right?"

"Yes, sir," the guards answered.

"Cut the sir," Marquis said with disgust. "Yeah, nah, or anything not ending with sir will work.

"And why weren't they stopped?"

"I saw them," one of the men spoke up. "And I just thought they were going to the restroom. One guy and another to watch his back. Seemed smart to me."

Marquis shook his head. "We are wasting time. They could still be alive. C'mon, let's find them." He headed into the woods.

"Sir, I mean, Marquis," a guard said.

"Mark is fine."

"Mark, we don't know what the threat is. We *think* its wild animals. We can't risk harm coming to you. You need to stay on the road. We will take a medic with us and radio you what we find."

It made sense, no denying that. Mark stepped from the bush and back to the road. "Fine, Ill be at the buses."

Moving to check on his wife, Marquis ignored the inquisitive "what happened" looks on people's faces. He appreciated their respect in not peppering him with questions. Getting to the first bus, he motioned for Renée, who sat by the window, to get off.

"What's going on babe?" she asked.

They edged away from the crowd. "I'm so pissed right now" Marquis hissed. Renée didn't say a word, she just listened.

"I can't even speak to the people right now because I want to cuss them out. Breaking out running like that? Not even knowing why! And people got trampled. I thought we were more disciplined.

But most of us are still just out for self." He sighed and shook his head as he walked around in circles.

"I think you need to tell them….tell US," Renée said.

"I know," Mark replied. "I just needed to tell you first. Hear the words come from my mouth. If I would have addressed them first, it may not have come out right."

Gunshots echoed in the distance and the crowd murmured. Marquis gave the ones near the buses a hard stare as if to say *you better not run*! Shortly after, the radio on his hip crackled. He pulled it from his waistband. "Go ahead," he said.

"We need you back here," the voice said.

"On my way". Marquis led his wife back to the bus. "I'll be back baby". He kissed her and started a jog toward the back of the group. Everyone's eyes followed his bounce. It seemed to Mark that they were starting to get antsy and impatient with curiosity.

Reaching the guards, he shot them an expectant look.

"They're gone. The dogs messed them up bad…"

"Go on!" Marquis prompted.

"Well…that's about it."

"There was shooting…where are the bodies? Y'all have to have more to tell me than just 'they're gone'!"

An older guard spoke up. "The dogs were eating them. We put them down. That was the shooting. We found a litter of puppies. Could be that the dogs were protecting them. We didn't kill the puppies. Really wasn't sure what to do about them. We got IDs off the bodies but they were so messed up. It would be a bad scene bringing them out on the road."

"What is your name?" Marquis asked.

"Briggs," the man replied.

"Thank you Briggs. From now on, I want you on point. When things happen, I need to be updated the way you just did it."

"Ok," Mark continued, "Find out if they had any family here, I will need to address the group. We can't have chaos if something happens. That was unacceptable. We need to form a better plan for emergencies, and going to the bathroom. No wandering off. Briggs, will you help me tighten this shit up?"

"Certainly," Briggs said.

"Great, let's get our fallen comrades buried. It will be dark in a few hours so I think we will go down the road a little bit, just to get away from this scene, then we will set up camp for the night."

Later that evening once they made camp, Marquis called a meeting at the head bus. Before food and rest, he wanted put something on their minds. As the crowd gathered Mark sat on top of the bus with his legs crossed. He appeared to be meditating, but wasn't. He waited, and after five minutes everyone had arrived. He stood. Breathing deep, he prepared to speak. He knew that without a megaphone, his voice wouldn't carry, but he'd do his best. He had to reach the people, instill teamwork and unity or they'd die out here.

CHAPTER 26

When Tina arrived at the pier in New Jersey, an official looking vehicle whisked her away to Dr. Jones' home. The whole way up, Tina meditated, reaching out, and trying to connect with Clifford's mind. She could not. Fighting despair, she sought comfort in hope. Hope that the Creator wouldn't strike down a great man before his work was done. She talked to her husband, encouraging him, threatening and bribing him, and letting him know that she was nearby. *I am in the city, my love,* she told him. *Hold on. I will see you soon.*

Arriving at the doctor's brownstone, Tina returned consoling hugs from the crowd outside. She was anxious, yet nervous about seeing Cliff. She had never seen him powerless. Sure he was a baby when he was sick, and she took joy in nursing her baby back to health. This was very different.

She clutched her purse, unconsciously protecting the Gullah medicine, as Delana led her to the guest bedroom. Dr. Jones met her at the bedroom door.

"Good to meet you sister Bishop," he greeted. "I'd shake your hand, but I've just sterilized. I understand you have a potion from down South to help break up the clots?"

Tina nodded.

"Great, I'd like to prepare it for intravenous delivery."

She handed the bag to Delana. "When can I see Cliff?"

"Right now. We'll go get this ready and give you some privacy."

"Thank you for everything you have done, Doctor," Tina said, and kissed him on the cheek.

Dr. Jones nodded and stepped away from the doorway.

The sight of her beloved husband unconscious and ill, stunned Tina. She staggered to the bedside and fell to her knees, sobbing loudly. "You see what this is doing to me?" she said to Cliff, practically arguing with him. "You are my rock," she continued. "You are our strength." She reached up and held his hand. "I know that we all die. We've talked about it. This isn't your time, baby. You have a mission to see through, General. You have another huge speech to give in a couple of months, your biggest yet! Most of all, baby, you have me. And I am not prepared to be without you by my side, in my bed, and in my life."

She continued talking, ignoring Dr. and Mrs. Jones as they entered and attached a pale red fluid to his existing IV. She continued to ignore them as they checked the machines and made adjustments. Tina even failed to notice them exit.

"Should we bring her out with us?" Delana asked. "We could get her some food, and get her set up in the other guest bedroom."

"It'll take an Army to pry her from his side," Dr. Jones said, "She will come to us. Let her be. We've done about all we can. Cliff is in God's hands now."

***

Marquis really gave it to the travelers about running off when the dog attack in the woods occurred. He did his best to censor his language due to children being present. Otherwise he would have cussed them out, up and down. Sweat tickled his brow by the time he was done. He didn't care too much about their bad attitudes either. What he cared about was that everyone looked out for one another and no one leave their brothers and sisters if the shit ever truly hit the fan.

They were only about a day out from the docks. When they boarded the boats and head south Mark figured that everyone could rest and put their minds at ease. They pushed forward. Those who were trampled in the previous melee were mended and back on the march as well.

Renée beamed with pride at her husband. She'd always felt that with true leadership someone should piss people off sometimes. And if it didn't, you were being soft and things could run more efficiently when a fire was lit under some asses. Now with the majority angry, wifey was happy!

The baby kicked from time to time and Renée had shown Justin the footprint on her belly. He drew back, disgusted. He looked at his mother like a space creature.

"Remember," she said, "you come from the same place." She pinched his cheek.

"C'mon, mom," he said. Justin had been trying to act grownup now that he was "working" more closely with his dad.

By nightfall, if they kept pace, they'd be at the river's banks. When Marquis spread the word, everyone felt a sense of relief. What a stressful trip it had been so far. No one was more relieved than Marquis. He couldn't wait to stop babysitting, as he called it. He looked forward to resting his tired feet, and hanging with his wife and son in a more relaxed atmosphere.

The plan was to board the boats by moonlight and get going under cover of darkness. With their proximity to the destination, the group would have to slow down to make it happen. Marquis called for a prolonged lunch break near a lake he saw off the highway. Once the group got to an adequate clearing Marquis requested that everyone gather. Once they had circled the buses Marquis took his customary place on top of the vehicle.

"Let me first say," he started, "that you all are doing great! Especially the little ones," he said as he looked at the children. "Now, although we are close to the boats, that doesn't mean we have arrived. We still have a good piece left. And I don't want any of you to become complacent."

"You are doing a great job too, brother!" someone yelled.

"That's right!"

"Sho nuff!"

"We love you!"

The outpouring of love warmed Marquis' heart. He figured he had made most of the masses hate him. It seemed they understood the pressure he was under. Once the cheering died down, Marquis continued. "I appreciate it. I'm not a bossy person and I'm out of my element with all this. I am doing my best."

"You're doing fine, brotha!"

"Thanks, again. Anyway," he said, wrapping up the love fest, "we got a couple of hours to rest. We want to get to the water's edge by nightfall so we can board and cast off. Relax, for now, but be ready when its time to pull out."

Marquis got some help climbing down only to find Renée waiting for him, smiling wide. She embraced him warmly and whispered in his ear, "Let's find some privacy."

He pulled back so he could look her in the eye. They were both blushing. "Ooh," he said with a grin. Then he took her hand. "C'mon!"

Marquis woke from his coma-like slumber and glanced down at his beautiful, sleeping wife. He thought about his unborn child and considered how different their life would be-raised in a liberated and self-governed state. Then he thought about Justin. *Where is Justin?* he thought. He stood and looked across the field. It didn't take long to spot a group of children, running and playing. Justin was right in the thick of it. Marquis was glad to see Justin able to do his thing without worrying about where his mom and dad were. The boy was maturing and his growing independence pleased Marquis. He feared Justin was so spoiled to his mom that he couldn't separate from her.

He kneeled to wake his wife. "Baby, I'm about to go. We gotta leave soon."

"Ok," she said, stretching and slowly sitting up. "Where's Justin?"

"Over there playing," Marquis pointed. "He's fine."

"Good. Alright," she said, "help my fat butt up." She held out her hand and Marquis pulled her up. He grunted like she weighed a ton! Renée wasn't amused. "Yeah, whatever!" she said. "I ain't THAT heavy!"

"Um, no comment."

Once she was standing, she punched her hubby in his arm.

"Ouch!" Marquis stressed. "You put your weight behind that one!" The last statement earned him another punch. "Ok, ok, I give," he said as he wrapped his wife up in a firm and loving embrace. "You know I love you, right?" he asked Renée.

"I know," she said. "I love you too, baby. It's been good to see your smile too."

"You always know how to make me smile," he replied. As they stood there, gazing into each other's eyes, Marquis knew he'd be content to lay back down with his wife all day. But there were things that had to be done, and Renée, sensing it, beat him to the punch.

"Boy, get off me," she said, pushing Mark away. "We got things to do."

Marquis stumbled back, staring at his smiling wife. "Aiight then," he said. "I'll see you in a bit."

Everyone was adequately rested and fed. After the length of the trip so far, the distance left seemed like a walk in the park. "Ten minutes," Marquis bellowed as he walked pass the buses and groups of people. "If you gotta relieve yourself, do it now," he warned. "We're about to pull off and we ain't stopping." He approached Carl Landry, who was talking to a group near the second bus. "Speaking of relief," he said to Carl, "I need to go myself. Anyone looking for me tell them I went to the head. I'll be right back.

"Gotcha," Carl said. Both men ignored the protocol that no one wander off alone.

As he sprinted for the woods, Marquis saw Renée and waved, then he continued toward the trees. Renée tried getting his attention. She wondered why he was alone. Marquis couldn't hear her.

Marquis had to do more than pee, and he decided to wander deeper into the foliage. He found a good spot behind some dense bushes, lowered his pants and squatted.

As he made himself somewhat comfortable he looked to the right and saw a nest of baby snakes coiling amongst themselves. Their slick, shiny bodies coiling around each other unsettled him. Even more unsettling, he wondered where their mother was. He couldn't identify what type of snake they were. If they were rattlers, their rattles hadn't developed yet.

Marquis finished his business quickly and reached to pull up his pants when he heard the hiss and then felt the fangs rivet into the back of his arm. Pain burned up his right arm. He stumbled and fell on his ass, but he quickly regained his composure. The snake had bitten him in his triceps, near the elbow. And it held its bite. Marquis dislodged the reptile with his left hand. "A copperhead," Marquis noted. Furious, the snake struck again, tearing Marquis' pant leg, but tearing no flesh.

Marquis high stepped and danced away from the nest and it's angry protector. He ran as the copperhead gave chase. After darting about twenty-five yards Mark stopped and turned only to see that he was running alone. Relieved, he twisted his shoulder and forearm, trying to examine the puncture wound. He couldn't see the holes but could see prominent swelling. He squeezed the wound, trying to excrete the poison. The swollen area burst like an overgrown pimple and yellow poisonous puss oozed from his arm. Lightheaded, Marquis looked around, trying to find the camp. Still squeezing the infected limb, he began a slow, stumbling jog toward daylight.

Renée had been focused on the tree line from the time Marquis entered the woods. She now had the "worry wrinkle" as Justin called it, between her eyes and firmly planted on her face.

"What's wrong, Mommy?" Justin asked.

She didn't attempt a feeble cover-up of her feelings. "Your dad's been gone too long."

"Maybe he had to do number two," Justin said.

"Too long for number two too," she replied. "Baby, can you go get…"

"There he is," Justin interrupted. Down the tree-line, far left of his point of entry, Renée saw Marquis just standing there.

Something's not right, she thought. "Baby," her voice was cracking as she spoke to Justin, "go get Mr. Carl." Before Justin could make a move Renée started yelling, "Carl! Carl!"

He heard her yelling. "What is it?" he asked.

"Mark…" Renée gasped. He wasn't at the tree-line anymore. "Marquis was by the trees over there." She pointed in the general direction. "He was standing there looking crazy. I think he may have fainted!"

Carl leapt from the steps of the bus and ran into the field. Briggs and a few others followed close behind.

Renée tried to disembark the bus but a couple of the elder women grabbed her by the hand and suggested she wait onboard. It was their woman senses. Some things, a woman just shouldn't walk up on. Renée saw the men kneeling. She knew Marquis had collapsed. *What happened in those woods this time?* she wondered. She recalled the little girl's warning.

The older women held Rene's hands and formed a sitting semi-circle. They began praying aloud. Renée whispered a prayer but didn't take her eyes off the scene in the field.

One man ran back. Another two ran out. Then a pickup truck sped toward the men with Marquis. Renée couldn't take it anymore. Once she saw the pickup truck coming back she broke loose of the prayer circle and made her way to meet the vehicle.

When Carl noticed Renée striding toward the truck he headed her off. "I want to see my man!" she was shouting to Carl before he even reached her.

"Ok, Renée," Carl said. "Let me talk to you first."

She stopped, arms crossed atop her big belly, her head cocked. "WHAT?!"

Carl didn't look Renée in the eye. He feared turning to stone. "Mark got bit by a snake. A poisonous one. Left him in real bad shape." Finally Carl glanced up to see her reaction.

Her eyes were big as saucers and one hand covered her mouth. "Will he live?" she asked softly.

"Honestly, it's hard to tell," Carl admitted. He couldn't take being the bearer of bad news. "Doc, could you come over here?"

The resident doctor looked up from Marquis. Seeing Renée standing nearby, he rushed over, issuing orders along the way. "Keep the pressure right there. And you, wet that rag again and keep his head cool." A crowd gathered near the makeshift triage, though they kept a respectable distance. "Let's walk over this way," doc suggested to Renée. He guided her by the arm as he glanced at Carl as if to say "I need you here with me." Carl followed closely.

"Your husband suffered a pretty severe poisonous snakebite. He has a fever and there are signs that the poison has spread. In order to increase his chance of survival we need to take his right arm. And even then, there are no guarantees."

Carl stepped beside Renée to give her something to lean on. "Someone bring us a chair or a stool," he yelled. Within seconds a small boy brought a folding stool and Renée sat.

"You can't save his arm?" Renée asked.

"Right now," the doctor said, "the greater concern is saving his life."

"You say that won't guarantee him living though, right?"

The doctor didn't hesitate. "No," he said. "There are a lot of variables in place. The biggest is simply his body's ability to fight the poison. With our limited supplies, it isn't a lot we can do but draw out as much poison as we can, keep him comfortable, and wait. If we are going to amputate the arm we need to do so ASAP."

**

Steadily the group moved along, and as they neared Louisville, the mood was upbeat. Crossing the state line gave everyone a sense of accomplishment. They sang more songs, and often, Mr. Chris Hill led the verses.

As dusk drew nearer and it got closer to the time where Ryan would normally call it a day, the group urged Ryan forward, asking to continue their march into the night. They were both energetic and unafraid. And march on, they did; day and night. Brandon was tasked with watching the line and gauging when, no matter what they said, it was time to take a prolonged break.

Ryan had planned an extended break in Louisville, but as they got closer, there were signs that maybe they should keep it moving. There were hand painted signs that said, "The Only Good Nigger is a Dead Nigger" and "Whites Traveling with Darkies are Traitors" and even, "Sleep with One Eye Opened, Niggers".

Nooses hung from trees, and animal blood stained the streets. It was all scare tactics, but they were pretty effective. Everyone held it together until, on the other side of Louisville, they started seeing bodies. They came upon a group of ten dead bodies. Mixed Black and White, but obviously they were traveling south. There was a note attached to the fallen. "Are they with you?" the note asks. "Don't worry. You will join them soon," it concluded.

The atrocity silenced their song, but hardened their resolve. It only confirmed their conviction that the exodus was correct and righteous.

It was past midnight, dark and moonless. Brandon sat on the hood of the lead car as it crept ahead. Peering through his night vision binoculars Brandon saw activity and light ahead. "Uncle!" he shouted.

Ryan jogged up to the lead vehicle. "What is it, nephew?"

"Look," he said, handing Ryan the binoculars.

Ryan looked through and saw the lights also, but couldn't make out exactly what it was. He held up his right fist, signaling the convoy to stop. "I am going up a bit further to see if I can figure out what we are looking at," he said.

"Oh no you don't," Brandon shot back. He jumped from the hood and guided his uncle by the arm to a spot where they couldn't be heard. "Unc," he started, "I know you like being one of the crew. But out here you are the leader. In manhood training I learned that a leader has to be able to delegate authority to others. I think this is a time for you to delegate." Ryan was about to speak but Brandon cut him off. "I know, I know. You weren't going far up the road. You can take someone with you. This, that and the third....save it Unc."

Ryan laughed. "Alright nephew, damn!" he said with a smile. "It ain't that big of a deal."

"We hope," Brandon responded.

"True, true..." The two of them walked back to the collective. Brandon took the lead, barking orders.

"Booker, McCray, Williamson, Dunn, front and center." Two Black men and two White hustled into a line right in front of Brandon.

Ryan stood transfixed. *Look at my little nephew*, he thought, *taking charge*.

"In diamond formation," Brandon continued, "I want y'all to get a visual up the road. Do not engage and do not be seen. Understood?"

"Yes, sir," they said to the teenager.

"Take these," He handed Williamson the night vision binoculars. "Only go as far as necessary to identify the light and it's source, got it?"

"Yes, sir," they said again, then they headed out.

Brandon produced another pair of binoculars to keep an eye on his men. Ryan sent word down the ranks for everyone to rest, remain quiet, and keep calm. Brandon watched the squadron. One in front, one on each side, and one watching the rear. They moved forward slowly for about fifteen minutes, then stopped. Shortly thereafter, they started jogging back.

"They're on their way back," he told his uncle. Brandon, Ryan and a couple more guys who had leadership positions, walked forward to meet them.

"What is the light?" Ryan asked as they approached.

"Torches," Williamson said.

"In the hands of the Klan," Dunn added. "Two or three hundred of em!" Out of breath, and nervous about the situation ahead, Dunn, Williamson, and the others looked to Ryan. "What are we going to do?"

"All children under age ten in a vehicle," Ryan ordered over the walkie talkie. "I want everyone to bring it in, and close the ranks around the women. None on the edges. And, NO VISIBLE WEAPONS!" he yelled. He realized his tone may be unsettling but if there were anytime to be unsettled, this was it.

The group quickly complied. The Klansmen had apparently stopped where they were. Undoubtedly, they could see the headlights in the distance. It was also possible that they had sent their own spy to see what the holdup was.

Once Ryan deemed the convoy ready, he said a quiet prayer to himself and then gave the order to move out. As they neared the Klansman they could hear them yelling.

"You don't wanna do that, boy!"

"Ya might want to turn on around, now."

The bed sheet covered cowards lined each roadside, not obstructing the convoy. Ryan realized that this was either a trap or a scare tactic. He readied himself for an ambush, confident in a victory. *We outnumber them 4 to 1, only counting our men*, he thought. *I wish a moth'a fucker would jump!*

As he and the convoy got close enough to see the eyes underneath the White masks, Brandon started up a hymn, "Lord it's so hard..."

And everyone joined in: "living this life, a constant struggle each and every day. Some wonder why I'd rather die than continue living this way."

The Klan continued their verbal assault. Eventually their voices were drowned out by the singing.

"Many are blind and cannot find the truth cuz no one seems to really know."

As they walked through, each person looked the torch bearing ghosts in the eye, showing no fear. "But I won't accept that this is how its gon be. Devil you gotta let me and my people go!"

The last travelers passed through the Klan's gauntlet unharmed and unbowed. Their overwhelming numbers deterred the hooded terrorist. They stood, furious and impotent. They would have to increase their numbers and head off the exodus further South.

As the travelers moved forward, no one glancing back, they finished their hymn: "Cause I wanna be free. Completely free. Lord won't you please come and save me. I want to be free, totally free. I'm not gon let this world worry me...."

CHAPTER 27

Jack regretted this excursion. Two days in the field and they were nowhere near seeing combat, as far as Jack could tell. They had marched from Kentucky to Illinois where a huge contingent of travelers were expected to pass. The militia didn't realize they had been spotted and now avoided by travelers twice already. Word was out that a militia group was out head hunting. Still, in their ignorance, the men pushed on.

They set up camp in the tree line, next to an open field. Most of the guys were having a great time drinking, playing cards, and telling stories. Jack was frustrated. He wanted one of two things: brown heads to bust, or home and health. Dicking around in the woods with his thumb up his ass was not his idea of a good time.

His boys saw him sitting alone, looking depressed. They went over and offered him some moonshine. Before long, Jack, like most of the other men, was so drunk that he could hardly see. He had ranted and raved about his past exploits against the "coloreds" and he bragged about what he would do when he saw them.

Jack didn't remember laying down, or going to sleep. At some point he must have passed out. The last thing he remembered was someone yelling "Make sure to sleep all that shit off, you drunk fucks! We got solid intel that we will see action tomorrow." Jack closed his eyes and smiled. Even though his head was spinning, he couldn't wait to work off his hangover tomorrow.

***

For a surgery conducted in a pickup truck with the worst medical instruments imaginable, it went relatively well. When it was over Marquis still lived, though he remained in a coma.

One of the travelers volunteered their tent for as an intensive care unit. Once Marquis was settled inside Renée visited him.

He lay on a pallet. Renée crawled in and lay on his left side. She didn't really look at him. She wasn't ready. She just felt him, and smelled his familiar mustiness. After five minutes, she sat up to examine him. His right arm was gone, from right below the shoulder. His shoulder and face were swollen and discolored. He looked like he'd been in a fist fight. An IV ran into his left arm. She felt his weakened heartbeat and noted his shallow breathing. Then Renée thought back to just a few hours before, when she and Marquis made love, laughed and joked with one another. She was doubtful of his recovery and imagined she may never have a moment like that with her husband again.

When Renée exited the tent the first thing she noticed was people again making camp. She saw Carl and motioned him over. "Why are they making camp?" she asked.

Carl looked confused. "Because Brother Marquis is down and unable to travel."

"We have a schedule," Renée reminded, "and people expecting to meet us. Delaying anymore puts both them and us at risk."

"Would you have us risk your husband's life, traveling in the condition he is in?" Carl asked, figuring it would jar some sense into Renée's head.

She recognized his attempt to appeal to her emotions and didn't like it. She was already an emotional mess. "Mark had this conversation with me several times," she said calmly. "And he was always clear that neither he nor I come before the cause." Justin ran over to her side. She rubbed his head and shoulder and kept talking. "I don't want to endanger him but we have obligations."

She looked down at her son. "Go on in and see your daddy, baby," she said. She and Carl watched Justin crawl into the tent, and they left the entrance open so she could keep an eye on him. Then she and Carl stepped away from the tent, just out of Justin's earshot.

"I am not trying to be cold," Renée continued, "but Mark gets overnight to rest from the surgery. In the morning, we head out. If he makes it through the night, and I pray he will, we can get him on a truck and move toward the boats. If he survives laying right here, then he should survive laying in the back of a truck."

Skepticism clouded Carl's face.

"This is not a request or a suggestion," she said. "It ain't up for negotiation. This is a Bishop order," she concluded, looking Carl right in the eye. "Make me go Harriet Tubman if you want to," she said, now getting irritated. "I damn sure will! Big belly and all!"

"Ase," Carl replied. "It shall be done, sister! Most definitely!"

Renée turned back toward the tent, Carl took that as his cue to leave. As she crawled back in to lay with her son and husband Carl went to inform the others of the plan to leave in the A.M. no matter what.

***

A dense fog laced the woods and lay heavy on the open field nearby. Jack awoke, but couldn't open his eyes due to a heavy mucus that developed overnight. *Guess I slept pretty hard*, he thought. Jack felt around for his canteen and got water to rinse his face and eyes. Once he cleared his vision and saw the fog he was amazed, and he hoped the fog would still be there when they went into battle. That would be fun!

He found Ralph, who was also washing his face. "Waddup, Ralphie?" Jack said.

"Man," Ralph grumbled, "I can't see."

"You too?" Jack asked. "I couldn't see either when I got up. Must be the fog. I had so much eye snot that it wasn't even funny!"

"Nah, I got all that," Ralph said. "My right eye is still real foggy."

"That's the fog, fool!" Jack joked.

"I'm serious," Ralph said angrily. "Look at it. Do you see anything?" He raised up and turned to Jack and awaited inspection.

"Wow!" Jack responded. Ralph's right eyeball was covered in a milky white film. The pupil wasn't as visible as it should be. "And that won't wash away?" Jack asked.

"Nope," Ralph replied. "What does it look like?"

"It's white," Jack said, "like you are wearing a funky contact lens in one eye."

"What the hell, man?!" Ralph was frustrated, and a little scared.

"Just give it time, brother," Jack consoled. "It will clear up. And if you need a Seeing Eye dog, I got you."

As more men stirred there were more complaints of heavy eye mucus. Some were completely impaired in one eye and by the end of breakfast, nine men were completely blind.

The fog lifted, and no matter how much Jack cleared his eyes, or wiped his face with a wet rag, the mucus returned. His vision faded too. And as realization that, whatever this was, was affecting everyone, panic set in. If everyone is blind, who will be left to guide?

Though the sun now shined bright, no one in the militia could see. Their skin felt the warmth but their pupils were cloudy white. The men wandered and stumbled in all directions while, just a short distance off, curious brown eyes watched the odd show.

"What's wrong with 'em?"

JoJo peered through his binoculars. "Man, you won't believe this," he said. "It looks like all those sucka's done gone blind!"

"Let me see!" JoJo's partner demanded. JoJo handed over the looking glasses to Maurice. He watched as the militia men tripped over their gear, and each other. They both listened to the men's wails of dismay.

"Ok," Maurice said, "I guess it's clear for us to move then. Let's go tell the others.

"Looks like some good supplies out here, chief," JoJo noted.

"Good point," Maurice said. "We will come back this way to scavenge. Not like these chumps can see us anyway."

Jack sat "Indian style" on the grass, wondering. Would his vision return? Would see his woman again? Would ever see his son or daughter? Why did he let his friends talk him into this?

He heard footsteps. Not the frantic, disjointed steps of his fellow blind brethren. No, these steps belonged to the sighted, someone with direction and purpose. In the land of the blind, the one eyed man is King…

"Who is there"? Jack asked. "Help me! Help me get home!"

The footsteps stopped, then continued.

No one replied to Jack. "Please, help me," he implored again.

A young boy with curly hair and a round, brown face looked up at his father. They both stood right over Jack. The dad held a finger to his lips, signaling for his son not to make a sound. Then he shook his head. They wouldn't be helping Jack today.

The travelers quietly and quickly picked through the supplies, grabbed things they needed for their continued journey, and they moved on, leaving their blinded would-be attackers whimpering, clueless, and sightless behind them.

CHAPTER 28

Tina didn't leave Cliff's bedside for three days, nor did she eat. "Either he would live or die," she had told the Jones, "but I'll be by his side."

The Gullah concoction had reduced Cliff's swelling and broke up any remaining clots, since there had been no artery blockage. Still, he lay there motionless and unresponsive.

"He's come through the worst of it, Tina," Dr Jones said. "He should live, barring any problems. Until he regains consciousness, I won't know how bad the damage is."

"You've done your best," Tina said. "The rest is up to Cliff." Tina kept praying and fasting. On the third night she heard singing outside. *What could that be*, she thought. Glancing out the window, she saw candlelight.

Delana tip-toed into the room. "Mrs. Bishop," she said softly, "could you step out here for a moment?" Reluctantly, Tina stood, adjusted and smoothed her dress and stepped outside. "First of all,

Tina, word about your husband's condition has not left Brooklyn, but it's hard for you to come into the city and your husband go missing for days and word not get out. People have been out praying since before sundown. And the numbers are only growing. May I offer a suggestion?"

"Yes, I'd appreciate it," Tina said.

"Channel that energy, honey," Delana said. "Go touch the people, lead a prayer, and lead a song or something. We know you are a vessel that channels energy to Brother Cliff. It's just a suggestion," she concluded. Delana spoke passionately but when she looked at Tina she feared her words fell on deaf ears.

"That is a great suggestion," Tina replied. "I need that energy. Cliff needs it, and I think that the Movement needs it too. I'll follow you out."

Delana smiled and led Tina toward the front door. As they walked down the hallway they passed Dr. Jones' office. He looked up, surprised to see the two figures passing by. Curiosity brought him to his feet and he followed them. Delana opened the door and stood there for a second, admiring the singing crowd as they held lit candles. Then she stepped to the side, exposing Tina. The crowd didn't treat her like a celebrity. They kept singing. Someone yelled out "We are here for you sister!" "We love you!" "Get well, our brother!"

Delana whispered to Tina, "They are around the whole house."

"The cypher," Tina said to herself.

"Huh?" Delana asked, barely hearing Tina.

"Let the circle be unbroken," she said to Delana. "Doctor," she said, addressing Dr. Jones.

"Yes ma'am?"

"Do you mind if we open the windows?"

"Which ones?" he asked.

"All of them," she said. "And I'd like to open the back door too, if that's ok."

"Sure, sister."

Tina pointed at four people in the crowd and motioned them forward. "Help the doctor please." She looked back to the crowd. "Keep singing," she said.

Tina then walked to the back door and opened it wide. Seeing the people out back, she gave a weak smile and wave. "Keep singing," she mouthed.

Tina returned to Cliff's room, opened those windows, and stood at his bedside. "Listen, baby. These people are here for you because they love you. Just listen, and find your way back to us."

The crowd was singing an old Negro spiritual called "Hold On". "Keep yo han' on-a dat plow. Hold on! Hold on!"

Tina said, "You hear 'em baby? Hold on!"

Delana stood in the doorway, checking on Tina. Tina saw her, motioned her over and whispered something in her ear. Delana took the message to her husband, and then she went to one door and Dr. Jones went to the other. They let the crowd finish their song, then they delivered the message.

"Brother Bishop hears your song," they said. "Now Sister Bishop has a request. We want to fill this house with the Spirit. That's why she wanted every window open. She asks that you pray. Pray for her husband, our leader. Pray for the Movement. Pray for Sister Bishop. Pray out loud, and if you speak any other languages, pray in that language too." The prayers began and the Jones' kept talking and encouraging. "Pray to God, to Allah, to YHWH, and to Jehovah. Pray your prayers and fill this house with Holy Spirit.

The prayer service was in full force. You could hardly make out the words, but every now and then Tina would hear what was being said:

"In the name of Jesus," "Namaste," "Allah Akbar," "Inshallah," "Ase," "Hallelujah," "Atakalo Iitajiri (What God wills, will happen)." Their prayers were physical, almost tangible energy.

Tina lowered her head and prayed along silently. She wanted Cliff to hear the crowd. Dr. and Mrs. Jones entered and encircled the bed, taking Tina and Cliff's hand (let the circle be unbroken). As Tina prayed Spirit filled her. Outside, tears flowed freely, and Tina cried too, but not the same mournful keening as before. Her tears were now hopeful, emotional.

Her tears landed on Cliff's hand. He flinched. Dr. Jones held Cliff's other hand. He felt the quick squeeze and opened his eyes, looking at Tina. She opened her eyes, as she felt it too, and she acknowledged the doctor with a slight nod and smile.

She was ecstatic at the reaction, and flooded with hope. Still, she needed to hear from him, in her soul. She kept praying, and they all, including the crowd outside, kept praying.

The next morning Tina awoke to Cliff laying there staring at her. His left eye was drooping and the pillow was wet underneath his face from the tears that he had been shedding. Cliff's mouth moved when he saw Tina awake, but no words came out. He tried again…nothing.

Tina smiled at the effort and fight from her man. She saw his struggle so she tried something else. *Good morning, my love*, she thought. She wanted to remind Cliff that they had a second language, a connection. *You can do it*, she projected. *I feel you. I sense you. Say it with your mind. I'll hear you.*

Cliff closed his eyes. *I'm sorry*, he thought.

Tina, extremely relieved to receive the words, shushed him "Don't be sorry," she said aloud. "You just needed a break. Welcome back, my love…"

CHAPTER 29

Though Clifford suffered paralysis on his left side, and currently couldn't speak, Dr. Jones determined that he was out of danger and now needed rehabilitation. He didn't have the technology to assess how much recovery was possible. Nor did he have the facilities for proper physical and speech therapy.

The doctor had OK'd Cliff for travel, though, and Tina wanted to take him back south, to Gullah country. She had confidence in their practices and believed they could offer great physical therapy. She wasn't sure about the speech therapy. Her husband didn't speak Gullah, yet, she would give it a try. The people there had said they were able to offer speech therapy too. If they were unsuccessful, Tina decided she would take up the effort herself.

"Thank you for saving my husband's life," Tina told Dr. Jones as they stood outside. "I owe you everything."

"Your presence and the medicine you brought did a lot," Dr. Jones replied. "I think we're even." They hugged. "I will see you down south," he told Tina.

Cliff sat in a wheelchair, waiting to be loaded into a nearby SUV. He motioned for Dr. Jones to come over. Cliff sat up proudly and straight in the wheelchair and he extended his hand to Dr. Jones. Dr. Jones shook his hand. Tina was speaking with Delana but she noticed the interaction, and she heard a message from Cliff. "He says 'thank you'," she said to the doctor.

"You are welcome, sir," Jones said with a smile. "I am honored to serve you."

Cliff continued shaking Jones' hand as tears welled. He struggled and pressed, and finally he was able to say, "thank you."

Dr. Jones was utterly surprised, but at the same time, not surprised. "You're gonna be just fine, brother," he said as he leaned down to hug Cliff. "I'll be seeing you soon in Florida."

Cliff wiped his tears, gave a crooked smile, and nodded his agreement.

***

Master Sergeant Runyon's intelligence officers informed him of a group of travelers heading South, about a day out from their current location. He passed the news to his troops. Most were happy. Some, like Jeb, faked happiness. It seemed that the moment he dreaded was upon him. He thought of his grandmother and her feeling that this was all a bad omen. He thought about protecting his wife and kids. Then he realized he wasn't protecting them from anything. They weren't being threatened or attacked. What was he doing this for again?

After a hard day's march, the militia prepared to attack. They were bunkered down in fighting holes in the woods, awaiting word to attack. Scouts were deployed with explicit instructions to radio Sergeant Runyon when the targets were an hour out. Time had passed. He should have heard from them already. Concerned,

Runyon radioed for their status, but he got no response. Radio silence.

Thirty more minutes passed and something rustled in the woods ahead. *Maybe they got past the scouts*, Runyon thought. He signaled for everyone to be at the "ready". The movement in the woods went silent and there was no other activity for ten minutes. Suddenly there was a rush of activity. Rustling of grass, breaking of dead tree limbs, but there were no people in sight. The noise approached fast. Staff Sergeant looked into his night vision goggles to identify the sound. "Rats!" he finally said. There were hundreds, maybe thousands of them about to overrun their position.

"It's only mice," he announced. "Stand your ground. They should run on by."

They didn't. The hungry rats gnawed and bit, attacking everything that moved. Panicked militia members ran in all directions in a very unorganized retreat. Some fell, and were quickly carpeted by vermin. When the rats moved on, dead, half eaten bodies were left.

Jeb grabbed his brother's arm, pulled him up and they ran frantically, outrunning the rats. These were some persistent pests. As Jeb, Micah, and others ran beyond their stamina's capacity to carry them, the rats kept coming.

Micah fell and was quickly bitten. Before too many were upon him, Jeb started knocking them off of his brother, and he pulled Micah to his feet. They ran and ran until it seemed like they were no longer being chased.

The two stopped running and looked around in the dark, trying to see how many guys were with them. "Guys, gather over here," Jeb said in a low voice as he waved a flashlight. A dozen men came toward the light.

"This is it?" Micah asked. "There were maybe, two-hundred of us!"

"It seemed like there were about *two-thousand* rats," one of the survivors said.

"Is Master Sergeant here?" Jeb asked. The men looked at each other. No Master Sergeant.

"We gotta go back. I know everyone isn't dead," Jeb said.

"We should wait till sunrise," someone stated.

"There may be men who need medical attention," Jeb replied.

"Is anyone here a medic? No," Micah said. "Hell, we need medical attention ourselves! Did anyone not get bit?" No one spoke. They all were bitten at some point during the escape.

"Jeb, you can go back there if you want to," one of the men said. "I am sitting right here until the sun comes up. I'm tired, bleeding and I want to go home."

"Same here."

"Ditto."

"Ok," Jeb said. "Start a fire, or light a glow stick or something so I know how to get back to you. Is ANYONE going with me?"

Not even Micah volunteered. Jeb was alone. "In the morning," they said.

Jeb's conscience would not let him stay at the makeshift camp. He had to check on his fallen comrades. As he got closer, he beamed his flashlight over the field and all he saw was the bloody, ravaged bodies. The rats were gone. *There is no way mice did all this damage so quickly*, he thought. *No way*!

Suddenly his stomach twisted and he broke into a sweat. Jeb fell to his knees and vomited violently. He stood and considered heading back. There was something he needed to do first.

"Hello!" he yelled as he partially covered his nose and mouth. "Is anyone alive? Make some noise if you are." There were no voices or noises. The night was eerily still. Everyone was dead.

Jeb's stomach started twisting again so he turned and headed back toward his brother and their wanton crew. He found them, but there was no fire or glow sticks lit. "What the hell, man?" he asked. "Micah, I almost didn't find y'all. What happened to making a fire?"

Micah didn't answer. Jeb could hear Micah struggling to breathe. He fell to his knees and to his brother's side. "Micah, what's wrong?"

His stomach turned and he had to lunge to the side and throw up again. "Shit!" he whispered, wiping his mouth.

"The rats," Micah struggled to say. "Something with those rats. The other guys are dead."

"What?" Jeb asked. He shined his flashlight on the others only to see their lifeless, pale faces.

"The rats, man," Micah said as he took his last breath.

"Micah, Micah!" Jeb shouted in vain. His brother was gone.

And Jeb was still sweating and nauseous, like he had the flu. He felt himself getting weaker and weaker. "The rats," he whispered. He lay beside his brother and sobbed as he thought about his wife and children. Then he thought about his grandmother's words.

"One day God's gonna bring down his wrath on us," she had said.

"Seems grandma was right," Jeb said out loud into the stale, foul night air. "Grandma was right…"

***

For about a week after the Klan incident everyone was at a heightened sense of alert. They stayed off the road at night and they picked up the pace in the daytime. But there were no other Klan sightings and that actually made the people nervous. They figured the Klan was mounting up for some large massacre.

The only thing mounting was a storm. On several occasions when it rained Brandon and Ryan were able to lead onward. Over the last few days the rain and wind were so heavy that the thousands of travelers were forced to find shelter. They found it off exit 231 in Bowling Green. It was once a thriving Interstate exit, but now it was rundown, like many other exits. They were able to commandeer three abandoned motels. A few days travel would be lost waiting for the storm to pass.

The rooms were hot, stale and moldy, a sign that no fresh air had circulated through them in a while. Brandon and Ryan, like everyone else, propped their door open, trying to circulate the air. It was day two at the motel and Ryan wanted to leave, even with the rain. But the solar panel cells on the vehicles were low due to the constant cloud cover. For now all they could do is wait.

Brandon took a walk to visit some of the crew, and Ryan was napping when he awoke to a knock on the open door. "Sorry to wake you, Ryan." It was one of the nurses.

"No worries, Anita," Ryan said as he sat up and stretched. "What's up?"

"You know we have been giving check-ups in the lobby, right? We have a few elderly that are critically ill."

"Critically? How many?" Ryan asked.

"Nine."

Ryan scratched his beard. "Ok, so when you say critical, how bad do you mean?"

"I mean that three may not make it through the day and the other six are in no condition to travel."

"Shit," Ryan said, surprised at the severity of the situation. He got up and prepared to head down to the lobby. Anita led him.

"We set up a triage in the conference room. This way," she said, as she led Ryan down a hallway past a few offices. Every doctor, nurse, or EMT traveling with them was in the conference room. There were even a few interns looking to learn and help however they could. They had wheeled in beds and nine were occupied. Anita discretely let Ryan know which patients were the worst off.

"Those three," she nodded to the right, "they have pneumonia. Severe cases, and we don't have the supplies to care for them. The others have flu symptoms. A younger person, I would say is ok to travel. But based on the age of the sick here, they really shouldn't be moving about."

"We may not have much to say in that matter," Ryan said softly. "How can I help? What do you need?"

Anita thought for a second. "There is probably no way to get ice," she said aloud, but she was really talking to herself. "We need water," she said, looking at Ryan this time. "Water and towels from the other motels. As well as any first aid materials we could scrounge up."

"I'm on it," Ryan said.

"And Ryan," Anita continued, "you may want to get a detail started digging some graves," she whispered to him.

He looked her in the eyes and solemnly nodded in agreement. "Is it ok if I go talk to the patients?" he asked. "I would like to lift their spirits if I can."

"They are all in good spirits," Anita commented. "Even the ones in the worst condition. Sure, you can talk to them. You will need this, though." She handed him a scarf. "That is to wrap your nose and mouth. We don't have any surgical masks."

"Thanks," Ryan said, taking the scarf and wrapping it around his neck and covering his mouth and nose. "Oh, can you send somebody to find Brandon?"

"OK," Anita replied. She watched as Ryan went to the first set of beds, pulled up a chair and sat and talked with the infirmed.

Ryan saw Brandon when he came in the door. He excused himself from the patients and walked over to his nephew. Unwrapping his face, he spoke, "Hey, nephew."

"Depressing, huh?" Brandon asked.

"Actually," Ryan replied, "No. You would not imagine the strength and resolve of these folk. They are so proud and excited that the day came that Black people wanted to take their destiny into their own hands. They are just proud to be a part of that. A couple of them even told me that they didn't expect they would make it. They never thought they would. But they would rather die trying. Some testimony, huh?"

"Sure is," Brandon said. "What do you need from me, Unc?"

Ryan's face hardened a bit. "I need you to get a crew to dig four graves," he said solemnly. "As I said, not all of them will make it."

Brandon opened his mouth to speak but nothing came out. A million thoughts crossed his mind. Instead, all he could say was, "Ok, Unc. I got you. Anything else?"

"Yeah, have someone bring in a case of water. That will be it."

As Brandon turned to leave, Ryan wrapped his nose and mouth again and headed back to converse with the sick, but courageous elders.

The rain subsided and the glow of a new day was rising in the east. The motel rooms were empty and everyone gathered in an open field by the highway. They were in a circle surrounding four graves. A team of men filled three of the graves, covering the bodies wrapped in White sheets. Family members and onlookers stood nearby, crying.

Once the graves were filled everyone sung a hymn and Ryan spoke. He never imagined that leading this leg of the Movement would make him a motivational speaker, a eulogist, a drill instructor, an enforcer, and a preacher. "Lord, give me strength," he whispered.

"I won't take long," he began. "We have lost a couple of days and we gotta get back on the road. I want to share a piece of my conversations with our two brothers and our sister that we have laid to rest today." He told the stories of how these soldiers only wanted to march. March toward this goal, even if they didn't make it. They had seen trials and tribulations in their day that led to Black people working together more. They all knew that the hatred still existed. They knew there was more work for Black folk to do. And they were proud to march toward that continued work…He spoke for about ten minutes before rallying everyone to board buses or get into their places, ready to continue the long haul further south.

The exodus continued. The group, still on their trek down I-65, crossed the Kentucky/Tennessee border, with Nashville being their next major city mark. There were six sick elders who continued the trip. Of them, three had recovered significantly, two had worsened, and one passed away. They stopped to bury him not far from Bowling Green.

They re-established the trip's groove, traveling deep into the night and awakening early to do it again.

CHAPTER 30

Renee watched intently as six men carefully lifted Marquis and positioned him back into the bed of the pickup truck that was used to transport his snake bitten body a little more than twenty-four hours ago. His one-hundred and three temperature was one degree cooler than the night before. One good sign, at least. Regardless, Renée was getting this convoy back on track today. She was nervous as hell about her husband's condition. A large part of her psyche had accepted Marquis dying, and she hated that feeling. But she knew it would fuel her forward.

The final comforting adjustments were made: padding on all sides, a place for a caretaker to ride in the back with Marquis, and the IV connected. Renée kissed her hand and placed it on Mark's forehead. "Fight, baby," she said. "Come back to me."

She then turned to Briggs and made the "round 'em up" signal with her index finger.

"Alright," Briggs yelled, "let's move out!"

As she headed back to the lead bus, Renée felt a pain in her stomach. "Lord, not right now," she whispered. "Bad timing, baby. This ain't a good day." She figured that the fetus might be feeling her stress so she tried to calm down. One of the women, noticing Renée's pause, ran to her side. Renée assured her everything was fine and simply asked for assistance to the bus.

The caravan passed through Greenwood and the old financial district. They saw more houses and abandoned storefronts as they made their way toward the heart of Shreveport.

Justin rode in the truck with his dad. He stared at the bloody stump where is dad's arm used to be. He looked at his dad's closed eyes and wondered if they would ever open again. As much as he wanted to cry at that very moment, he held back his tears. He didn't want anyone trying to take him to his "mommy". Justin thought about Brandon and lessons he learned from his big brother. How to be a big boy. A soldier, and how to be strong like daddy. Justin didn't want to be strong. He wanted to be a kid-sad because his dad is wounded. Sad because his mom is sad. He wished they had never left Richmond. He wished they had never left Oklahoma. He couldn't help it when a few tears fell but he quickly wiped them away. One of the men walking with the truck saw him, roughly rubbed his head, and told him that everything would be alright.

On the bus Renée explored Marquis' backpack and discovered a notebook with his handwritten plans. She studied them, preparing to lead, even if she didn't feel or look like a leader, with her big stomach. After a while, she spaced out and found herself staring at the words on the page, but not reading them. Two wayward tears hit the pad, smearing the ink. Quickly, she wiped her eyes and closed the notebook.

She sat it in the empty seat beside her and began rubbing her belly. Her thoughts turned to her unborn child. Keeping her focus on one thing was becoming damn near impossible. There was too much going on! Renée wanted to look out the window and see her man walking beside her, protecting and leading her.

As they approached the cities epicenter, tensions ratcheted skyward. Every now and then they spotted a person watching, then scurrying into the shadows, like rats. Faces peered from office buildings, but no one greeted. No one shouted. No one said a thing.

As unnerving as it was, Renée departed her bus and walked at the head of the convoy, walking cane in one hand to support her added weight, and a 9mm Ruger in the other hand. The pistol was just for show. Or at least she hoped. She had no intentions of shooting anyone, but sought to project power and confidence to her group and any potential attackers. She wanted both her people, as well as those watching, to know she wasn't playing.

A few blocks later Renée saw figures walking toward them far in the distance. She asked for a pair of binoculars. When a young man brought her a pair, she handed him her cane and pistol and she took the lenses. She saw five twenty-something Black men and women, waving white bandanas. Three women and two men. Their facial expressions did not look tense, angry, or threatening. "Looks like our welcoming party," she announced aloud.

Briggs, Carl and two teenagers jogged ahead to meet the greeters. They asked Renée to stop several feet behind while they made brief introductions and verified identities. They wanted to make sure these people were who they should be.

Minutes later, they turned and led the greeters toward Renée. Soon, her front line was face to face with the smiling strangers. Renée exhaled and her mind went to Marquis...

The five were crew-members of three Black Star Fleet ships: The Oprah, The Mahalia, and, most fitting, The Sojourner. They were only a mile and a half from the casino, where they could wash off the road grime and sleep in real beds.

One of the crew members, a nurse, wanted to transport Renée and Marquis driven ahead to the hotel for medical attention. "Take my husband, but I will stay," Renée said.

"It's just for a checkup, Mrs. Bishop," the nurse told her.

"Honey," she replied, "I'm not the only one here who needs medical attention. And I am no better than them."

"Well, ma'am," another crew members said, "If anyone needs immediate attention, we can take them ahead too. Aside from that, we have a triage set up on the ships and in the hotel. We'll address the bug bites, blisters, dehydration, whatever they need, taken care of."

Renée nodded her approval.

"Could we please get you and your son to escort your husband on ahead? We can see if there's anything else we can do to better his condition."

Renée knew this was still a way for them to get her ahead for examination. She reluctantly agreed. She would only go after a call went out to the group to get anyone else experiencing any issues to be jettisoned to the hotel as well.

CHAPTER 31

The three modified steamboats were stuffed with humanity. The Captain prayed that the waters would be high enough to avoid scraping the bottom. That would be bad.

Finally, they embarked. Outside, the muggy air made above decks unbearable. Below deck, the stale, hot air made it impossible to get comfortable. Especially for a nine month's pregnant woman. During the day Renée lay as still as possible and Justin spent most of the day fanning his mother. At night she, and most everyone on board, went outside, hoping to find just a bit of relief from the South's oppressive heat. Every now and then someone would remind the travelers that they could still be walking and that they should remain thankful-which they were. It didn't make enduring the awful heat any easier.

They'd escaped the road, but the winding river brought its own challenges. Low hanging tree branches threatened the boat from above, sonar often indicated submerged tree branches or sometimes, whole trees, and if they couldn't be avoided, they had to be cut up and removed. A daunting task without scuba gear or any real underwater tools.

The baby had been kicking Renée even more than usual. At this point, she was past due. It was as if Renée was purposely holding the baby back, waiting until they settled in their new land. The baby no longer wanted to cooperate.

Renée felt a poke. Then another. Justin was sleeping wildly and if Renée took one more knee she was gonna choke him. She was half awake anyway, so she rolled to her feet and headed outside.

The deck was crowded. Nighttime being the coolest, and outside being the best place to feel the coolness, many slept. Others walked and talked. And some star gazed, meditated or prayed.

Everyone recognized Renée. They waved or nodded when she walked by. Some asked if everything was ok. She appreciated the caring and support. It made her miss Marquis more and more. She stopped at a spot on the railing to listen to the waves and the crickets, to look at the fireflies, and to think about her husband and cry a little. Someone politely, and quietly, brought her a chair. She thanked the man as he assisted her. He nodded, and faded back into the background.

After 30 minutes of feeling sorry for herself she noticed the glow of a new day breaking the horizon. Renée had no idea of the time when she came out, and was surprised to see that the dawn was upon her. She said a prayer of thanks and slowly stood. Once she was up, she felt moisture run down her leg. She looked down at the chair to see that it was also wet. She felt her butt. Yes, wet too. Her water had broken. "It is truly a new day," she said.

Renée knew if she was standing then someone was watching her. She waved her hand and soon two men were at her service. One was the man who had brought her the chair earlier. "Guys, I am going into labor," she said. Both men started talking at the same time. "Wait, she said. "Listen to me." Renée was calm outwardly; she knew what she wanted. The thoughts had run through her mind a million times.

"Take me that way," she pointed. "Where my husband is. You," she said to the chair guy, "please go to my cabin and wake my son. Let him know where I am and he will have a bag to bring to me."

The man remained quiet, waiting for more orders. Renée looked at him oddly. "Ok, let's go!" The men broke from their trances and went into action.

The nurse who changed Marquis' IV bags was surprised to see Renée at the infirmary so early in the morning. She stopped Renée at the door. "Good morning, Mrs. Bishop. Would you mind giving us a few minutes to change your husband's bandages, and get him settled?"

"Bitch, I am in labor," Renée said, trying to stay calm, but she was getting close to losing it. Pain was kicking in.

"Oh, god!" the nurse exclaimed. She got a wheelchair. "Sit here. I have to get the doctor." She started out the room, but then stopped and came back in. "Wait a minute," she was obviously shaken up. "Let me get you to this other room."

"No," Renée abruptly, but politely declined. "I want to be in here with my husband when our child is born."

The poor nurse didn't know what to do. She looked at the man who had helped Renée to the infirmary. He shrugged his shoulders. "We can probably do that," she told Renée. "This room is very unsanitary right now. We don't want to bring the baby into this world like that. We have to clean your husband up before we can consider birthing a baby in here. Make sense?" Her eyes were pleading with Renée.

"Ok," Renée said. "I'm not having this baby without my husband there!"

"Of course," the nurse said as she led Renée to the secondary treatment room.

Renée held her husband's hand as she lay in bed waiting for baby to arrive. Her early morning excitement had turned into early afternoon melodrama, as it was now a bit after 1pm. The birth of her boys was an all-day affair so she wasn't surprised.

Justin left the crowded little room and went outside to play. Though he stayed nearby and he would peek in several times to assure his mother was fine. Once he saw how his mom was positioned in the bed, Justin decided he didn't want to be in the room for the birth. He saw his mom squeeze Marquis' hand. The pains were coming and Justin didn't care to see what might happen next. As he now played outside, he also paced back and forth like an expectant father waiting on the news.

Renée was exhausted. It was shortly after five and still, no baby. She was fully dilated and the doctor encouraged her to push. Renée was tired of pushing. "He will come when he wants," she told the doctor. Suddenly a pain hit that caused her to let go of Marquis' hand, the first time today. "Ok, I think he's ready," she said.

Renée reached over, looking for Marquis' hand. Once it was firmly back in her hand, she pushed, and pushed. After twenty more minutes of pushing her new baby girl entered the world. Upon hearing her little girl crying Renée relaxed her neck and closed her eyes. She smiled and tears ran down her face and wet the sheets.

As she lay there panting, eyes closed, she didn't see what her daughter's cries had awakened. As the newborn's shrieks filled the room, Marquis opened his eyes. He didn't move, and no one noticed that he was now staring at the ceiling, listening to his seed. He turned and looked at his wife, her eyes still closed. He gave her hand a gentle squeeze and Renée opened her eyes and turned to Marquis. She figured a nerve may have caused his hand to squeeze but to her surprise she turned to see him staring right at her. Marquis moved his lips to say "Good job, mama."

Renée replied, "Thank you…welcome back."

The doctor and nurse, who had been tending to the baby, turned back to Renée and they were elated to see Marquis awake. They lay the baby between them. Renée was so full of emotion that all she could do was cry. She wanted to jump on Marquis and kiss him like crazy! She also wanted to squeeze and love all over her baby girl. It was too much for her senses to handle!

She could see that Marquis wanted to roll over and embrace them, but he couldn't. No one had told him yet that he had lost an arm. And before anyone could, in burst Justin. He first ran to his mother. He looked at her, then his sister, and then to his dad's open eyes and smile.

"Hey, champ!" Marquis whispered.

"Daddy!" Justin screamed, and he ran to the other side of the bed and hugged his father's neck. Marquis tried to hug his son in return, but couldn't.

He looked over to his wife, his voice slowly returning. "Am I tied down or something?" he asked.

Renée motioned for the nurse to come get the baby, which she did. She lay the little one in a make-shift bassinette. Seeing that the newborn was secure, Renée turned toward Marquis. "Do you remember being bit by a snake, baby?" she asked.

"That's the last thing I remember," Marquis replied.

"You almost died," Renée continued. "You have been in a coma for a while now. We are on the boats heading south."

"And what aren't you telling me, babe?" Marquis asked impatiently.

Renée took a deep breath as Justin looked on. "The doctors had to amputate your other arm so the snake venom wouldn't kill you," she let the words spill from her like water. It was the only way for her to say it, just letting it flow.

Marquis turned away and stared at the ceiling.

"Good thing God gave you two arms, right Dad?" Justin chimed in, breaking the silence. He hugged his dad again.

Marquis couldn't help but smile. "That's right, big fella. That's right."

The steamboats were buzzing with conjecture. It was known that Renée went into labor. Word spread that Renée died in childbirth. Others said the baby died. Extremists said both had died. Lastly, there was a rumor that Marquis died as his baby was born. All three ships were more active than they had been.

Justin exited to get his dad some clothes and was overwhelmed when he left the solitude of the medical facilities. He was bombarded with questions, and on the verge of tears before a middle aged lady made everyone leave him alone. He thanked her and ran to his cabin. After Justin gathered some clothes, he ran all the way back to the wellness center. "Dad," he said, still catching his breath, "it's crazy out there. They think someone died. I think you need to tell them something."

Marquis was glad to see his son was ready to lean on him again so soon. But he didn't know if he was prepared to face the world yet with only one arm. He was nowhere used to it himself and Marquis hadn't even taken a moment to really process. He felt compromised. In the short time he had known he was missing an arm Marquis had already thought about his ability to hold his daughter, who they had not yet named. He thought about playing ball with his sons, and he wondered how much help he could be rebuilding Florida.

Renée knew her husband. She saw the worry on Mark's face and she knew what bothered him. She guided his chin toward her so he could look her in the eyes. "Count your blessings, baby," she said. "Not your stumbling blocks. You used to tell me that a lot," Renée smiled. Marquis returned a forced grin.

"You're right, babe," he replied.

"Justin, go get the nurse," Mark requested. When the nurse entered Marquis gave her a message: "Spread the word that the Bishops will be out in an hour. If they ask questions, don't answer. Your only message is that the Bishops will be out in an hour. Got it?"

"Yes, sir," she said.

"And hurry back," Renée added. "The quicker you return, the less pressure they can put on you."

The nurse left and returned almost immediately. "You were right!" she exclaimed. "It's crazy out there. But I delivered the message."

"Good," Marquis said. "Is there any other way out of here?" he asked.

"No, sir," the nurse said, apologetically. Marquis thanked her, and she left.

He then turned to his wife and son. "J," he said to Justin, "we will need you to take the front and lead the way when we go outside. Make some space so your mom and little sister aren't crowded. Ok?"

"Ok, daddy," Justin replied.

"And now," Mark said with a sigh as he turned to Renée. "What do we name this pretty little girl?"

"Make way, make way!" Justin was all business. No one was going to touch his little sister. He stood in the doorway of the clinic and made it clear that no one would come out until there was adequate space. "Make a path to the stairway," he said. The word passed and an opening was created leading to the stairs of the observation deck. Justin walked the path to see if it felt wide enough to him. "All clear," he yelled back to the clinic.

Shortly thereafter, Marquis emerged from the darkened doorway holding his daughter.

"Oh my God!"

"It's Bishop!"

"He's awake!"

"He's alive!"

The word spread like wildfire and the crowds on all boats grew louder as they tried to get a glimpse of Marquis and the baby.

"He has the baby!" People leaned on the rails, and practically piled on top of each other.

Renée followed her husband. Justin fell back as they reached the steps and he held his mother's hand.

"Welcome back to us, Brother Bishop!" someone yelled. With that, all the boats broke into shouts and yells of celebration. Marquis smiled and nodded his appreciation. He felt the baby jump a little. All the noise had woke and startled her.

Obadiah Holder

"Sorry, little one," Marquis whispered into the blanket bundle he carried.

They moved up the stairs. Once they were on the observation deck Marquis handed the baby to Justin. He held her gently. This was Justin's first time holding his little sister. Renée made sure he secured her head while Marquis searched for the microphone so he could address the crowd.

"Bishop! Bishop! Bishop!" they chanted.

Before picking up the mic Marquis wiped tears from his eyes, which was a waste of time because the dam was broken. As much as he hated it, today, everyone would see him boo hoo, which in turn made Renée cry. Several people in the audience also shed tears. Not Justin. This was his "strong" moment. He was in centurion mode.

Marquis motioned for the crowd to quiet and picked up the microphone. "Happy birthday!" he exclaimed. "I've always felt like every day we wake, we are reborn. Today, that idea holds a stronger meaning. My awakening to a new reality for myself," he said, looking down at his stump. "Which pales in comparison to the actual birth of the Bishop's new baby girl." He motioned Justin forward and whispered in his son's ear. Justin carefully changed the position in which he held his sister, and he slowly hoisted her into the air. "Ladies, and gentlemen," Marquis said, "I would like you all to welcome Jewel Johanna Bishop into this lifetime!"

All three ships sounded their large steam horns and everyone on board sung Stevie Wonder's version of Happy Birthday. Both Renée and Marquis could swear they saw little Jo smiling.

CHAPTER 32

They'd avoided violence with the KKK, but Ryan needed better warning about potential incidents. He dispatched a reconnaissance team ahead of the bus. They stayed a half mile ahead. Just south of Nashville, the scouts saw an all too familiar scenario. Just off the highway at the Hermitage exit they saw a group of Black guys hanging out at a dilapidated gas station eyeing them suspiciously.

"What up, nigga!" one of the gas station attendees yelled.

"Oh shit," one of the scouts mumbled, "niggas!" The scouts waved at the guys.

"Y'all come here," someone else at the gas station yelled. "Let me holla at you."

"Got somewhere to be," they yelled back.

"Nigga, y'all ain't got nowhere to be. Let us holla at you a sec."

The scouts knew what would happen if they went over. Ever since things went bad and Black people separated from the niggas that wanted to be, well, niggas, the Blacks made it a point to stay out of the nigga's hoods. And, after a few failed attempts at robbery, the

251

niggas decided it was best to stay away from the Black people's neighborhoods. Now it appeared that the Black and White convoy was on a direct path, a collision course if you will, with some niggas.

The scouts turned their bikes around and headed back toward the convoy. "Where you going? What y'all scared of?" The scouts just kept it moving. "They will be back. They traveling south. They gotta come this way."

The ringleader, a short, bright-skinned guy, with cornrows and a full beard, called a long legged fifteen year old boy over to him. "Lil nigga," he said, "go get the crew and tell 'em to tool up. We about to come up today!"

The scouts didn't bother to radio Ryan. Instead, they just hauled ass back to the convoy. When Ryan saw them coming, he knew something must be happening. He held up his fist, signifying for the group to stop walking. "Break-time, y'all," he announced. By that time, the motorcycles arrived.

"Brandon," Ryan said into the radio, "come up to the front, sir." Ryan signaled his appointed leaders forward for a pivotal discussion. "Gentlemen," Ryan said to his sergeants, "can you go over there with the scouts? I am just waiting on Brandon."

Brandon arrived shortly thereafter. "What we got now, Unc?" he asked.

"I don't know," Ryan said. "Let's go find out together." They walked together over to the scouts. "What's up, guys?" Ryan asked the scouts.

"I think we have a problem about a mile up, sir," the scout said.

"Klan again?" Brandon asked.

"Worse, maybe," the scout replied. "Niggas!"

Ryan frowned hearing the word. "You mean there are Black folk up ahead?"

"No, sir," the scout said, "I mean there are niggas up ahead. Looks like we have to go through their part of town."

Ryan, as a kid, was always taught to stay out of "nigga town" as it was called. The places where miscreants dwelled. He had always been protected from the nigga element so he didn't know what to expect. "Did they say anything?" he asked.

"They called us over, but that wasn't nothing but a setup for a robbery. So we came back here."

"How can you be so sure?" Brandon asked.

"No disrespect, Brandon," one of the sergeant said, "Have you had any dealings with niggas?"

"No," Brandon admitted. Ryan was glad that his own ignorance wasn't revealed. They both listened intensely.

"I am sure you have heard stories," the sergeant continued. "Niggas can be wolves. Predators. When they catch someone in their territory they turn vicious. I don't doubt," he continued, "that if these four scouts would have gone over, they would have been stripped buck naked and sent back to us walking. And if they would have resisted, they would have been killed. That's how niggas do," he concluded.

"And now they are expecting us," another of the leaders said. "What is our best play?" The first sergeant who spoke looked to Ryan.

Ryan looked back at him and nodded. "What do you suggest?" he asked.

"Niggas don't care about non-violence," Sarge began again. "They will crack you in the head and laugh at you for not defending yourself. We can't treat them like we did with the Klan. Hell no! These niggas need to see our guns! They need to see that we are packing and not afraid to go to war with them. If they feel outmatched they will scurry back to their rat holes.

"There could still be a possibility of them circling back on us, and honestly, sir, we have to be ready and willing to blast on 'em!"

Ryan shook his head. "I don't know if that is the play," he said, thinking about his father's order for no use of guns. "Maybe they will see how many of us there are and leave us alone like the Klan did."

"I doubt it," Sarge said. "See," he went on, "the Klan uses fear as a weapon. Niggas use weapons as weapons. And fear is just a bi-product of their violence. They think that if people see two or three people killed then the rest will fall in line. In my experience," he concluded, "the only thing niggas respond to is the threat of violence coming right back on them."

As they did before, the children and women were shuffled into the vehicles. Unlike before, the men packed their weapons, pistols on hips and AR15s, AK's and shotguns in hand. A couple of snipers darted into the tree line and disappeared. Once the ranks were re-arranged they began moving forward again.

Ryan decided to swallow his pride, and he let Sarge know of his inexperience in dealing with niggas. "I figured as much," Sarge replied.

"What do I do?" Ryan asked quietly. "What if they got the street blocked or something? Do I negotiate with them, barter a trade, or what?"

"Do we have anything valuable to offer that we don't need ourselves?" Sarge asked.

"Well," Ryan thought for a second, "no."

"Then, no, we do not fake negotiations."

"What is the play?"

Sarge didn't hesitate to answer. "We stand strong. We don't back down and like I said before, we blast if we have to."

"Then we would be looking at a bloodbath on either side," Ryan said with apprehension. "That is not a good look."

"Ryan," Sarge said impatiently, "what are our choices? Give them whatever they want, which will be everything, or what else, young Bishop? What are our other options?"

"We negotiate," Ryan reiterated.

Sarge let out a sigh. "You are the boss. I am just giving my opinion based on past experience and I really suggest you take it. Or be prepared to take it."

Ryan stared at Sarge, then looked into the distance with his binoculars. He could see people starting to take up positions in the middle of the street. Yeah, confrontation was imminent.

Per Sarge's instructions, Ryan had put military trained and battle tested men in the front of the convoy. Packing heat, and mean mugging, they marched forward, ready for action.

Down the road, the niggas lined the highway. They numbered seventy, give or take. And although numerically inferior, they were armed to the teeth, on their own turf, and fierce. The ringleader and his counterparts stood front and center. *Shit*, the ringleader whispered, *it's a lot of them motherfuckers*. Still, he was undeterred. He waited until the convoy was in earshot and he yelled, "Tax time niggas. Time to pay the toll."

Sarge walked beside Ryan. They were in the second row. "We got the numbers, big time," he said. "Don't back down, bruh."

Ryan agreed. They marched forward and moved within fifty feet from the nigga's line. Ryan held up his fist and the convoy stopped.

"What up nigga?" the leader asked, directing his question toward Ryan.

"Aim!" Ryan yelled, and the front row fell to one knee, while taking aim. The next row raised their rifles. Guns emerged from bus windows and truck beds. People were on top of the buses taking aim. "Bullets," Ryan said calmly. "We got bullets for ya, brother. Now, we have some place to be. If y'all don't mind moving..."

"What we don't mind is dying," the leader said. "We ain't scared of y'all. And we hungry!"

"Niggas been dying for years," Ryan said. "I guess today wont be any different. This is your last chance. You are outnumbered and out gunned. Yes, some of us will die. Hell, I may even die. But I promise you, ALL of you will die, and you won't get shit, and we will continue marching."

"Marching to glory, nigga!" the Big Bad Wolf said. "Marching to meet your maker! We ain't playing!" and he ordered his handful of soldiers to raise their weapons.

For the first time, Sarge noticed the glassy look in the Big Bad Wolf's eyes. "He is high on something," Sarge whispered to Ryan. "This may get out of control."

"What up? We ain't gonna be standing here all day." The Wolf was getting antsy. It looked like his crew was probably high too, but they didn't have the conviction of the Wolf. While they realized they were outnumbered and may need to stand down, the Wolf didn't seem to care. He was ready to die, ready for a bloody standoff to end it all.

Ryan whispered into the walkie talkie, "Bird's Eye, standby." He then commanded the convoy to lower their weapons. Confused, but obedient, they lowered their guns. "Key in on the loudmouth, Bird's Eye," he said to the walkie talkie. "Ok, my man," Ryan said, speaking to the Wolf, "if y'all can lower your guns and we can discuss how to make y'all happy-then we'll be on our way."

The Wolf, now emboldened, ordered his guys to lower their guns, and they did. In his boldness, the Wolf started barking at Ryan again. "Alright, bitch! What y'all…"

"Fire," Ryan said into the radio, and a single shot rang out in the distance. A hole appeared in the Wolf's forehead, and the people behind him were sprayed with a pink and red mist. The Wolf's body dropped and some of the women on the bus screamed. The Wolf lay there, spread-eagle in the street, eyes wide open, a grim snow angel with a halo of blood. His body twitched, as red and gray matter oozed from his shattered skull.

The gruesome scene was a small price to pay to avoid a greater bloodshed and tragedy. The blood splatter on the people behind the Wolf was the worst part. Even that was effective, based on the reaction of the Wolf's minions. Without a word from Ryan, they vacated the street. They realized they would end up on the losing end if they bucked.

The courage of Ryan's decision impressed Sarge. He broke ranks, grabbed a couple of men, and they removed the Wolf's body from the highway.

Before moving on, Ryan addressed the niggas, as some of them were meandering about. "Our goal isn't violence. It is a shame that blood had to be spilled. We will pray for y'all. And if you ever get your heads on straight, you can join us in Florida. But don't bring none of this bullshit with you. WE ARE NOT NIGGAS! And YOU don't have to be niggas! Elevate, y'all!" he yelled.

"Ok," he said to the convoy, "let's move."

Ryan saw desire in some of the niggas eyes as they passed. Beneath the glassiness and drugs, he could tell they wanted to join the movement. Ryan opened his mouth to extend the invite when Sarge cut him off.

"Nah, young Bishop. They're not ready," he said. "Maybe someday. Maybe even soon. Not right now."

Ryan was not surprised that Sarge knew what he was thinking. Nothing about Sarge surprised Ryan anymore. "Why not?" he asked.

"Look into their eyes," Sarge said. "See the haze? They are junkies, addicts. When we get to Florida we still have a lot of infrastructure to set up, right?"

"Correct," Ryan replied.

"A junkie isn't the best worker," Sarge continued. "And they aren't very dependable. Plus since we won't have any drugs, eventually they will go into withdrawal. Are we setting up drug treatment in Florida?"

"Not right off," Ryan said.

"There you go!" Sarge said as he patted Ryan on the back.

Following Sarge's lead, Ryan averted his eyes from the junkies that lined the road. Instead, he focused on the road in front of him.

CHAPTER 33

When Cliff departed the boat, rolling down the ramp, the first face he saw was his daughter, Denise. A tear rolled down his numb left cheek. "Baby!" he stuttered.

"Hi, daddy," Denise said as she jogged toward her father. "Oh, daddy," she stopped Cliff's momentum as she wrapped her arms around her dad's neck. "Oh, I love you! I love you!"

Though Cliff wanted to share the sentiment, he could not produce the words. Since waking, he hadn't tried to speak very much and he really wasn't aware of his limitations. Cliff visibly struggled to find words to say to Denise. It didn't take long before he visibly showed his frustration.

Cliff's struggle at speech startled Denise. As her mom walked down the pier, their eyes met. Tina picked up her pace as she noticed the distress in her daughter's eyes.

"Hey, baby," she said as she kissed Denise's forehead. "What's wrong?" she continued as she looked down at Cliff.

Again, he struggled with his words. Finally, giving up, he mentally shared with Tina.

"It's gonna be a struggle, baby," she spoke aloud. "We will be in therapy trying to get you back to your old self while we are here. Ok?"

Cliff gave an accepting, yet defeated look. He didn't have a choice.

Denise and Tina sat at a round wooden table in the middle of the dilapidated kitchen, sipping tea. Cliff slept comfortably in a nearby bedroom. He would begin speech therapy tomorrow.

"Any idea how much speech and movement they think daddy will get back?" Denise asked.

"No," Tina replied, "Dr. Jones in New York couldn't make a judgment. Really, it is going to be a matter of working the therapy and Cliff getting the most out of it that he can, no matter how long it takes."

"And you think this is the best place for therapy?" Denise asked as she gave a doubtful expression. "I mean," she continued, "most of them speak Geechy. I don't know if you understand them, Mom, but I know I don't."

"They all don't speak Geechy, child," Tina replied with a grin. "They have established speech and physical therapy down here for a couple of reasons. For one, they have a lot of elders here. They got into physical therapy years ago to aid their aging population.

"And in regard to speech, they started teaching speech so that the youth could understand both English and Geechy to relate at home, and still compete in the outside world. They have experience and I think Cliff will benefit. Still, aside from that, it's not like we have a whole bunch of choices. We are where we are, and I believe God has us in the right place."

"I sure hope so," Denise said as she sipped her tea.

Tina and Cliff sat in the living room of a classic Victorian home. White, paisley furniture filled the room. The type of room where only "grown folk" could hang out. They waited patiently carrying on a mental conversation.

A fifty-something aged gentleman wearing a dashiki, and using a walking cane entered. His bald head caught the morning sunlight coming through the window. "Good morning," he said.

"Good morning," Tina replied. "And Cliff says good morning too."

"Oh, does he?" the man asked. "He should tell me himself. Cliff," he said, "how about you tell me 'good morning'. It's the polite thing to do."

Cliff tried, struggling and stuttering on the letter "G". He looked the man in the eye, exasperated, and signaling that he gives up.

"Clifford," the man said, "I am Dr. St. Croix. I wasn't trying to humiliate you. I will be your speech therapist and in a week you will be telling me good morning. If…." He left his sentence hanging right there, waiting for someone to take the bait. Tina bit.

"If?"

"I'm glad you asked, Mrs. Bishop," he said. "If you will cease, for a while, with your telepathic conversation."

They both grimaced, but continued listening. "Go on," Tina said.

"Your telepathy provides an escape from the need to communicate verbally. It is a crutch. It's an awesome crutch, mind you," St. Croix added. "But," he said, looking directly at Cliff, "if you want to regain your verbal speech, you have to work here, at home, and always. And when I say work I mean talking. I will give you the tools and teach you how to use them. With that, I am sure you will rebuild that masterful vocabulary of yours. Agreed?"

Tina looked at Cliff. This was his call. Cliff held up one finger, looked at his wife, and was obviously saying something to her mind. Tina blushed and laughed out loud. Cliff then turned back to Dr. St. Croix and nodded his head in acceptance.

CHAPTER 34

Corey listened from the other room as his wife, Mary, home-schooled the 10 year old twins, Monte and Madison. Mary, a skinny bleached blonde who really needed glasses, had a Confederate flag laid out on the kitchen table. "And what do the stars mean?" she asked.

"Thirteen states!" Monte yelled.

"Very good," Mary said. "You don't have to yell, son. Lastly, what is the original name for this flag?" Both children thought, but neither could remember. "The…" Mary hinted.

"Battle flag," Monte said, not yelling this time.

"Good! Battle flag of what?" she prodded.

"Of Northern Virginia," Madison completed.

"That is awesome!" Corey said as he entered the kitchen. "Y'all are doing well! Hun, is that all of today's lessons" he asked Mary. "I need Monte's help."

"That's it," Mary said. "Madison and I need to start cooking anyway. Y'all go ahead."

"Go get your work gloves, son," he told Monte, "and meet me outside." Corey kissed Mary and Madison and headed out the back door.

Grabbing ax, he headed for the wood pile. Waiting for him was his buddy, Thomas. "Hey, Tom," Corey greeted.

"Hey man," Thomas replied as the two shook hands. Tom was of average height with an above average gut.

"What's up?" Corey asked.

"Nothing. Wife is cooking so I just figured I'd get out of her way. So," Thomas continued, "I know you got that flyer last week. The meeting is tonight, and word is, they gonna want us to head out by the weekend. You thought about it?"

Monte had come outside, Corey instructed him to stack some of the wood that had already been cut. "Yeah, I've thought on it," he said to Tom. "You heard any of these crazy stories about what's been happening though?"

"Those are just stories," Tom said.

"Nah, there is some truth," Corey replied. "My wife's cousin's husband went out with a group up north. His group went blind. All of 'em! And most of them died. Hell, no one went to track them down for a week! They had just been stumbling around the woods."

"What happened to your cousin?" Tom asked.

"My wife's cousin's husband," Corey corrected.

"Whatever, man!" Tom laughed. "What happened to him?"

"They got him back home," Corey said, "and he is still blind."

"Shit!" Tom said. "I'm going to the meeting. Can't hurt anything. Go with me! I know you are down for the cause."

"You are right," Corey replied. "I'll go. I'm down."

"Just scared of a few ghost stories, huh?"

"Shut up and grab an ax, asshole! If you gonna be out here bothering me you may as well help me chop some wood."

The meeting left Corey impressed and excited. They were gathering the largest force, yet, to combat the exodus. The group leader did a good job encouraging the fence sitters, like Corey. He couldn't wait to get home, tell his wife…and clean his pistols.

As he walked, Corey felt a sharp pain in his right foot. It hurt and soon he was limping. At his front porch, he stopped and removed his boots, expecting to see a rock fall from inside.

His daughter's cries drew him away from his pain. He kicked his boots aside and stepped toward the door. "Oww!" he said aloud. His foot ached. *Must be a blister*, he thought. Ignoring his foot, he went inside. His wife looked worried. "What is wrong with baby girl?" Corey asked.

Mary fought back tears. "Madison has a rash, or something," she said. "She has a big boil on her arm and she said it hurts."

Corey examined Madison. She had a gruesome, puss-filled wart of some type on her forearm, and it appeared to be spreading. "It hurts, daddy," she said.

"Daddy will bring you some medicine, ok?" he asked.

"'Kay."

Shortly thereafter, Corey brought Madison a small shot of corn liquor to help her sleep. Medicine wasn't easily attained these days. Once she was quieted, Corey slipped into the bathroom to look at his own foot. Like Madison, he had a wart-looking, puss-filled abscess near his big toe. Bumps and pimples always annoyed Corey and he was quick to burst them. This growth would be no different. He reached down with his thumbs, squeezed the growth. Pink, white, and red puss gushed out. When it popped, Corey felt like he'd been hit in the stomach. Light-headed, he slumped over on the toilet. As he worked to shake off the sick feeling he looked down at his toe. The abscess was already refilled with fluid, it was bigger, and there was a new one beside it. *What the…*

There came a knock at the door. "Babe," Mary said, "I need to show you something." Corey put his sock on, cleaned the mess from the floor, and went to see Mary. She was in the bedroom with her back to the dresser. She held a small mirror and she used it to look into the mirror on the dresser so she could see the back of her head. "Come, look," she told Corey.

She turned and he looked at her hairline. He could see that some of her hair was missing and as he looked closer to the scalp he saw that she had a wart on her head. He moved the hair near the wart so he could get a closer look, and the hair around it came out in his hand.

"I am trying to not freak out here," Mary said calmly. "But I am seriously freaked out!"

"I have one on my foot," Corey confessed.

"What is this?" Mary asked. "Bedbugs?"

"I never seen bedbugs before," Corey said. "I don't know. Monte, come here." His son ran into the bedroom. "Do you have any new bumps or pimples?" Corey asked.

"Nah, Dad," Monte said, looking at his arms and hands.

"Ok," Corey said. "Run down to Tom's. See if he has any ointment."

"Anyway," Mary said to Corey, "how'd the meeting go?" She was trying to keep her mind off of her discomfort and her hair loss.

"Productive," Corey said. "Everyone is ready to go."

"Sounds exciting," Mary said, cutting the conversation short. She could tell Corey was deep in thought and really didn't feel like talking. Twenty minutes of uncomfortable silence later, Monte walked back into the house.

"No one will let me in," he began, "I went to three houses."

"Were they home?" Mary asked.

"Yes," Monte replied. "They yelled for me to go away. I yelled back to Mr. Tom, telling him what we needed. He said they have warts too and that they need their medicine. Same at the other two houses. One of them sent their daughter to the door. It's like one person in every house isn't getting those bumps."

Corey pondered the information and he thought about the other things he had heard about from groups that had tried to interfere with the Black movement. "Plague," he muttered.

"What, honey?" Mary asked.

"Monte," Corey said, ignoring Mary, "In the morning, go to town, and try to find some medicine. Then find out how widespread this is. Until then, all we can do is try to get comfortable and get some sleep."

Corey slept on the couch. His feet ached and he didn't want to suffer the discomfort of walking to his bedroom. Mary slept with Madison. She didn't want to sleep alone. Corey woke when he heard the door close. Was it Monte coming in? No. Monte was leaving.

Corey pulled his blanket up to examine his throbbing feet. *There's no way I could walk,* he thought. His feet were grotesquely swollen with warts. Some were open sores. They hurt, but the appearance of his feet and their condition hurt Corey more than the actual pain. He lay his head back on the pillow and let the tears fall from his eyes.

Monte came in the front door. Again, he startled Corey, who had fallen back to sleep. "Hey, son," Corey said.

"Hi, Dad," Monte replied.

Mary walked in. She had a bandanna on her head, covering the overnight hair loss and wart spreading. "Morning, boys," she said. They both replied. "So?" she asked Monte, bluntly.

"Ok," Monte began, "there was like, one member of every family in town. It seems that we were the only ones that didn't break out. They said all their families have it, on their hands, feet, faces, all over," Corey said.

"You have to go over to the next town," Corey said.

"It's there too," Monte told his dad. "There were kids from the other towns. They said that every town that had people in that meeting yesterday, all of those towns are infected.

Is that really the connection? Corey thought.

"You think that's it, Pop?" Monte asked, breaking Corey from his thoughts. "Maybe someone there was sick, and they spread it to everybody."

"Could be," Corey said.

"How does that explain one member of every family not getting sick?" Mary asked.

"It doesn't," Corey said.

Everyone was silent for a second. "Go ahead and say it," Mary said to Corey. "I know what you are thinking. Be the one to say it out loud."

Corey let out a sigh. "The stories are true…the plagues are real."

CHAPTER 35

Marquis lay back in the infirmary with Renée and baby Jewel, his head turned away from them as he pretended to sleep. He was in pain, his right hand throbbed, even though he had no right hand. Marquis tried to reconcile with his brain that the pain was imaginary. It wasn't working.

How could he have been so dumb, he thought, to let himself be bitten by a snake? He recalled the little girl who had come out of the woods with the ominous message. *I should have been more careful with everything after that.* And he had been careful. He hadn't taken any unnecessary risks. He was just going to take a dump, for god's sake. Was that so risky? Then he remembered. He didn't follow the protocol that he had recently fussed at the group about. He had gone it alone into the woods. He shook his head, bit his lip and cursed himself.

Renée reached around and put her hand on Marquis' chest, feeling his heartbeat. "It is just dumb luck baby. Crazy circumstances," she said.

"You know what I'm thinking about?" Marquis asked.

"Yeah."

"How?"

"We're connected baby," she replied. "Like your mom and dad are connected. Like your whole family is connected. Plus you haven't had a lot of time to process your accident, so it only makes sense, really."

Marquis turned toward his wife, allowing her to see that he had been crying. "How can I be your 'everything'…like this?" he asked.

"Who am I talking to right now?" she asked back, rhetorically. "I am talking to you. I don't talk to your arm, or your hand."

"That hand used to talk to you sometimes," Marquis said, giving a devilish grin.

Renée smiled back. "You have another hand," she replied. They both laughed. "Seriously though," Renée said, "I know the new 'you' will take some getting used to. What is important is that there is a 'you'! You are our leader and I know you saw how excited everyone was to see their leader. You are their inspiration, and even more, you are mine, your son's, and you will be your daughter's too! I am glad that I didn't lose you! I need you." Tears ran down Renée's face. Marquis was speechless. Renée continued.

"Now, we been on this river for a while. We should be hitting the Mississippi, or the Gulf, or something soon. I'm gonna need you to get well enough to find out what's going on, and report back to mama. I've had my Harriet Tubman moment. You missed it. Now its time for me to just be the woman who recently had a baby."

"I can do that, babe," Marquis said.

"Don't rush yourself," Renée added. It looked like Marquis was about to get up right then. "Give it time. You stay right here with me for now." She rested her hand back on Marquis' heart.

"Damn, make up your mind, woman," Marquis replied. They laughed again.

Soon they would reach the Mississippi River and they would change boats so the ones they were on could head back to Shreveport to transport others south. It was anticipated that they would have to make the trip at least once more. Marquis stood in the wheel room, guiding the boat and watching the ripples glide over the water. Justin slept in a chair behind his dad. The sun was rising behind the trees ahead. A beautiful day was in store.

The captain returned to the cabin. "Thank you for the break, Mark," he said, taking his place behind the wheel again.

"Not a problem," Marquis said as he sat next to his son. "How much longer on the river?" he asked.

"I'll show you," the captain said. He set the auto pilot and motioned Marquis to a nearby map table.

Auto pilot? Marquis thought. He figured the captain probably didn't even need him to guide the ship. *He just wanted to get me involved, which I appreciate*, he reasoned. He didn't want to be treated like he was handicap.

Marquis went to the table and the captain pointed to locations near the Gulf. "Of course, open water is our final destination," he said. "We are here," he pointed to the lower points of the Red River. "After those two bends we will reach the Mississippi. Should be there by sunset."

"That's great!" Marquis exclaimed. "I thought we were further out."

"No, sir. By this time tomorrow, you should be headed down the Mississippi."

Marquis examined the map closely as the captain took his seat behind the wheel. Marquis looked at the distance they had traveled and thought about the fact that he was unconscious for some of the time. He felt guilty. "Cap," he started, "this whole trip, we haven't run into any issues?"

"Had to remove some snags (submerged tree branches) here and there. Our water levels have been good and we haven't had any major rafts blocking our way."

"I mean, attacks," Marquis asked. "Shots fired? Traps? Anything?"

"Nope," the captain assured. "It's been the damndest thing. A couple of times there was radio chatter that we might see some trouble. Nothing ever came of it. Praise God!"

"Indeed," Marquis agreed, thinking of his arm. "We've certainly been under his protection."

The riverboats wound through a short waterway that connected the Red River to the mighty Mississippi. Reaching the end of the waterway, they could see a bevy of activity. Boats traveling in all directions. Some headed south, full of passengers, either just arriving at this checkpoint, or continuing the journey to the Gulf. Others were empty and headed north. It was a sight to behold. In total there were over a dozen riverboats present.

As Marquis and his crew got closer they could see a multitude of Black, brown, and some White faces on shore, obviously waiting for their ship to come in. "Captain," Marquis said, "this is where we part ways?"

"It is," the Captain replied. "We are sending one of our boats south, but it won't be this one. Most migrants have been channeled down so we don't see the need for as many boats up North for transport anymore."

When the boats received the "go ahead" to dock they made announcements informing the passengers to retrieve their belongings. They were told that if they wanted to stay with particular groups, it was up to them. Everyone on the shore was heading in the same direction. Their best bet was to try to get on a boat south as soon as they could. The passengers were also reminded to be patient, as some people on the dock had been waiting for days and deserved to board before others who were just getting to this location. The boarding ramps were lowered and the passengers began departing.

On shore, things were a loosely organized cluster fuck. Those who had been waiting for a while were impatient and they jockeyed for position on the next boats going south. Others made their way to the road where buses were taking people to New Orleans. There weren't many buses though. The decision to choose one mode of transportation over another was a tricky one.

The stench of garbage was overbearing. Trash was placed in designated areas but no garbage men were coming to pick it up so the foulness remained. And with that comes rats, flies, and disease. After a long and trying journey, this was quite a depressing place to end up.

That is, until a Bishop showed up. Word spread that a Bishop was aboard one of the recently docked boats. No one knew which Bishop, exactly, but knowing one of them was there lifted the spirits of the travelers. Marquis and family had been guided to a first aid tent where they could stay together and sit. Soon, though, Marquis saw heads stretching to get a glimpse of him. He realized there was a buzz and sensed he may be the reason. "Son, how bout we walk for a bit; see if we can help anyone," he said to Justin.

"OK, Pop," Justin said as he stood. "We'll be back Mom," he said, beating his dad to the punch. He looked at Marquis and smiled. Marquis smiled too.

"That's right, babe, we will be back," he said as he kissed his wife and daughter.

"Ok," she said. "Just stay together."

"Yes, ma'am," the men echoed.

Exhausted, Marquis didn't feel up to playing politician, but he knew that any opportunity to lift morale needed to be seized. He plastered on a smile and commenced to shaking hands and giving half hugs with his one good arm. Since news didn't travel at the rate it once did, the people on shore were surprised to see Mark's limb loss. He assured them he was fine. He implored everyone to keep the faith, stay patient, stay strong, and pass the message. There was no podium. No mic. Mark knew he could not personally touch everyone so he certainly hoped his message would spread.

As Marquis and Justin made their way back to the first-aid tent Mark could see Renée laughing and having a jovial conversation with someone. As he got closer he saw she was talking to a tall, afro'd brother. Renée saw Marquis and she must have said something to her guest, because he turned around. It was Stephen from L.A.

"Marky Mark," Stephen shouted, "Good to see you, man!" He went over and hugged Marquis.

"Likewise, brotha," Marquis said, returning the embrace. In these strange days it always felt good to see a familiar face. "You look healthy and happy."

"I try to stay that way," Stephen replied. "And I'd say this journey has left you a changed man," he continued, as he patted Marquis' left shoulder.

"Indeed it has. I am a changed man," Marquis said with a smile. "I'm adjusting."

"The baby isn't keeping you up all night?" Stephen asked with a smile.

"The baby?" Marquis asked. "Oh, I thought you were talking about..." he looked down at his missing arm.

"I was, I was," Stephen said with a laugh. "Just trying to lighten the mood."

Marquis laughed. "I can dig it. Hey, let's go somewhere we can have more than just small talk."

"Baby, y'all can sit in here," Renée said. "Unless you need privacy from me too."

"No, I don't have any secrets to tell," Marquis said.

"Me either," Stephen echoed. Both men pulled up plastic folding chairs.

"So..." both men said at the same time. Stephen gave way for Marquis to speak.

"...how was your trip?"

"Man," Stephen started, "a trip!"

"Y'all had some incidents?"

"We had internal beefs, but nothing from the outside," Stephen said. "And that was the most trippy part, homie! I mean, we saw White people, groups of angry looking White men! But none of them were F'ing with us. They actually looked like they had already been through hell and couldn't deal with any hell we would have brought them."

"That's crazy," Marquis said.

"You're telling me! What about y'all?" Stephen asked. "Is that what happened to your arm?"

"Nah, man," Mark replied. "Damn snake bite. It's almost embarrassing. We got attacked by a pack of wild dogs. Nothing racial at all. Not to say I was looking for trouble, but still, I expected it."

"You haven't heard the stories?" Stephen asked.

"I guess not. Something they are saying around here?"

"Yeah," Stephen said. "Word is, militia, Klan, haters, whatever, they were gearing up all over to ambush our routes. And some of our groups were killed or scattered. There were some crazy gunfights. For the most part these militias and hating asses were getting it with biblical type shit! Oops, sorry little man," Stephen said to Justin.

Marquis was puzzled. "What do you mean?"

"Like biblical plague shi....stuff," Stephen continued. "I heard that three fourths of one of the groups just dropped dead on the spot! One group's babies went blind. I heard some other people's fingers and toes fell off. It was bad to the point that they decided to leave us alone! And that is why we ain't had to deal with much more than our own personal problems."

"Are you serious?" Renée asked.

"We didn't see any evidence of anything like this," Marquis said. "Did you? Or did anyone who is telling these stories?"

"You know how that goes," Stephen said. "He said that she told him that so-and-so had direct contact...Still though, them mad ass White boys looked like something was holding them back. And it wasn't us."

"Yeah," Marquis added, "and it would explain why we haven't been caught up in either a race war or a massacre."

"On another note," Stephen began, "we need to get y'all moving."

CHAPTER 36

Word spread that the groups scheming to divert the Exodus were suffering tremendous casualties. The operational planning meetings had a different feel. Some were cancelled outright due to a lack of participation. Others had such poor attendance that there weren't abundant numbers to plan any effective offensives.

The general mood amongst the militia and racist groups was to stand down. For what they were trying to accomplish, the pain and suffering they saw others going through wasn't worth it.

President Reynolds was incensed. Already an international pariah, and now the laughing stock of the world too. He met with the Joint Chiefs, but found it hard to concentrate. He felt distant and uninterested.

"Sir, are you with us?"

Reynolds nodded. "Unless you have any good news to share, why should I be anymore engaged than this?" he asked. No one answered, and the meeting continued.

A few weak ideas were tossed around, and dismissed. Someone even suggested small-pox blankets or airborne chem-trail viruses. Outside of direct military action, their options fell short. Still, President Reynolds was unresponsive. The men in the room looked at him. Then they looked at each other. The Secretary of Defense shrugged.

"Maybe we just gotta let them have ole hurricane plagued Florida," someone said. President Reynolds lifted his eyes quickly, scanning the room for the voice who had spoken.

Reynolds stood and spoke, "We do not give up! We do not quit! If you all can't think of a damn thing then maybe I need a new staff! You have twenty-four hours. I want to hear something practical and effective! If you don't have anything, don't show yourself in this room tomorrow, and consider yourself dismissed, permanently!" He exited before those in the room could offer the customary courtesy of standing.

Outside the door, the President paused and shook his head. "These mother fuckers are gonna get away with this shit," he said lowly. "Ok, time to start thinking about the next plan."

***

Once they reached Atlanta the group exited the highway at Exit 248 and headed down Auburn Avenue. It was only right that they pay homage to the fallen soldier, Martin Luther King Jr, and his wife Coretta, at their final resting place. None of the travelers had made the pilgrimage before. Interstate travel wasn't as frequent as in times past. Many of the travelers had never left their respective cities.

As they walked down Auburn some Black children took notice, then disappeared in different directions. Undoubtedly letting some adults somewhere know what they saw. Brandon, walking beside Ryan asked, "Should we be worried?"

Ryan glanced at Sarge, deferring to his wisdom. Before Sarge could speak they saw about twenty five people ahead of them. And down side streets, more were coming from homes and into their yards. They were holding signs, "We Shall Overcome," "A New Day is Here," "We Will Endure". "Black folk," Sarge said.

"Nah," Ryan finally said, in reply to Brandon. "Looks like we are amongst family here." At that point the march was more like a parade. The people who had joined in walked to the side of the caravan and they offered gifts of water, tea, bread, whatever they could provide. And the convoy waved and greeted the onlookers. Then the onlookers joined the ranks. They blended right on in, with smiling faces and open arms. They hugged, greeted and introduced themselves like they were at church and it was time for the recognition of visitors.

What a loving community, Ryan thought. He wondered if they would be joining the convoy for the rest of the trip.

When they arrived at the entrance to the King Center, a dozen elders waited to greet them. Some wore Kente cloth. Others wore traditional European suits. It was obvious they had put on their best clothes to meet the travelers. "We are so glad the Spirit led you this way," an elderly man standing in the center of the twelve said. He wore a brown suit and tie. A worn brown fedora adorned his head. "My name is Conrad Abernathy," he said. "Welcome to the A."

Ryan smiled and extended his hand. Conrad ignored the hand and pulled Ryan in for a full embrace. "Hello," Ryan said awkwardly. "I am Ryan Bishop and my nephew Brandon is over there."

Conrad let go of the hug but he kept both hands on Ryan's shoulders, like he wanted to admire him from afar. He looked at Ryan from head to toe. Then he looked over at Brandon. "The Bishops!" he said excitedly. "It is indeed an honor. Make yourselves at home. If anyone wants to bathe, play, or just soak their feet in the water, it is fine. Folk from the neighborhood will be bringing food and water until someone tells them to stop. Eat your fill and take plenty with you."

"Your hospitality is appreciated," Ryan said. "This is a big surprise. We thought we might be the only ones here."

"I hope you aren't disappointed," Conrad said with a laugh.

"Far from it," Ryan laughed back.

"Excuse me one second," Conrad said as he noticed that the people had not yet dispersed. He stood on a low brick wall, just high enough for him to be noticed by the crowd. "Ladies and gentlemen," he boomed in a voice that seemed much larger than himself. "Make yourselves at home. If you need anything, first aid, new shoes, anything, just ask. My warrior brothers and sisters, enjoy your time in this place of positivity and good spiritual energy. I am sure you will feel it." He smiled warmly and waved at the crowd with both hands. Then he stepped off the wall.

"Ok, brother Ryan," he continued, "Where were we?"

Brandon, Ryan, and Conrad sat on a bench near the Eternal Flame. They watched the children splash in the water and the adults simply relax. It was good to see everyone relieved from the tensions of the trip, though it wouldn't last much longer. "Conrad," Ryan began, "I take it y'all have no plans to come to Florida?"

"Some do," Conrad revealed. "Most don't, I'll admit. We were hoping y'all would choose Georgia. We got a nice setup here. But we understand the advantages of being right there on the water."

"Hopefully we will expand, eventually," Ryan commented. "And we will be doing business all over, so this makes for a natural collaboration."

"Florida, Georgia, South Carolina, Alabama…from the South, on up!" Brandon mumbled to himself as he visualized how the results of the Exodus could influence America as a whole.

"I hear you Nephew, I hear ya!" Ryan turned back to Conrad. "It is good to know we have allies to the north," he concluded.

"We have been tracking the progress of your travels as best we can," Conrad said.

"Met some White people who told us the same," Brandon said. "How?"

"I am sure you saw candle lit windows along the way. Even if you didn't stop for assistance, they were watching for you. And they have posted whatever information they could."

"Wow!" Ryan commented. "Any word on the other groups? They seem to be getting along ok? I am surprised we haven't had more problems with racists."

"Word on the wire is all good. The ones further west have been making their way to the Mississippi River," Conrad reported. "From there, the Black Star Line carries them down river."

"Makes sense," Ryan said. "I remember reading about Marcus Garvey's Black Star Line. I like that!"

"Have y'all heard about the plagues?" Conrad asked. Brandon and Ryan looked at each other curiously, their faces showing their confusion. Conrad continued. "The Klan and different militia groups intended to disrupt this movement. Praise the Creator for his protection, they've caught all kinds of hell. Their children died. There were freak hail storms that only popped up where *they* live. I even heard that in one place all the men's 'Johnson's' fell off." Conrad chuckled, slapping his knee. "I'm not sure how true it is. The point is, they got so much hell from heaven that they saw the light and decided to back off."

"Damn!" Ryan said. "You serious? That's crazy!"

"Yeah, so the biggest obstacles y'all gonna face is the elements, and yourselves. White folk scared to bother us."

"That's good to know," Ryan said with relief.

"Y'all gonna stay the evening?" Conrad asked, reading Ryan's mind.

"At this point in the day, it would make sense for us to," Brandon commented.

"If we aren't imposing," Ryan said. "And if there is room for us all. We have, and will, sleep pretty much anywhere."

Conrad smiled. "Don't worry about that," he said with a laugh. "We look forward to it. Now, if you excuse me, let me make preparations." He stood and walked away. On seeing Conrad stand, his inner circle joined him. Conrad spoke to them. Brandon and Ryan watched, amazed by Conrad's level of command and respect.

After receiving directives, the 12 separated and addressed subgroups of their own. Who, in turn, addressed others or went to their assigned tasks.

By sundown food was prepared and bedding had been arranged for everyone. Ryan was in awe at the organization. As they sat and ate, a choir sang. Then a preacher stepped up to offer a word. It was a good ole impromptu revival. And at this point in the journey, everyone needed some food for the soul.

CHAPTER 37

Exhausted, Cliff slept in the wheelchair as a burly, Black as night assistant pushed him toward their temporary home. Tina watched from the window. It had been two weeks and Tina decided in the beginning that it was best for her to stay away from the therapy. Seeing her husband struggle, and often fail, was hard for her.

The bumpy handicap ramp didn't wake Cliff, but he stirred from his slumber once they entered the front door. "Hey, baby," Tina welcomed.

"Hey, baby baby!" Cliff answered back. It was good to hear him forming words, though, at this stage of his rehab, EVERYONE was "baby".

"How was physical therapy today?" Tina asked.

Cliff shrugged, and thought for a minute, "Hard!" he finally exclaimed. "Yeah, baby, hard!"

"You are going to show me what they had you doing though, right? "she asked.

Again, Cliff searched for the words. "Tired," he said. "Going to bed."

"Ok," Tina accepted. "Nap time. Show me later?"

"Ok," Cliff agreed.

"You want a sandwich or something before you lay down?"

"No," he replied. "Just go to sleep."

Cliff was never a big man. Since the stroke, his naturally thick and muscular frame had withered. He looked skinny and frail. Slowly his appetite was returning and hopefully he would regain the weight soon.

The burly assistant lifted Cliff and carried him to the bedroom. He then came and sat with Tina at the breakfast table. "Mr. Bishop did well today," he started.

"Did he?" Tina asked, perking up from her previously slumped posture.

"Yes, ma'am. He still isn't using his right side, but he is learning to swing his body weight and walk some. Hopefully, he will show you later. Here," the assistant handed Tina a White plastic leg brace. "This goes in his shoe. It keeps his foot from dragging."

"That's great. Thanks," Tina said. "And thank you for everything. You have been great. It is hard for me to move Clifford's big ass around!"

"I'm honored to serve," the assistant said. "Is there anything else I could help you with before I take a bit of a lay-down?"

"No," Tina responded. "Go get you a nap. I will have dinner ready when you two hard working men wake up."

A full month passed and Clifford improved greatly. He walked with the aid of a cane and a foot brace, though still partially paralyzed. He exercised daily, hoping and praying for a twitch in his big toe, or a feeling of arthritis in his fingers. The therapists encouraged Cliff and explained that it would take time. "One day it could come back like THAT! Like a light switch." Cliff didn't argue. He gritted his teeth and put in the work.

His speech, though, was another story. For a natural orator, accepting the inability to express himself verbally would never happen. Yet, the struggle was breaking him. "Relax Mr. Bishop," the speech therapist would say. "You are trying too hard. You have to let it flow." Too often when Cliff tried to let flow the words in his head, he failed.

He did make the breakthrough of speaking to his therapist telepathically. The therapist, amazed and amused, still insisted that Cliff only speak-verbally. "We need the words to come from your mouth, Brother Bishop".

Tina wasn't the least bit amused. She believed the telepathic bond to be strictly between Cliff and her, that is, until the children showed signs. She was fine with that. *All in the family*, she figured. When the therapist told her that Cliff both spoke to her telepathically and was also able to hear her thoughts, Tina was furious. She smiled, laughed, and remained courteous to the therapist. Inside though, she couldn't wait to let Cliff know how she felt.

He was still outside, making his way in. "Thank you for the update," Tina was saying as she held the door for the therapist to depart, and for Cliff to enter.

"I will see you tomorrow, Mr. Bishop," the therapist said in passing.

"O, o, ok," Cliff stuttered.

Everyone gave warm and encouraging smiles. But Tina's smile was fake. As soon as the door closed it disappeared, and Cliff saw her disposition change. "What's wrong?" he asked.

"What are you doing all up in the therapist's head?" Tina accused.

Cliff's speech had not returned enough for him to find the suitable words for an argument, and he knew it. He didn't even try to reply. And the silence only pissed Tina off more.

"Mmm hmm," she said. "If you really wanted to tell me you would have said it in my head. You don't seem to have a problem talking all up in other people's heads these days."

"She said to work on talking, not arguing," Cliff said telepathically.

"Did you even try to speak just now?" Tina fired back. "No you didn't. If you don't have anything to say for yourself, I have plenty to say…"

"Wait," Cliff said aloud, stopping his wife from her tirade. Then he went back to speaking telepathically. *"I have to talk to you like this so I can explain. Ok?"*

"Fine," Tina answered.

"You have known me forever," Cliff began, *"and all this time I've been a talker. What did you used to call me?"* he asked.

"Silver tongue devil," she replied.

"Exactly," he said. *"My best tool has always been my words. This is killing me right now. You have to know that, first and foremost."*

"I can imagine," Tina said.

"I don't have to imagine," Cliff replied. *"This is my life. And communicating with the therapist was actually an accident. In my frustration, in my mind I said, 'this is some bullshit.' And she heard me. She looked up, directly at me, and asked what I said. I told her 'nothing' but she insisted she had heard me. Then I purposely spoke to her mind and, yep, she heard me. We didn't go any deeper than that because she wants me talking. Really, I just want to be heard. I was in no way trying to disrespect you or our thing, baby."* Cliff stood, extending his one good arm for a hug. Tina walked over to oblige.

"I am sorry," Cliff said out loud. Tina felt bad for going ballistic about the situation.

"No," she said, "I'm sorry. I blew it out of proportion. I was trippin'."

"Yyyyeah," Cliff stammered with a lighthearted smile.

"Don't get cocky," Tina shot back.

Cliff responded with the only words he could get out, "I love you, baby baby."

"And don't try to be all sweet either," Tina said with a grin. "I love you too."

***

President Reynolds fidgeted with boredom and frustration in the budget meeting. The Bishops were ignoring him, or so he felt. He let it be known that he wanted a word with Clifford Bishop three days ago-to no avail. When an aide whispered that Mrs. Bishop was on the line, his pulse quickened.

"Excuse me everyone," Reynolds said, "but I have to take this call." He excused the head economist but asked his Chief Strategist to stay. Reynolds then answered and put the call on speaker. "Mrs. Bishop," he started, "it's a pleasure. I expected to hear from your husband."

"He is quite busy," Tina said. "What's up?"

Reynolds didn't like her Tina's tone. It lacked respect, which he knew he may not get from the Bishops anyway. He swallowed his pride and continued. "It appears that your big move is going along well, aside from a little skirmish here and there."

"In this racist country, that's to be expected," Tina said bluntly.

"It could be a lot worse though," Reynolds replied.

Oh, could it?"

"I'm not implying anything," Reynolds interjected. "What I'm doing is congratulating you and offering the White House's assistance, if there is anything we can do."

"Why now?" Tina asked.

"Because Florida will not cease being in America. Its sovereign soil. To me this isn't about race. It is about our nation. Unless you plan on making Florida a sovereign nation?"

"If we get to that point we will let you know," Tina said. She was rolling her eyes listening to the President with his political B.S.

"I hope not. I think we all could benefit from working together. I am extending an olive branch and I want to help, if at all possible."

"Thank you," Tina said, "I will let my husband know. I have to go now. If the time comes we will be in touch." She hung up without saying goodbye.

"Bitch," Reynolds growled. "I hate this," he admitted. "Regardless, sometimes you have to sacrifice a battle to win the war."

CHAPTER 38

They were about 250 miles from their destination and the convoy dragged with exhaustion. After spending the day in Atlanta, everyone longed to be settled and going about their daily duties. Many of the travelers were on a short fuse, no one spoke very much. No one sang songs. Every now and then a child cried and a parent fussed. Over the last few nights, arguments erupted between spouses.

The days grew hotter, now that they were in the South, and the nights were not much better. With the day's heat and humidity, traveling at night became the only option. Not far past Macon, three travelers died from the heat. One of them was only six years old. Brandon and Ryan feared that if they didn't make it to Florida soon, people would indeed start dropping like flies.

Rations were low, and with the extra notches he'd poked in his belt, Ryan figured he's lost twenty pounds. Looking around, he saw loose, scarecrow fitting clothes draped on many others. The exodus extracted it's toll, but it was a worthy sacrifice, and people of color had suffered worse.

On a positive note, they neared the Georgia/Florida state line- still a decent distance to cover, but, a visible light at the end of the tunnel.

***

The ride down the Mississippi was a lot less stressful than the trip on the Red River. Stephen's news that White detractors had given up the hunt eased everyone's nerves. Also, having Marquis back on his feet and Renée giving birth were joyous occasions worthy of celebration. although they didn't stress as much everyone held off on celebrating.

Marquis, Stephen, and Justin stood at the bow enjoying a moment of peace and tranquility after weeks of chaos and stress. A warm breeze caressed their skin. "Where are we now daddy?" Justin asked.

"Just passed Baton Rouge," Marquis replied, "approaching New Orleans. Soon we will be in the Gulf of Mexico."

"Is that where Florida is?"

"Not quite. But the next time we get off the boat we will be in Florida. Just a few more days now."

"I never thought I'd see this part of the world," Stephen remarked. "With the way things are now, I never imagined leaving Cali."

"And here you are in bayou country," Marquis said, "making history!"

"I guess I am," Stephen remarked with pride. "Thank you! Thank you, and your family!"

"Man, thank you! You took care of my little brother out west. You took care of me and my family and got us moving again. No need to thank us. You're playing a vital role."

Justin glanced over his shoulder. He thought he had heard something. And sure enough he did. His mother was holding his little

290

sister and motioning for the men to come to her. Justin tugged his dad's shirt and then took off running in his mother's direction.

"The Captain wants to speak to your dad and Mr. Stephen," she said.

"Dad!" Justin yelled, "The captain wants you."

"What's up?" Marquis asked Renée.

"He wants to brief you on our whereabouts and ETA before he announces it to the rest of the ship. We will be there soon. Can you believe it?"

"I can't," Mark admitted. "After all we been through, I'm so thankful to be able to say and hear those words though."

The steamer passed other boats in the Gulf. They were heading back toward the Mississippi for another round of pickups. Seeing the boats Renée imagined the number of people already in Florida. She and Marquis looked out onto the open waters, trying to spot land, many people were. Everyone anticipated docking and being on solid ground once again.

Stephen approached Marquis with some news. "Excuse me, Mark," he said, "the captain said we are in radio range of Rosewood, in case you want to try to reach any of your family."

"Do you mind doing it, Steve?" Mark asked. "It would be great to see my kin as soon as possible." Marquis wasn't feeling his best. The non-existent arm still pained him. One moment it burned, next it tingled. And his medication left him sluggish and *off*.

"Sure," Stephen said. "Any specific instructions if I reach someone?"

"Yeah, let them know we have a new baby."

"And what about for you?"

"What do you mean?" Mark asked.

"With your condition, do you want me to give a heads up so we can have a doctor on the ready or a transport for you or something?"

"Nah," Marquis replied. "Man, I am fine."

Stephen looked at Renée. She had a frown and with her eyes and body language she told Stephen, "Yes, let them know about my husband."

Stephen's gut told him to follow Renée's instructions in this case. "I got it boss! I will let you know the outcome."

As he departed, Renée turned to her husband. "Are you ashamed, baby?" she asked. "You have nothing to be ashamed of."

"I laid out an order for how we would conduct certain things, then I disobeyed my own order, got snake bit, and almost died. Yeah, that's a bit embarrassing."

"And look where we are now," she reminded. "In the Gulf, soon to make landfall in Florida. You got our people here. You had to expect some casualties. It sucks that one of them is you, but you are still standing and you are coming through with getting our people here. You can bet no one in Florida will allow you to walk with your head hung."

Marquis hugged Renée with his good arm. While holding her and looking into the distance, he saw land. "Land, ho," he whispered to Renée and he let her go to see for herself.

"Hallelujah," she replied.

An announcement boomed over the speakers: "LAND, HO EVERYONE! LAND, HO!" Soon they'd dock in Cedar Key, then journey to Rosewood.

CHAPTER 39

After crossing into Florida, Ryan wanted to reach out to his sister, Denise and her husband, Lamar. He wanted to let them know his group had arrived in the state and receive further instructions, if needed. After again traveling all night, they made camp in the shade of the woods. Ryan directed Brandon to work on getting his Aunt D on a radio, or phone, or something. Thirty minutes later, Brandon returned. "Got her Unc," he said, handing a phone to Ryan. Ryan nodded his thanks and took the receiver.

"Little brother?" Denise said.

"Big sis!" Ryan almost yelled. "God, it is good to hear your voice!"

"Same here," she said. "How y'all holding up?"

Ryan walked to a secluded area, not wanting eavesdroppers. "I am tired as hell, sis! My arches fell. I've lost weight and feel dehydrated. Basically, everyone, in one sense or another, feels like I feel. Nevertheless, we are in the Sunshine State!"

"Where are y'all? Denise asked. "You here already?"

"We just crossed the Florida border not long ago," Ryan reported. "We are traveling at night to avoid this heat. We're camped out right now." Ryan then told his sister how many died along the way, and tallied the injured or sick, as well as their ration status.

"When you can," Denise said, "let me know what mile marker you are at. We'll send a team with more food and water."

"Sounds good. I'll do that within the hour."

"I am so excited, Ryan," Denise finally said. She'd held back her feelings while Ryan reported. "We are really doing this! And I miss you!"

"I miss you too, sis," Ryan replied. He was much more tired than he had let on to anyone. Even though he told his sister, he didn't want to quell her excitement with his fatigue. "Are we the first here? Is Daddy there already?"

"Groups are arriving every day," she said. "Your brother's group is here." She didn't mention Marquis' condition.

"I can tell there is a lot you aren't telling me, big sis," he said. "I won't press. I am too tired, and I have enough on my plate."

"You're right," Denise admitted, "and thanks."

"Let me send a scout to get that mile marker information and I will hit you back soon. Love you."

"Love you back," Denise said, and disconnected the call.

Word spread throughout the processing center in Rosewood. A huge contingent from the north would be arriving within days. Not only that, but this was one of the groups being led by one of the Bishops. This was a big event, the arrival of the last Bishop child. Processing staff were beefed up, room was made to handle the inflow, and the infirmary prepped to care for the sick, dehydrated, and malnourished.

Their entrance into Rosewood was a lot like their exit from Indianapolis. The streets were lined on both sides with excited faces. Some held signs with instructions to point the newcomers in the right direction. It looked like a career fair, or the first day of class registration for a college freshman.

Ryan, still leading the pack, finally saw his family. He saw his sister, arms open wide, eager to embrace her little brother. Upon seeing her, Ryan felt like he was able to finally release all the emotion he had been holding onto for so long. He let out the fatigue, the pain, the sadness from all the death he had witnessed—he quit fighting these feelings and let them overtake him. Ryan collapsed into his sister's arms. Lamar appeared out of nowhere to help her support Ryan's weight, and all three of them went down to one knee.

"Hey, big sis," Ryan said in a voice barely over a whisper. His head was down and he watched his own tears moisten the brown dirt, turning it to clay. "We made it."

"Yes, you did," Denise replied, as she started to cry too.

Lamar glanced up to see that everyone was falling to one knee or simply taking a seat in the dirt. They kneeled because of fatigue, joy, pride, and thanks. He saw his nephew, Brandon, standing tall, head and hands stretched to the sky, and tears streaming down his cheeks.

Brandon, caught up with Spirit and emotion, began bellowing out a prayer.

Lamar bowed his head to join all those around him in thanks. The air was filled with praise and gratitude to the Creator. No one held back any longer. No one tried to keep a brave façade. The end was here! Just in time for a new beginning...

CHAPTER 40

"The homecoming isn't complete," Ryan said. "Where's my brother?" Denise looked upset. "And I don't care about your look either, D. Tell me that he's dead, or get us together."

"Alright," she said.

"And go ahead and tell me what you have to tell me."

Her hesitation caught Brandon's attention. "What's wrong?" he pressed. "Where are my Mom and Dad?"

"Everybody is fine," Lamar said.

"Your dad had an accident on the way here and he has issues with his arm. I'll take you to them now."

"But everybody is ok? Really?" Brandon asked nervously.

"Yeah your mom, brother, and sister made it without a scratch."

"Wait. Sister?" Brandon's eyes lit up, and Ryan's mouth gaped wide.

Denise didn't mean to spill the beans, though it was good to sprinkle in some good news in the midst of delivering bad news.

Lamar looked side-eye at his wife. "C'mon, y'all," he said. "They're at our place. Let's go."

***

Tina got word from Denise that all her children had made it successfully to Rosewood. "Yes, Momma," Denise said, "we are all reunited and having a big family reunion. When will you and Daddy be coming? And how are you getting here?"

"I will talk to the therapist today," Tina said excitedly. "Your Daddy is improving. He's speaking and mobility are better. I don't know if they feel like they can do much more if he stays here. I'm ready to go," she admitted. "I want to see my children! It has been way too long."

"I know Momma! The boys have got so big! And your new granddaughter is so adorable!"

Tina paused. "Oh, you just being mean now, little girl."

"I'm sorry," Denise said, smiling. "That was below the belt, but I want y'all to come on! We can keep therapy going here. And Lamar has been working on something special to get you here as soon as possible."

"My kids and grandkids are enough reason," Tina said.

"No, it's not a 'what', it is more of a 'how'," Denise vaguely explained. "And the 'how' should be there in a couple of days."

"You are being too cryptic for me, girl. I'm getting off this phone. I will talk to you soon to tell you what's up."

"Ok, momma. Love you, and can't wait to have you here!"

"Love you too, and tell everyone that Momma and Daddy love them and we'll see them soon."

Tina was waiting at the therapist's home when her husband's therapy was finished. "Hi, Doc," she said. "Think we could talk for a minute?"

"Sure," the therapist said.

Tina kissed her husband and they all sat on the porch. "Doc, I wanted to know how much more progress you think Cliff can make here? And if he has reached his limits, I would like for us to go on to Florida and we can keep doing exercises or whatever from there."

Cliff looked surprised. He and Tina had not talked about this. He couldn't say for sure that he was ready to be in front of other people.

"Actually, I was about ready to sit you both down and tell you the same thing. Cliff has done well with both his speech and movement. We can only hope that the paralysis someday reverses itself. Until then, Cliff has adjusted to the foot brace and getting the swing of walking the way he has to now. I can give you a list of daily exercises. And speech wise, Cliff you have to talk. You can't depend on your awesome telepathy. Ok, sir?"

"Ok, doc," Cliff said with ease.

"When would you leave?"

"I am not sure," Tina said, "My daughter is cooking something up to get us down there sooner than later. I may expect that we will be gone before weeks end."

"I will get some exercises to you by tomorrow evening. Cliff, there is no need for you to be bothered by us anymore, fine sir. It has been a pleasure, and I will see you two tomorrow." They stood and exchanged pleasantries before going on their way.

"Why the hurry?" Cliff asked as they walked home.

"Why not?" Tina asked in return. "Florida is the mission, and if our work is done here its time to get on down there. All the kids are there and they been developing the place. I think it is time for the next phase."

Cliff didn't disagree. He didn't say a word. Tina could sense his feelings. "You're nervous about your condition."

"That's right," Cliff replied.

"Baby," Tina began, "don't be selfish. You said on more than one occasion that this whole thing is bigger than you. And the fact that everyone is already there without you leading a step shows it. They made it! We made it! Now to get to the next phase the people need their leader. They need you there in body and spirit. You can talk. They need to hear your voice. Yeah, the trip was one of the hard parts, but now we have to put in more sweat and tears every day. Its time, baby."

"I know," Cliff admitted. "The last time they saw me I was healthy and together though."

"Honey, most of the people there have never seen you in person. It is what it is. And you still are who you are. Be that person, that's all."

"Yes, ma'am," Cliff replied. "I see there is no talking you out of leaving soon. You just ready to see your children aren't you?"

"And grandchildren," Tina said. "And our new grandbaby girl."

Cliff looked at Tina and smiled. "Ok baby. I am ready too. Talk to Denise and see what she has up her sleeve. It's time for us to make it to the mountaintop."

***

Many were still going through registration lines. Citizens were added to census rolls and questioned about skills and abilities for critical job placement. Lamar and Denise, now seasoned veterans of the intake process, wanted to move people to cities where they were needed. But Tina sent word to hold fast, and for those in surrounding areas to make their way to Rosewood. She and Clifford would arrive soon.

Denise, Marquis, and Ryan wondered how they'd arrive: by foot, caravan, or convoy? Marquis worried about their safety and proposed sending out escorts. Lamar, smiling, said, "Don't worry. They will be safe. I sent my Cadillac."

"Boy, Cadillac went out of business a long time ago," Denise said.

"Wait and see," he replied with a wink.

That evening as people worked in the town a Black helicopter flew over and then circled. Marquis and Ryan were inside with the boys and they all came out and looked skyward. Then Denise and Renée came out from the house across the street. The helicopter caused nervousness but since it was only one, no one felt threatened, only cautious and curious.

Lamar, busy rebuilding a desperately needed truck, heard the blades-*twop-twop-twop-twop*-chopping through the air. "You hear that purr?" he asked one of the mechanics. "Sounds like my baby!" He exited the maintenance shop, and, looking up the hill, saw Denise and the family staring.

Denise wondered why Lamar was smiling. He said something but she couldn't hear him. He was still too far away. The chopper was landing in a field in the distance. Lamar started to the landing and motioned for the family to follow.

Once Denise caught up, he told her, "That's the Caddy! My chopper I use to get across the state. You forgot, huh?

"I did!" she exclaimed.

Denise broke into a grin, motioned for her siblings to come on, then sprinted for the landing site. Following their lead, the curious townspeople started jogging toward the general direction as well.

The kids stopped at a safe distance while the propellers slowed and the co-pilot jumped out.

"Completely solar powered," Lamar beamed with pride. "I had this baby worked up a while back so I could get around the state faster. And so I could get to my lady!" Denise blushed.

The door opened and the co-pilot assisted Tina as she stepped down. Then they both assisted Clifford from the chopper. Seeing Cliff in a bit of a helpless state, and needing a cane and assistance was a big shock to everyone except Lamar and Denise. Ryan and Marquis' hearts sank a bit.

Likewise, as they walked forward and Tina saw that her big boy, Marquis had lost an arm in the travels, she too was hurt to the core and her eyes watered. The emotional moment felt surreal, filled with joy, but tinged with sadness and hurt.

Clifford exclaimed with a big crooked smile. "My babies!" His smile, warmth, and palpable joy removed mountains of sadness that were building. His words said to the family, *everything is ok*. They felt it and they smiled. Those that followed saw the family's smiles and they rejoiced.

"The Bishops are here, the Bishops are here!!" The cry went out and spread through the community like wildfire.

The family: children, grandchildren, and in-laws, formed a circle hug. "Let the circle be unbroken," Tina said.

"Ase," they echoed.

They prayed together, and Cliff spoke. "Kids, we need to catch up. I want us to have family dinner tonight. Spread the word that tonight is for celebration. Spread the word throughout the state. Let everyone know.

"Get the audio and transmissions ready for the morning. I want to address the group here and anyone in receiving range at 9:30." He stopped giving orders. "Damn, it's good to see all of you! And who is that little girl?" he asked, looking at his new granddaughter. He held out his good arm and Renée handed him the child. "Hi, little girl! I am your Granddaddy. And this is your Maw Maw." He handed her to Tina who was flowing rivers of tears.

Cliff then focused on Marquis. "Looks like you earned your stripes, son," he said. "I am sorry to see your battle scars."

"And I am sorry to see yours too, Dad," Marquis said. "But I am happy to see you!"

"Likewise, son! And you too, Ryan! And my Grandsons, I hear you played a big part too!"

"We are Bishops," Brandon said. "Most definitely!"

"Come on," Denise urged. "We can get out of this field and go get situated. We have so much to catch up on." And for the first time in a very long time, they walked as a family toward town as they prepared for a long evening together.

***

Tina and Clifford walked the grounds, enjoying the morning. It wasn't as quiet as they expected. People were already up and about, doing their work, which Cliff was glad to see. "The people are serious!" Tina noted.

"Yes, they are, and that is a very good thing," Cliff added. "Things are looking great here, and Lamar said he will take us on a tour of the state in his solar powered 'Caddy' as he likes to say." They both laughed.

"It is amazing what he did with that helicopter though," Tina said. "He is extremely handy!"

"Yeah, good pick baby girl!"

By the time their long walk got them back to the center of town, it was almost time for Cliff to speak, so they had to get to the open fields, where the masses were already gathering. Their grandsons, Brandon and Justin drove by in a golf cart and gave them a lift.

The crowd eagerly awaited. They sang songs and kept a vibe of positive energy flowing. But if one paid close attention you could see signs of discontent. There were whispers and finger pointing from some members of the crowd. They were pointing out the interracial couples and mixed children. Not everyone agreed with ANY Whites being able to join. At this point in the new adventure, it was too early to tell if it would be a problem. But looking into the eyes of some of the Blacks who seemed bothered, it would be a subject that needs addressing.

An air horn blew. Cow bells rang. Fireworks went into the air, all signaling that it was time for their leader, Clifford Bishop, to speak, not only to Florida, but to the Black nation, for the first time in their new home.

"We are here!" Cliff began, and automatically the crowd went bananas. The whooping and hollering went on for five minutes and Cliff did not try to stop it. It was a praise session. Tina danced on stage. Cliff tapped his hand and his good foot. People throughout the crowd praised God and celebrated. When they died down on their own, Cliff continued.

"Before we go any further, let us have a moment of silence for those that did not make it. We know that some of our elders died along the way. Militia groups got some of us. And disease got others. Let's bow for a silent prayer for those fallen."

After the silence, he continued. "Thank you. And for those still traveling.....I see a group coming into the city square now. Y'all come on up here! They are still coming! WE are still coming! To those on the way, come on! This is real, it has happened and it is thriving!

"My family stands here with me and as you can see, we are scarred too. I had a stroke. My son lost an arm. And we have all seen trauma and pain. At the same time, we welcomed a new baby girl into our family. You see, life continues, it thrives, and it grows! All we wanted is a safe place for the cycle of life to do its thing. And guess what y'all? THIS is it! We are HERE!

"We have something that the original Black Wall Street didn't have. We have security. And they will be put to use. I don't want any of you to think that we have it easy now. There is hard work ahead and we will constantly face the threat of attack so we have to be ready.

"I am not going to concentrate on such negative things now though. We have seen enough negativity, and like our ancestors who survived the Middle Passage, only to endure the hardships of slavery, we too have survived a passage. We too are the cream of the crop. And we too will survive and thrive through all and any adversity!"

The crowd lost their minds! The excitement was ridiculous. Across the state, groups listened on radios and celebrated with the ruckus crowd they heard in the background. On the road, travelers listened on radios and put a little more pep in their steps, ready to be in Florida themselves.

In California, Former President Teddy Jones celebrated his sister and brother in law's victory. "Way to go, family."

At the White House, President Reynolds sat alone in the Oval Office listening to the broadcast. His mind kept drifting toward thoughts of unification, but he resisted it. Stubborn pride and sheer hatred kept him focused on revenge. "That's ok Bishops. The war is just beginning. You will see me again..." he cut off the radio, turned his chair toward the window, and silently watched the new day.

The Bishop family huddled into their familiar circle on the stage. "Let the circle be unbroken, y'all," Tina said.

"And let the circle grow," Marquis added.

"The circle has grown, my son," Cliff added. "And from here it can only expand; to all parts of Florida, to Georgia, Alabama and the whole south. On to the Caribbean, South America, and back to the Mother Land.

"We have finished, and so we must begin anew. Doors close, new ones open....ok, family," Cliff concluded, "let's get back to work."